"Okay, that was weird," Audie said aloud in the car. "You were getting off like you were in junior fucking high." She was nothing short of stunned by the sensations that had surged through her as she held Beth's hand. Something was wrong here, because she didn't think of Beth that way.

It wasn't that Beth wasn't worth a second look. She was. Nice body . . . pretty face. If a woman like her ever walked into the Gallery, Audie knew she would go out of her way to meet her. And if they hit it off on the dance floor, she would be more than willing to try out the horizontal version. She just didn't think of Beth that way.

Beth was older. Okay, so she wasn't that much older. And it wasn't really her age. It was that she acted so serious all the time, so settled. A woman like Beth wasn't ever going to walk into the Gallery looking to get laid. What she probably wanted was a relationship, a monogamous deal where you both came home for dinner and talked about your day. That was all fine and good for some people, but Audie wasn't one of those people. She liked excitement and adventure. And freedom. Besides . . . she didn't think of Beth that way.

Visit

Bella Books

at

BellaBooks.com

or call our toll-free number

1-800-729-4992

Sumter Point

KG MacGregor

Bella
BOOKS

2007

Bella Books, Inc.
P.O. Box 10543
Tallahassee, FL 32302

First Edition

Editor: Cindy Cresap
Cover designer: Stephanie Solomon-Lopez

ISBN-10: 1-59493-089-9
ISBN-13: 978-1-59493-089-8

This one's for my Grammaw, for Mary Louise, and for the professionals who take care of our loved ones in their later years.

Acknowledgments

Many thanks to Cindy Diamond for her technical expertise on nursing home care. Thanks also to Cindy Cresap for her usual editing magic, and to Jenny for cleaning me up in the grammar department.

About the Author

Growing up in the mountains of North Carolina, KG MacGregor dreaded the summer influx of snowbirds escaping the Florida heat. The lines were longer, the traffic snarled, and the prices higher. Now that she's older and slightly more patient, she divides her time between Miami and Blowing Rock.

A former teacher, KG earned her PhD in mass communication and her writing stripes preparing market research reports for commercial clients in the publishing, television, and travel industries. In 2002, she tried her hand at lesbian fiction and discovered her bliss. When she isn't writing, you,ll probably find her on a hiking trail.

Chapter 1

Thelma Haggard's death was not unexpected.

The ninety-year-old woman had died peacefully in her bed yesterday during her afternoon nap, just missing an early evening performance by the First Christian Church choir. The decision to let her expire without intervention had been difficult for her family, despite her obvious decline. But while they had mourned her passing last night, another family no doubt rejoiced at the news of an empty bed at the Sumter County Long-Term Care Facility, known by everyone in town as the nursing home.

Beth Hester smoothed the linens on the bed before she ripped open the plastic package on the new pillow. The room's next occupant, Violet Pippin, was due to arrive by ambulance from the hospital any minute. According to the briefing this morning, Mrs. Pippin had suffered a serious stroke, and home health care would not be sufficient to meet her needs. Many patients ended up at the nursing home under similar circumstances.

Beth knew Mrs. Pippin, as did most people who had grown up in Sumter, Tennessee. The elderly woman retired several years ago as a county librarian. She lived in one of those old frame houses two blocks off Sumter's main street, the ones the yuppies were buying up for outrageous sums and renovating. Her husband had died six or seven years ago, Beth recalled. And they had raised their granddaughter, a girl who had gone to school with Beth's younger sister.

The room was ready. All it needed now was—

"Slow down! You're not hauling a sack of feed." A young woman's angry voice boomed throughout the wing.

Beth stepped into the hall to check out the commotion. She recognized the irate woman at once as her sister's former classmate, Mrs. Pippin's granddaughter. Audie—that was her name. She instantly recalled that, as a high school student playing basketball, Audie Pippin had a fiery streak, much like the one on display now.

"I'm okay, sweetheart. They didn't hurt me."

"Lucky for them."

The old woman reached out to take her granddaughter's hand. "You need to take it easy and not get so upset."

Audie leaned over and met her grandmother's eye. "They shouldn't have taken that corner so fast. They could have tipped you over."

Beth hurried up the hall to meet the ambulance crew. "Can I help here?"

Audie jerked her thumb in the direction of the attendants. "These guys act like there's a checkered flag at the end of the hall."

Beth made it a point to smile at the jibe, hoping an understanding look would dispel a bit of the young woman's obvious ire. "You're Audie Pippin, right?"

She nodded, seemingly startled to hear her name.

Beth drew closer and followed Audie's eyes to the nametag on her light green uniform. "I'm Beth Hester, Kelly's older sister. I recognized you from when you two played basketball together at Sumter High."

2

"Right." Audie looked back at the elderly woman on the gurney. "This is my grandmother, Violet Pippin. She's supposed to be here for a few weeks while she gets better. She had a stroke."

"Hello, Mrs. Pippin. We're very glad to have you here." Beth shot the youthful attendants a scolding look. This wasn't the first time someone had complained about their careless manner. "Why don't I lead the way to your new home away from home?"

"Temporary home away from home," Audie interjected.

Beth gave her what she hoped was a reassuring look. "I can get her settled in her room while you check in at the office." She pointed toward the nurses' station. "They'll give you an information packet with some forms. Bring it down to room twenty-three if you want and I'll help you fill everything out."

"Hear that, Grammaw? I need to go do some paperwork. I'll be down there in a minute." She looked directly at Beth. "You'll make sure she's okay?"

"Of course." Despite Audie's challenging tone when she first walked in, Beth was touched to see the young woman's unabashed devotion to her grandmother. She would take this attitude any day over what she usually saw—families who tucked away their elderly relatives with empty promises to come visit. Some of the residents here were lucky to get one visitor a month.

Beth watched as Audie turned and walked stridently toward the office. Then she patted Violet's hand and bent low to whisper in her ear. "Do these guys drive an ambulance as bad as they drive a gurney?"

Violet chuckled. "You have to forgive my granddaughter. She's been upset about this ever since Dr. Hill put me on the list to come here."

Beth strained to understand the garbled words, a hallmark of strokes that paralyzed some of the facial muscles. "It's a difficult time, Mrs. Pippin. Change can be hard on everybody. But Audie will feel better once she sees how well we take care of people here."

She led the attendants to the empty room where they backed the gurney into the space between the bed and the recliner.

"Let's have you try out the bed first, okay? I want to get it adjusted just right and show you where everything is."

Beth stepped out of the way to allow the young men to make the transfer. Then she followed them back into the hallway as they prepared to leave. "Hey, guys." She lowered her voice, and her tone was serious. "You need to slow down when it's not an emergency. Imagine how you'd feel if you were already afraid of coming here and that was your first experience."

One of the men nodded sheepishly as the other looked away, a childish smirk on his face. Without another word, they continued slowly down the hall and disappeared around the corner to the ambulance bay. Beth returned to Violet's room, her cheerful demeanor back in place.

"This room has a pretty nice view, Mrs. Pippin." She flung back the curtain to reveal a sprawling lawn lined with oak trees. "When it's not so hot, people sit out there and visit with their families. I tell you, this has been the hottest August of my whole life."

"Call me Violet," the woman rasped.

"Excuse me?"

Violet cleared her throat. "You can call me Violet."

"That's going to be pretty hard for me after calling you Mrs. Pippin all those years at the library."

The old woman laughed. "Then call me Miss Violet. That's what the children in the neighborhood call me."

"I'll try, but it's going to take some getting used to." She walked over and stood between the two doors on either side of the entrance to the room. "Okay, you ready for the grand tour of your temporary home?"

Miss Violet's eyes twinkled as she smiled. "You have my full attention, Miss Hester."

"If I'm going to call you Miss Violet, you have to call me Beth. In fact, you have to call everyone on the staff by their first names because we aren't trained to answer to anything else." Beth laughed as she opened the closet door first. "This is your closet. You can keep your skateboard in here." She flashed a mischievous grin. "And there is an extra blanket on the top shelf if you get too cold. All you have to do is ask for help and someone will get it for you."

Miss Violet smiled and nodded to indicate her understanding.

Beth then opened the other door. "And this is your private bathroom. The charge nurse on second shift—her name's Norma, she's the boss here at night—she'll come see you after dinner this evening to do an assessment. She needs to know what sorts of things you need help with and what you can do on your own. Don't be afraid to speak up anytime you want help. That's what we're all here for."

"My left leg doesn't work much anymore . . . or my arm." Then she gestured toward the left side of her face, which drooped slightly.

"I saw that in the chart Dr. Hill sent over this morning. In fact, he wants you to get some physical therapy and speech therapy to see if we can improve that a little. We'll probably start later this week."

"Whatever you say."

"And here's the last thing." Beth picked up the remote that controlled the bed. "I need to show you how to work all these buttons." She deftly looped the remote around the top of the bed so that it rested on the other side. "But it wouldn't do us any good if we left all the buttons on that side, would it?"

"Useless."

"Okay, the top ones with the picture of the bed make you sit up or lie down, and the bottom ones control your knees. Just press whichever arrow you want. The light bulb picture turns on the light over your head like this." She demonstrated. "And this red button is to call the staff. We come around pretty often anyway to make sure you're comfortable and have everything you need, but you can press this whenever you want someone to come help. Got all that?"

"Grammaw?" Audie came into the room with her packet and her grandmother's overnight bag.

"I was just showing your grandmother where everything is so she can make herself comfortable."

Audie spun around to take in the features. "Well, at least this room's a little nicer than the one Grampaw had. You've got a window." As she peered out onto the lawn, she slapped the concrete block wall and added, "But it's just as depressing, isn't it?"

Beth studied the tall, lanky woman from across the room. Audie was Kelly's age, about twenty-four, but she still had the shape of a teenager, slender and straight. Her reddish-brown hair was tied into a ponytail that hung through the hole in the back of a plain black baseball cap. Her purse was a small, ragged backpack slung over a shoulder, and she wore frayed jeans and a tight black T-shirt.

"It always looks pretty drab at first. But after you bring in some pictures for the bulletin board and personal items to decorate, it starts to look a little more like home."

"Home looks like home. I told you, Grammaw's not going to be here that long, just till she can get around on her own again."

Beth held up a hand and nodded. "Right, I understand. I'm just thinking that even if your grandmother is only going to be here for a little while, she'll probably enjoy having some of her things. What could it hurt?" She looked at Miss Violet for confirmation. "Right?"

"I wouldn't mind having a few pictures . . . and maybe my flowerpot off the back porch. At least then I won't have to worry about who's watering it." She said the last bit with a chuckle.

"Hmpff! You're worried about those old weeds?" Audie smiled and walked over to sit on the edge of the bed. "All right, I guess I can bring a few things over. But don't get too comfortable, 'cause I don't plan on leaving you here in this . . . crappy place."

Beth felt her defenses go up, but she bit her tongue. She reminded herself that Audie probably didn't know enough about the nursing home for that to be a real assessment. She was just reacting to the difficult circumstances.

"You want me to bring Buster over to see you?"

The mention of Buster brightened Miss Violet's face.

Beth softened as she saw the love that passed between the old woman and her granddaughter. "I take it Buster's your dog?"

"Grammaw's dog," Audie corrected. "He's half lab, half border collie."

"He's a border mutt," Miss Violet corrected. "But don't listen to Audie. Buster knows whose dog he is."

"You should bring in a picture of him and we'll put it on the bulletin board. Oh!" Beth got up and went to the window. "And he can even visit out in the backyard."

"That's a good idea." Audie addressed her grandmother. "You haven't seen him since you went into the hospital. I can bring him tomorrow morning and play Frisbee back there."

"Mornings aren't all that good for visiting," Beth said. "There's a lot going on . . . breakfast, baths, medication. Two to five is probably the best time to visit."

"I work eleven to seven at the animal shelter. Morning is the only time I can come, except on my days off."

"It's okay then, we'll work around it. Regular visits are best, no matter what time of day."

"Oh, I'll be regular. I'll be coming by here every single day to check on things, so you might as well get used to seeing my face."

Though it sounded like a challenge, Beth wouldn't rise to it. "Believe me, I'd love to see family members coming by every day. Our residents do so much better when their families visit. And it gives them something to look forward to."

"She's not going to be here very long, just until she can get around again."

"Nothing makes us happier than to see people go back home." Though it rarely happened. "Would you like some help with that packet?"

"Sure." Audie sat on the edge of the bed as Beth perched on the arm of the recliner. "This one says . . . inventory of personal items. It's a checklist."

"Right. It's just for special items, like TVs or CD players, or any

7

furniture you want to bring in. The next page is a list of things we like to have on hand, like gowns, socks, robes, things like that." Beth turned to Miss Violet. "We write your name in your clothes so we won't get your things mixed up in the laundry. Don't bring in anything you don't want your name on."

"Grammaw, do you want me to bring your TV?"

"Maybe the little one from the back room."

"Okay." Audie jotted herself a note at the bottom of the sheet. "So you need me to bring all these things, seven gowns, seven pairs of socks, two pairs of slippers . . ."

"That's right. Just go down the list at home and check these off."

"And what's this part?" She pointed to the bottom section.

"Those are things we recommend our patients leave at home or with family members. Jewelry, cash, important papers."

"Can I keep my wedding ring?" Miss Violet asked.

Beth sighed softly. "We'd prefer that you give it to Audie, Miss Violet."

"Because they're afraid somebody that works here might steal it," Audie said gruffly.

She cocked her head and looked Audie directly in the eye. "Because people often lose a good bit of weight when they first get here while they're trying to get used to the meal and snack schedules. We would feel awful if it became lost for any reason."

With her good hand, Miss Violet tugged the small band from her ring finger and handed it to her granddaughter. "You can put this in my jewelry box with your Grampaw's for now, honey."

Audie dropped the ring into the front pocket of her jeans.

"But don't run it through the wash. You might tear up the washing machine."

"Think you're funny, don't you?" Audie shot her grandmother a devilish grin before continuing through the packet. "Okay, what's this one?"

"That's the durable power of attorney. It designates someone to

8

be in charge of your grandmother's affairs, like paying bills and managing property."

"We already signed one of those in the hospital."

"I know, but this one's durable. That means it continues even if—" Beth stopped short. "You know, you should probably go over these next couple of forms with Clara. She's our social worker."

Audie ignored her, flipping over to the next form. "What's this one?"

Beth took it from the packet and swallowed nervously. She had a gut feeling this page wouldn't go over well at all. "We call this a DNR, for Do Not Resuscitate. It's for you to specify the level of care you want in certain circumstances. Like I said, Clara can explain—"

"What the hell are you talking about?"

"Audrey Jane, watch your mouth!" Even after her stroke, Miss Violet's scolding came through loud and clear.

"Grammaw, they want permission to stand by and do nothing when you're just choking on a grape. You got here ten minutes ago and already they want your bed for the next person."

"Behave yourself!"

Audie stared at her shoes, her face growing redder by the second. It was clear she didn't want to erupt again in front of her grandmother, so it was no surprise to Beth when she suddenly slammed the packet down on the bed and stormed out of the room.

Beth took notice of the car keys still on the windowsill and knew Audie would be back after she cooled down. "I'm sorry, Miss Violet. I can send Clara down here to go over this. She's better at explaining all the technical parts. Or maybe Audie would prefer to talk to our director, Hazel Tilton."

"You have to forgive my granddaughter, Beth. She was hoping they would find a full-time nurse and let me come home, but Dr. Hill said I needed to be here." The old woman's eyes misted. "This is hard for her because of what happened to her Grampaw."

9

"Her grandfather?" Beth was having a little trouble deciphering the words, but she thought she had gotten the gist of it.

"We had to put him in a home up in Nashville. He had Alzheimer's."

"I'm so sorry."

"He was doing all right at first, but after a week or two, he was sleeping all the time. And then they called us and said . . ." Miss Violet's eyes had clouded with tears. "They said he died in his sleep."

Beth could feel her own tears pooling. "That's so sad. Losing a loved one is such a heartbreaking thing."

"But Audie says it wasn't right that he died. She thinks . . . she thinks they killed him. That's why she's so upset about me having to come here."

"She really thinks they killed him?"

"She took his chart after he died and showed it to a doctor friend of hers. He said he thought they might have given Lewis too much medicine."

Horror stories like that one gave nursing homes a bad name, but Beth could offer nothing to refute the Pippins' suspicions.

"Look, Miss Violet. I can't say if that other home did something wrong or not, but I can promise you this—we will take very good care of you here. We'll try our best to make you feel good and to make your stay here as pleasant and comfortable as it can be. And we will talk to you, and to Audie too if you want us to, about everything we do."

Miss Violet pursed her lips as best she could and nodded.

"Do you want me to go talk to your granddaughter now?"

"She doesn't usually listen when she's upset, but it's worth a try."

Audie kicked a rock as she exited the building, then spun around and leaned against the brick wall. She had been from one end of the nursing home to the other searching in vain for a private place to stew. What she really wanted right now was a cigarette, but she had given up smoking a year ago as a Christmas present to her Grammaw.

She had a bad feeling about her grandmother being in this place. Her only consolation was the possibility she would improve enough in the next few weeks to come back home. Dr. Hill didn't think that would happen—he had said the damage from a stroke of that magnitude was irreversible—but he didn't know Grammaw the way Audie did.

Out on the back lawn, an aide strolled beside an elderly robe-clad man as he labored with a walker. He grimaced in pain with every movement and stopped at three-step intervals to rest.

"That's Mr. Andrews." Beth Hester's gentle voice seemed to come out of nowhere. "He has advanced arthritis, but he's getting around pretty well for eighty-six, don't you think?"

Audie looked back at the struggling man. "Grammaw's only eighty-one. She shouldn't even be here."

"Strokes can be very cruel." Beth folded her arms across her chest and leaned against the wall, shoulder to shoulder with Audie, so that neither had to look at the other as they talked. "It's always sad to see older people fighting their bodies to get them to do what they used to do, but it's even more difficult to watch when they're as vibrant as your grandmother."

"Do you think she'll ever get to go home?"

"I'm not really qualified—"

"But you must have an opinion." Audie looked directly at Beth, not missing her reluctant expression. "I know you've seen others like her come in here."

Beth sighed, prompting Audie to brace for her answer. "I'd say it's unlikely she'll improve enough to be able to use her left side again. The best we can hope for is that she gains strength on her right side to compensate, but to be honest, it probably wouldn't be enough to make her independent again."

Audie turned away to hide the tears that burned her eyes. "But she might be able to, right?"

"Yes, she might."

She would cling to that glimmer of optimism, no matter how small.

"We're going to take care of her, Audie. You don't have to worry."

Audie was surprised to feel Beth's hand on her forearm.

"And I meant what I said about wanting you to come every day. If there's one thing that makes being here easier, it's having people who love you come visit. Do you have any idea how many people put their family members in here and forget about them?"

"I won't do that."

"I know you won't. It's obvious how much you love your grand-mother."

"She's all I've got." A tear dripped from her eye and she quickly wiped it away.

"And I bet you're all she's got too."

Audie nodded, but still wouldn't make eye contact.

"But she has us now. We aren't her family, but I promise you we're going to do everything we can to keep her healthy and happy."

The hard lump in the back of her throat made Audie swallow her words for fear she would sob. The last thing she wanted to do was appear vulnerable and trusting—that attitude had led the people at the other home to take advantage of them. Finally, she mumbled, "I'm going to hold you to that."

"Okay." Beth started toward the door, but stopped short. "Do you want me to ask someone to go over the other forms with you?"

"No, I don't want to deal with that shit today. I need to go get that stuff for Grammaw."

Audie returned to the room to go over the checklist one more time, promising to return with everything her Grammaw needed. As she walked out the front door of the nursing home, she caught one last look at Beth Hester. She had seen her not long ago, but couldn't recall the circumstances.

Chapter 2

Audie could hear Buster's greeting as she pulled into the drive. The poor dog had been home alone for much of last two hectic weeks in the wake of her grandmother's stroke. Audie had spent practically every free moment at her Grammaw's bedside in the hospital, stopping at the house only to shower and sleep. Buster was willing to forgive the neglect, but he wanted it to end today.

"Hey, boy. What's the matter with you? You not getting enough attention?" She squatted to scratch the dog briskly behind both ears and deliver a kiss to his snout. She had picked up the black-and-white mutt at the shelter after her grandfather died, thinking he would provide companionship and security for Grammaw when she was at home alone. That way, Audie wouldn't have to worry when she was at work or out late with her friends. Buster served his caretaker role well, but it was clear he considered Audie his real mistress.

"You smell like a dog."

Buster licked her nose as though thanking her for the compliment.

"I'm going to put you in Grammaw's tub tomorrow because she isn't here to say no." She made as if to grab the tattered Frisbee from the counter and Buster began to bark. "Wanna play?"

He barked again and started for the back door, just as Audie's cell phone chirped in her backpack. She smiled when she checked the display as she headed outside to the backyard.

"Hey, Tinkerbell!"

"Why do you always call me that?" Dennis whined. She had known Dennis Bell since middle school. He was the only other person in her class she identified as gay. Not so, Dennis had bragged, proceeding to list several so-called straight boys with whom he had traded hand jobs.

"Well, for starters, you always answer to it." She tossed the Frisbee and grinned as Buster caught it on the fly. "Besides, you like it whenever we're standing in the middle of a meat market."

"I'll answer to anything that gets me laid."

"You're such a slut."

"You say that like it's a bad thing. How'd it go today?"

"It wasn't as awful as I thought it would be. It's a nicer place than the one Grampaw was in, and Grammaw's nurse is pretty nice." Audie snatched the Frisbee from Buster's mouth when he relaxed his bite and she gave it another toss. "It was still hard though."

"I hope you told her I'd be out there to visit."

"You better. She always liked you. Of course, she hasn't heard all the stories about your perverted sexual exploits with hundreds of men."

"Ah, yes . . . the granddaughter she never had."

"Bitch."

"*Moi*? So anyway, I was calling to tell you they're having the amateur drag show tonight at the Palace. Dwayne's going to be in it."

"What does Joel think of that?"

"I think it was his idea. Anyway, it's my turn to drive so you can drink all you want."

"I don't know." Buster barked at her because she had waited too long between throws. "I have to work tomorrow."

"We all have to work tomorrow. But at least you don't have to be in until eleven. My ass has to be in that chair at eight, so I don't want to stay out all night either."

Audie flipped the Frisbee. "What time are you going?"

"About nine, but I want to get home by midnight."

"Okay, I'll be ready."

Two hours later, Audie bounded down the front steps of her house. She still wore her favorite jeans, but she had changed into a white shirt that bared her midriff. Where the baseball cap had been earlier, her hair was now full and flowing.

"Not too shabby, Audie," Dennis said as he flung open the car door for her. "I predict you'll get lucky tonight."

Audie snorted. "Not everyone needs to screw to have a good time."

Dennis's jaw dropped in mock dismay. "Then why the fuck are we going?"

"Because I need to get drunk."

"I'll say. You haven't been out in ages."

"Not since Grammaw's stroke."

"You ought to relax tonight and cut loose. Here." He reached beneath the seat for a plastic bag. "Roll us one."

Audie opened the road atlas to the centerfold and pulled out one of the rolling papers and a dollar bill. Bit by bit, she crumpled the dried marijuana leaves into flecks and removed the twigs. "You remember Kelly Hester from high school?"

Dennis frowned as he thought about the name. "Short girl? Kind of plump?"

"Yeah, we played basketball together."

"Woof."

"Her sister sure isn't a dog. She's Grammaw's nurse, the nice one I told you about."

"Oh yeah? I remember her. Her name was Beth or something, wasn't it?"

"Right. I think she's a lot older than us, eight or nine years. That would put her at about thirty-two or thirty-three."

"Don't roll that so tight! I have to save my sucking muscles."

Audie rolled her eyes. "Whenever you roll it, it goes up in flames before we can smoke it." Nonetheless, she dumped the dried leaves and started over. "Anyway, about this Beth Hester, I think she might be a dyke."

"I didn't know they made flannel nurse's uniforms."

"You're such a turd. I was trying to remember when I saw her last and it came to me while I was in the shower. She and this other woman showed up at the shelter a couple of years ago and adopted a dog together."

"Could've been a roommate."

"We don't get that much . . . roommates adopting, I mean. Besides, I remember when I saw them together I thought they were acting like a couple." She finished rolling the joint and put everything back into the plastic bag before lighting it and taking a deep draw. "Anyway, she's cute."

"So get her to come with us sometime." Dennis reached out to take the joint.

"Nah, she's not my type."

"No pussy?" He squeaked his words as he fought to hold the smoke deep in his lungs.

"Jesus, what's gotten into you tonight? You're full of piss and vinegar."

"What's that mean?"

"I don't know. Grammaw says that to me when I'm sassy."

"Ooo, I like being called sassy. Will you say that in front of the guys?"

"Why? They already know what they're getting with you." Audie took another toke and held it before exhaling loudly. "Hell, they've probably all had you a half dozen times. So how come you're not doing the drag show?"

"Because I needed a dress and you don't have one."

Audie began to giggle, knowing full well that Dennis's joke wasn't all that funny. It didn't matter, though. It felt good to laugh.

Beth emerged from the theater with Ginger, both shedding their sweaters immediately as the humid air engulfed them.

"Why is it always so cold in there?" Beth groused.

"Because it's calibrated for all the bubbas with high blood pressure."

"You'd think there would be more of us than there are them."

"Yeah, but who wants to be around them when they start to sweat?" Ginger answered sardonically. "So what did you think of the movie?"

"Mmm . . . three stars, I guess."

"Wow! You never give anything three stars. You must have loved it."

"I wouldn't say I loved it. I just thought it was well done, well acted, all that. I prefer a happier ending, though."

"Me too! Hey, speaking of happy endings, the bookstore's open till eleven. You up for coffee?"

"How can you drink coffee this late? I'd be up all night."

"There's always decaf."

Beth chuckled. "Admit it. It isn't the coffee you care about. It's who's pouring it."

Ginger grinned. "Doh! Let's at least see if she's working." They walked along the storefronts of Sumter's quaint downtown, finally spotting the woman in question through the window of the mega-bookstore.

"Do you even know her name?" Beth asked.

"Mallory."

"Isn't that a duck?"

Ginger punched her shoulder. "That's mallard, you jerk."

"Speaking of hot young lesbians, did you ever run across a girl by the name of Audie Pippin?"

17

Ginger squinted as she thought. "Wasn't she one of the ones at the Fourth of July picnic that Shelby got so uptight about?"

"Now that you mention it, I think she was." Her sister had told her years ago she thought Audie was a lesbian, but Beth didn't know it for sure until Audie had shown up at the informal lesbian gathering. "Shelby didn't need an excuse to get uptight."

"Talk about an understatement! You couldn't have crammed a needle up her ass with a jackhammer."

Beth chortled. "Tell me about it. I can't believe I lived with that for three years."

"At least now she's Tonya's problem."

Both women had long since gotten over any feelings of heartache and loss when Shelby had left Beth for Ginger's girl-friend, Tonya. The ugly memory still colored their respective outlooks on romance, but their shared history made for a solid friendship.

They entered the bookstore and approached the coffee counter, hanging back just a bit until Mallory was free to serve them.

"Hi there," Ginger said as they stepped up to place their order.

Beth smiled inwardly at the bright look on the young server's face when she recognized her customer. It was nice to see Ginger excited about someone and have that interest returned. She took a table to give them a little privacy while they chatted. When Ginger finally tore herself away from the counter, she deposited two coffees and two enormous pastries on their table.

"Hey! I didn't order this."

"Don't be an ingrate," Ginger whispered. "Mallory gave us these for free. She said she's closing soon and would have to throw them out."

"Sugar at this hour would be as bad as caffeine."

"Come on, lighten up. One little pecan twirl won't kill you."

Beth took a bite of the taboo sweet and nearly swooned. "So are you ever going to ask Mallory out?"

"I just did. Dinner on Sunday night." Ginger flashed a satisfied smile.

"Way to go! I guess you didn't tell her about being a serial killer," she mumbled with her mouth full.

"Nah, I figured I'd save something for us to talk about over dessert." Ginger took a bite of hers too. "So why were you asking about Audie Pippin?"

"No reason, really. She admitted her grandmother into the nursing home today."

"Is she still hot as ever?"

Beth shrugged. If she said yes, Ginger would be all over her to ask Audie out. "I guess. She looks like she always did."

"Then she's still hot. Say, there's one for you. She seeing anybody?"

Prediction confirmed. "How would I know? Besides, she's just a kid. She and Kelly were in the same class."

"Kelly's not a kid. What is she, twenty-four?"

"Yeah, and she's married with a baby. But Audie still looks like a teenager."

"Well, in case you haven't noticed, the pickings in this neck of the woods are pretty slim. I wouldn't rule out anybody that wasn't jail bait."

"You wouldn't rule out anybody, period," Beth teased as she took a sip of her coffee. "What was it exactly that happened at that picnic? I went to the restroom and came back to find Shelby in the car, ready to go."

"It wasn't much. Audie was there with some tattooed woman and they were holding hands and kissing, nothing vulgar or anything like that. Shelby just went nuts thinking everybody in the park would see them and know we were all lesbians."

"Oh, that's right. How could I forget? She always thought nobody knew." Beth chuckled. "Like sixty women arriving at the park in pairs wouldn't be a clue."

"She and Tonya are perfect for each other."

"Hear, hear." She held up her coffee for a toast. "Anyway, I felt sorry for Audie today. She looked like her heart was breaking. She loves her grandmother a lot. I thought it was sweet."

"You should find out what she's up to. Maybe you two could be friends."

"I'll probably be seeing a lot of her out at the nursing home. Maybe she'll want to come to a movie with us sometime."

"And I'll bring Mallory. We can double date."

"Very funny."

The Gallery was the hottest spot in Nashville for gays and lesbians. The atmosphere was always festive, and the owners sponsored a variety of events to make it entertaining. Situated on the south side of town, it was only twenty minutes from Sumter, making it a regular haunt for Audie and her small group of friends.

Besides Dennis, there was Joel Petrone, a pediatrician with a practice in Sumter, and his partner Dwayne O'Neal, an organizer for the Tennessee Democratic Party. Joel and Dwayne were in their late thirties and respected as the unspoken leaders of the group. Audie knew them because they had taken Dennis in several years ago when he was kicked out of his parents' house.

In addition to the group of guys from Sumter, there were a handful of women from Nashville Audie usually connected with, including a few she enjoyed as bed partners. Nothing serious, just a good time without strings.

"Hey, look who's here!" Joel got up and walked around the table to deliver a warm hug. "I was sorry to hear about your grandmother, Audie. How's she doing?"

Audie looked down at the floor, afraid she might lose her composure. "Dr. Hill wouldn't let her come home. I had to put her in the nursing home today."

"At Sumter?"

She nodded.

He tilted her chin up. "I'm sorry, sweetie. But for what it's worth, I hear a lot of good things about that place. It's not going to be like what happened to your Grampaw."

"I know. I was out there most of the day getting her settled in. They're pretty nice."

"Do you want me to go pay her a visit? It wouldn't hurt to let them know that she has a lot of people watching out for her."

Audie was so grateful she nearly cried on the spot. Grammaw had always liked her friends, and this was a good example of why. "I think she'd like that a lot."

"I'll try to get out there this week when I'm doing rounds at the hospital. Don't tell her, though. I want it to be a surprise."

"You're the best." Audie hugged him again, clinging to his shoulders as she fought back tears.

"Come sit by me. Dwayne's going to be hilarious tonight."

"Sure." Audie knew this was Joel being protective, and she appreciated it more than she could say. Dennis headed straight for the dance floor as soon as they came in and had already identified his quarry for the night. No way would they get out of here by midnight.

But it didn't matter to Audie, as long as someone kept the margaritas coming.

Beth waved goodbye to Ginger as she let herself into her condo. The light from over the kitchen sink cast a glow through the dining area and living room, enough that she could see her way to hang her sweater in the closet by the door.

She had the upstairs corner unit, the nicest one in the building, which she had purchased with her half of the proceeds from the sale of the house she and Shelby had owned for only two years. That house had been huge—Shelby's style was to make a big show of things—but Beth had all she needed with a master suite, a guest bedroom and bath, and a balcony. Best of all, the smaller mortgage made her feel more financially secure.

The space was perfect for one person. After the royal screwing from Shelby, all she wanted was time to get her life back on track—

alone. In the three years since Shelby left, she had not had a single date, outside of a clunky affair with Ginger.

Now all of a sudden, Ginger was going out with a pretty girl named Mallory, and all Beth could think of was that she needed to put herself back out there on the social scene again. Trouble was, she had never been one to get out and socialize. Sure, she might get lucky and actually meet someone at a club, but then it would be someone who enjoyed going to places like that. Clubbing wasn't her thing, so they probably wouldn't get past more than a few dates.

The lesbian community in Sumter was a tightly knit group, mostly professional women who had dinner parties or self-important organizational meetings. As an attorney, Shelby had fit in perfectly, and had somehow managed to keep all their mutual friends, despite being a lying cheat. And on top of that, she also took Diva, the rat terrier they had adopted together at the animal shelter.

"I should get another dog," Beth said aloud.

Thoughts of dogs led to thoughts of Audie Pippin, which she wrote off as merely an interesting coincidence.

Audie stumbled through the front door and was immediately greeted by Buster, who nearly knocked her off her wobbly feet. She stepped aside to allow him out the front door. At this hour— one-fucking-thirty, she noted by the clock on the mantle—there was no traffic out there to worry about, and besides, Buster was so excited to see her that he would pee and race right back through the door.

As she started down the hallway, she stopped to take a gander at her reflection in the full-length mirror. She looked like hell . . . on garbage day. Her eyes were bloodshot from the tequila and pot, and her hair was stringy from being inside the sweaty club all night. And thanks to Dennis's clumsy fuck-buddy, her white shirt now sported a strawberry daiquiri stain that covered her left breast.

"Think you got enough to drink?" she asked herself, already

knowing she would swear off tequila forever all day tomorrow. "Doesn't matter. There's nobody here that cares."

She interrupted her pity party to let Buster back in. As he danced in the hallway, Audie stared through the doorway of her grandmother's darkened room. "How am I going to do this, Buster?" She slid down the wall to crumple in a heap, letting herself cry for the third time that day.

Chapter 3

"Good morning!"

Miss Violet turned in her bed and smiled at seeing Beth's face in her doorway.

"So how was your first night?"

"I don't think I slept much," the old woman confessed. "I'm worried about Audie being all alone in that house."

"You shouldn't worry about Audie. She looks like she can take care of herself." Beth pulled the covers back on the bed.

"She can but she won't."

"What do you mean she won't?" She held out her forearm so Miss Violet could use it to sit up. Then she helped her put on her robe. "I'm taking you down to the dining room for breakfast, in case you're wondering."

"First, I need to . . ." She gestured toward the bathroom.

"I thought you might. That's the first thing everyone wants to do in the morning." She guided Miss Violet from the bed to the wheelchair, showing her how to position her feet so she could twist in the right direction and fall gently into her seat. "It's a little trickier in the bathroom, but I'll show you what to do in there to make it easy." Beth coached her through climbing onto the toilet and excused herself to strip the bed.

After a few minutes, Miss Violet emerged, using her good hand to grasp a rail and pull her wheelchair through the door.

"So what were you saying about your granddaughter? She doesn't take care of herself?"

"No, she doesn't eat right. She never was a very good eater, except for hotdogs and hamburgers."

"Too much of that isn't good for you."

"I know. I used to make her eat vegetables at home, but I bet she doesn't eat any with me not there to fix them." Miss Violet leaned over to slide her slipper over her feeble foot. "And she's gotten so skinny since I went to the hospital."

"That happens to some people when they worry. I'm just the opposite. I eat junk food when I get that way." She pushed Miss Violet down the hall into the dining room. "I have a surprise for you this morning."

"Edith Platt!"

"Hello, Violet."

Beth scooted the chair up to the table so the two women could renew their acquaintance. It had occurred to her last night that Edith Platt was only a little older than Violet Pippin, and had worked for many years at a drugstore near the library. It was hard to imagine they wouldn't know each other. Terribly pleased with herself for making the connection, she smiled as she headed back down the hall for Mr. Wortman. Lost in thought, she never saw what hit her, as Audie burst from her grandmother's room on a dead run.

"Whoa!" Beth grabbed the young woman's shoulders to keep them both from sprawling.

"Where's Grammaw?" Audie's eyes were wild with panic.

"Relax. I just took her to breakfast."

25

"Is she okay?"

Beth was close enough to get a strong whiff of stale alcohol, and she backed away. "She's fine. Wish I could say the same for you."

"What?"

"It's just that . . ." Beth knew it wasn't her place to say anything, but she thought Audie should know about her grandmother's concerns. She waved her hand in front of her face. "You really reek."

Audie looked away sheepishly. "I went out with some friends last night. I just needed to unwind a little."

"What you do is your own business. But you should know that your grandmother didn't sleep well last night because she was worried about you. And if she gets a whiff of you right now, she isn't going to sleep tonight either."

Audie stepped back and put her hands on her hips. "So I should just leave. Is that what you're saying?"

"It isn't up to me. I'm just telling you that it's going to bother her, but it'll probably be worse if you don't visit at all." She rustled in her pocket for a tube of mints. "Here, at least take one of these."

"Think it'll be enough?" Audie unwrapped one and popped it into her mouth.

"I doubt it. Does she like your friends?"

"Most of them."

"Then be sure to let her know they were looking out for you. Maybe that'll help."

Audie nodded.

"But if you make a habit of this, she's going to worry."

"I guess I screwed up." She sighed heavily. "Just one more thing that's all my fault."

Beth could see the defeat on Audie's face and thought maybe she had carried her admonition a little too far. "Audie, what happened to your grandmother couldn't have been your fault."

"I called her the day she had her stroke to tell her I wouldn't be home for dinner, but she didn't answer. I should have known something was wrong."

"That still doesn't mean you could have stopped it." Beth glanced at her watch. "I've got to run. Why don't you go grab some breakfast and come back in an hour or so?"

Audie made a face. "I don't think food would be such a great idea."

Beth chuckled. "Boy, you really are in bad shape. But your grandmother also said you were too skinny, and I think she's right."

Audie tugged up her jeans, proving their point. "No fair both of you ganging up on me."

"We'll make it our mission to straighten you out."

"Not much chance of that." Audie smiled for the first time.

"Not that kind of straight," Beth answered with a grin of her own before turning and heading down the hall.

Even the idea of breakfast was causing turmoil in Audie's stomach, but it made sense that a bite to eat would probably ease her hangover and take away the odor of tequila leaking from her pores. Besides, she had an hour to kill before going back to the nursing home.

That last little exchange with Beth sure was interesting. She had picked up on that straight joke very quickly. Audie wondered if her Grammaw had said anything about her being a lesbian. It was obvious she had been the subject of their conversation, but it wasn't like Grammaw to talk about that with people she didn't know very well.

Not that Audie's sexuality was such a big secret. Even back in school, she had been pretty up front about the fact that she wasn't interested in boys, but she had kept her distance from the girls too. Not many of the kids at her high school had been mature enough to grasp the fact that people like her and Dennis were different, not depraved or hedonistic, just different.

Audie laughed to herself as she amended her thought. Dennis

was definitely depraved and hedonistic. And to a lesser extent, so was she. But she behaved herself most of the time, except for the occasional wild nights like the last one.

But why had Beth grinned at her on her way out the door?

In a way, it was as if she was making it a point to let Audie know that she knew. Audie thought again about seeing Beth come into the animal shelter with that woman. If her hunch was right that the two women were lovers, Beth's easy reaction made perfect sense.

Moreover, it gave her tremendous satisfaction to know that Beth was taking care of Grammaw, and she would see her practically every day.

"Doesn't this feel good, Miss Violet?" Beth shielded the woman's eyes from the spray as she rinsed the last of the shampoo from her permed white hair.

"I feel like a new person."

Beth gently touched a wrinkled cheek. "I know. I can see a little dimple right here when you smile." She took two towels from the shelf, draping one across Violet's bare torso and using the smaller one to fluff her hair. "Are you warm enough?"

"Yes."

Beth gently dried her from head to toe and helped her into a blue gown and housecoat. "How would you like to sit in the sunroom for a while?"

Miss Violet nodded. "Can I take one of my books?"

"Sure. That was a great idea Audie had about bringing all those library books."

"She's a good girl."

Beth had to hand it to Audie. Coming back with an armload of books was a great distraction from her smelling like a distillery.

"Okay, here we go again. You ready?" Beth braced her legs to help Violet from the shower stool into her chair.

Finally they exited the bath and headed down the hall to the bright sunroom, stopping along the way to pick out a book.

"I'll come get you before I leave for the day. That's about an hour and a half. Will you be okay for that long?"

"Yes."

Beth parked the wheelchair in the corner of the room so Violet would have plenty of sunlight to read.

"Thank you."

"You're welcome." It was easy to be nice to patients like Miss Violet, who were sweet and appreciative of the attention to their needs.

Mr. Skelly was a whole different matter. He complained about everything at the home, and often took his anger out on the staff. It was sad, Beth thought, that his family didn't visit him much, but she couldn't blame them. It was very tiring to be around someone with such a bitter disposition.

She took a deep breath and started toward his room.

"Must have been a late night. You're dragging around here like you're hauling a house trailer." It was Hazel Tipton, the nursing home administrator.

"That's because it's time for Mr. Skelly's bath."

"Ahhh, but he likes you."

"He doesn't like anybody."

"True enough, but I think he hates you less than the others. You got a few minutes? I want to talk to you about something."

Grateful for the temporary reprieve, Beth followed her to the small office off the nurses' station. She liked her boss a lot. In fact, it was Hazel who had convinced her that an LPN wouldn't cut it if she wanted a worthwhile career in nursing. So at her boss's urging, she had continued in the nursing program at Sumter College and was set to graduate with her BS in nursing in December.

Hazel closed the door and gestured toward the love seat that sat opposite the cluttered desk. She was an attractive woman for her fifty-nine years, tall and elegant, and her professional demeanor left no doubt who was in charge of the nursing home. "I hear you tangled with the ambulance crew yesterday."

Beth dropped her jaw in surprise. "How do you do that?"

"Do what?"

"You weren't even here yesterday, and there wasn't anybody else around when it happened. How do you manage to know every little thing that goes on?"

Hazel smiled wryly. "It's my job."

"Are you telling me we don't get away with anything?"

"Not much." She sniggered and pushed a candy dish across her desk. "I had an interesting conversation with Francine this morning—a private conversation."

Against her better judgment, Beth took a miniature chocolate bar. She could never refuse chocolate. While she was curious about what Francine had said, she was even more curious about why Hazel would be telling her.

"She wants to move to third shift."

This wasn't a big surprise to Beth, or to anyone else who worked seven a.m. to three thirty. As first shift charge nurse, Francine had many administrative duties, and it was obvious to everyone she couldn't handle the paperwork.

"I asked her if she could hang on until December and she said yes."

"Why that long?"

"So I can get the charge nurse I've been wanting for the last seven years."

It suddenly dawned on Beth who she was talking about. "Me?"

"Don't act so surprised."

"Oh, my God!" Beth had never imagined her nursing degree would pay off so quickly. But the best part was if she did a good job as first shift charge nurse—and she knew she would—she would be at the top of the list to take over as administrator when Hazel retired in six years. "Are you serious?"

Hazel nodded and smiled. "You know there isn't anyone else in Sumter County who could do this job better than you. You understand how everything in this place works, and you're good with the families."

"I can't believe this. I don't know what to say."

"Don't say a word—not to anyone, even Francine. I think the

30

county has rules about hiring people for vacancies that don't exist yet."

"I won't, I promise. But are you sure it won't be a problem with the county? You're bound to get a lot of applications."

Hazel waved her off. "I've been here long enough to know where all the bodies are buried. I can hire whoever I want."

"I won't let you down, Hazel."

"I know you won't." She smiled her congratulations. "So did you get Mrs. Pippin settled in all right?"

"Sure did. She's got good use of her right side and her mind is sharp as a tack. She's down in the sunroom right now reading a library book."

Hazel nodded. "I guess that explains why she didn't think she should do a POA or a DNR."

Beth cocked her head to one side. "Yes and no. I think she was ready to sign—at least the power of attorney—but her grand-daughter's pretty insistent that she's going to get to go back home."

"Norma says there isn't much chance of that."

"I'm afraid I agree. And I told Audie—that's her granddaugh-ter—that it was pretty rare for someone to go home after a stroke that severe. I just think they both need a little time to adjust to the idea."

"It's always hard at first, at least for some people." Hazel stood and smoothed her skirt. "I suppose I should go introduce myself."

"She's a sweetheart." Beth looked at her watch and groaned. "You didn't keep me long enough."

Hazel laughed. "I didn't want poor old Mr. Skelly to miss his bath."

Audie removed the last load from the dryer, her bed sheets. She had spent the entire evening cleaning house, concentrating first on the dishes that were piled high in the sink. Once she and Buster smelled better, she had been compelled to get rid of the rot in the kitchen, along with the colony of ants that had taken up residence.

Her Grammaw would have been mortified at the state of the

house, but Audie rationalized that she hadn't spent much time at home since the stroke. Still, if the health department had dropped by this afternoon, the property would have been condemned. And if her Grammaw had actually been released to come home, she probably would have had another stroke at seeing the condition of her kitchen.

Audie was exhausted, she realized, as she tucked the sheets into the corners of her bed. Maybe tonight she would sleep for a change. It was ridiculous that she had come home totally shitfaced last night and still hadn't been able to get a good night's sleep. That's why she had gone to the nursing home so early—and why Beth had picked up so easily on the fact that she had been out partying.

The more she thought about her morning at the nursing home, the more embarrassed she became. She wanted to appear tough and demanding when it came to her Grammaw's care, and instead, she came off looking like an irresponsible fool. She didn't want those people at the nursing home—especially Beth Hester—to say things like, "Audie Pippin must not be too concerned about her Grammaw, or she wouldn't have been out partying all night." But that's probably what they did.

She would have to erase that impression, starting tomorrow.

Beth slid between her cool sheets, still giddy from today's news. She was bursting to tell somebody—Ginger, Kelly, anybody—but Hazel had sworn her to secrecy. She could live with that for now.

The fall semester started next week, and she had one last class to take for her RN degree, a three-hour course in geriatric care management. For someone with her background, it should be a breeze.

Beth was more worried about her nursing board exams, which she had already scheduled for October. She had never done very well on standardized tests, but she needed the state certification to step into Francine's job. Lots of people failed the exam on the first try, and Beth's stomach knotted with anxiety every time she imagined that day she would open the envelope with her scores.

While her age and experience served her well when it came to course work, the younger students always seemed more relaxed at test time. Beth envied not only their laid-back approach, but also the fact that most of them were full-time students. It had to be easier that way, but she hadn't had an opportunity like theirs.

From high school, she had gone straight to Sumter Vo-Tech to get certified as a nursing assistant. Then she went to work at the nursing home, taking more classes at night at Sumter College to earn her LPN. All the while, she served as a surrogate mother to her younger sister Kelly.

Beth tried not to think back on those years too often. She loved her sister dearly and was glad to have spared her what would have been a dreadful life at home with their stepmother. But she couldn't help having regrets about all the things she had missed out on, like going to college with her peers, enjoying the nightlife with friends and dating. Kelly hadn't been too keen about having a lesbian sister, so Beth had even put that part of her life on hold until Kelly moved in with her boyfriend six years ago when she turned eighteen.

No wonder Beth had made such a miserable choice when it came to Shelby. She had virtually nothing to compare the feelings to. At least now she knew better. No more closet cases. No more control freaks. No more monster egos. Beth wanted to feel real love for a change.

And she wanted someone who could make a promise and keep it. Someone responsible. She wasn't going to find a woman like that cruising the lesbian bars with Ginger and Mallory, that's for sure. Bars were full of people like . . . well, like Audie Pippin.

Chapter 4

Audie balanced perilously on the arm of the recliner, stretching to tape the wire to the wall at the highest possible point.

"Okay, that should do it."

She hopped down and turned on the small TV, flipping channels as she worked the rabbit ears. Two channels were relatively clear, and that was an improvement. But her Grammaw's favorite channel remained snowy, no matter how the antennae were positioned.

"Dang! I think that's as good as it's going to get, Grammaw."

"That's too bad." Since she entered the nursing home ten days ago, Violet had missed her favorite programs. "At least I have my books."

"No, we should get you hooked up to cable. I know they can do that because there's a man down the hall that has his TV on the country music channel all day."

"That's too much fuss."

"No, it isn't. Just because you have something to read doesn't mean you can't watch your shows too. Beth said we should try to make living here as much like being at home as we can."

Speaking of Beth, Audie hadn't laid eyes on her since last Friday. When she hadn't appeared over the weekend, Audie assumed those were her days off, but it was now Wednesday.

"I can make do with it like this. No sense in spending money on cable."

"Why not? Besides, I can disconnect the cable at home if you're worried about how much it costs."

"You don't want to do that."

"It doesn't matter to me. I hardly ever watch TV anyway, and if there's something I really want to see, I can go over to Dennis's."

Audie crumpled into the recliner. "Do you sit in this chair much?"

Her grandmother frowned. "It's hard as a rock."

"No kidding. Beth said we could order another one if we wanted, an electric one that changes positions like the bed."

"I wonder how much they cost."

"Quit worrying about the money! What good does it do to have it if you can't use it to be more comfortable?" If there was one subject in the whole world Audie hated, it was finances. Not that she ever had to worry about it much. Living at home rent-free meant she had lots of spending money from her paycheck, so she was rarely pinched for cash. She had a car payment and insurance, and she managed to put about a hundred dollars a week into her savings account. But most of her cash went to fast food restaurants, the Gallery, or whoever the guy was that supplied Dennis with pot.

Her Grammaw threw up her hand in surrender. "Okay, I guess we can ask Beth to order one."

"Beth must be on vacation. I haven't seen her in a while."

"She's here today. I guess she's busy."

Audie was surprised to hear that. She had been here almost an hour and hadn't seen anyone at all but her Grammaw. "Maybe I'll go see if I can find her. Then we can order it today."

After a quick tour of the nurses' station, the day room, and the sunroom, Audie found the object of her search in another patient's room. Beth gave her a bright smile and wave, which she automatically returned.

"Hi," Beth said, stepping out into the hall.

"Hi. I thought maybe you were on vacation or something."

"Vacation? I wish." She looped her stethoscope around her neck. "No, just my usual days off, spent cooped up at home by myself getting ready for my nursing boards."

"You're off four days in a row?" Not that she was counting or anything.

"It's our usual rotation. I work ten days straight, then the next four I'm off. That way, we all get to have two free weekends a month."

Audie nodded her understanding. "That sounds like a good schedule."

"It's not bad once you get used to it. I've been doing it for fourteen years."

"That's a long time to work in one place. I've been at the animal shelter for six years."

"What do you do there?"

"I'm a vet tech. I take care of the animals that come in sick or injured, unless it's something serious."

"Then I guess you have to take them to the vet."

"Yeah." Or put them down. "I like it. My boss wants me to take a promotion, though, doing some work out in the community, like talk to schools and clubs."

"I bet that would be fun."

"I have mixed feelings about it. For one thing, I'd have to dress up for work every day. I don't think I could stand that."

"We all have our crosses to bear. At least you wouldn't be stuck in one place all the time."

"True." Audie was glad for the chance to talk as they walked slowly down the hall. "So what's this about nursing boards? Do you have to take them every year?"

"Oh, no," Beth answered with a chuckle. "Just once, if you're lucky enough to pass on the first try."

"I don't understand. Why do you have to take an exam if you're already a nurse?"

"I'm a licensed practical nurse, not a registered nurse. They're different. I'm getting a bachelor's degree in nursing and I have to pass the state boards to get certified as an RN. I finish up the program at Sumter College in December, so I have to take my boards this fall."

"Well, good luck."

"Thanks. I'm pretty nervous about it."

"I'm sure you'll do great." They were nearing her grandmother's room. "I was looking for you because Grammaw wants to order one of those recliners you told us about, the one that adjusts."

Beth entered the room. "I don't know, Audie. If I give in and let her get a recliner, she'll probably want a motorcycle next."

Violet laughed, clearly delighted by the teasing.

"Actually, what she wants next is cable TV," Audie said.

"We can work that out, but I've got a better idea. Why don't we put you down to move into one of the rooms that's being renovated? They already have cable hookups." She pulled a blood pressure cuff from her large pocket and wrapped it around Violet's good arm.

"When are they going to be ready?"

"In a week or two, I think. Maybe your chair will be here by then."

"Does that sound all right, Grammaw?"

"It's fine with me. Will I have a window like this one?"

"Sure. We'll even put you on the back side like you are here." Beth turned to Audie. "I heard you and Buster put on a show for everybody on Sunday."

"Oh, yeah! He was in rare form. Everybody clapped and cheered when he caught the Frisbee. He ate it up."

Everyone went silent as Beth pumped up the cuff and pressed

37

her stethoscope to the inside of Violet's elbow. Finally, she said, "I bet it was fun. I wish I had been here."

"I can bring him again next Sunday if you're working then."

"You should. I'd love to see it." She folded the cuff and put it back in her pocket, turning back to Violet. "Did you get a sponge bath today?"

"No."

"Let's do that then."

When Beth went into the bathroom for her supplies, Audie grabbed the short stack of library books that her Grammaw had already finished.

"You're not leaving, are you?" Beth asked, checking her watch as she returned. "I thought you didn't have to be at work for another hour."

Audie shrugged. "I have to go by the library before I go in. Do I need to do anything about the chair, or can you order it?"

"Can you jot down your credit card number? If I call it in, they'll ship it out right away."

Audie gave her Grammaw a questioning look then turned back to Beth. "I don't have a credit card. I always pay cash for everything."

"Hmm . . . we'll have to figure out something else then. Maybe we can charge it to the county for now and then take it directly from Miss Violet's patient fund." She helped Violet sit up and remove her gown.

"Or I could write a check," Audie offered, sidling to the doorway.

"That'll take longer. Let me look into my idea first. I'll let you know tomorrow, okay?"

"Sure." Audie was practically standing in the hall. "I'll see you then. Love you, Grammaw."

Beth soaped a cloth and began to wash the old woman's torso. "Was it my imagination or did your granddaughter just tear out of here like her pants were on fire?"

"I think she's a little shy about seeing me without my clothes on. She did that at the hospital too."

"Oh, I see."

"It was even worse when I had to get her to help me with her Grampaw."

Beth was growing accustomed to the cadence of Miss Violet's speech and now found her easier to understand than she had at first. "I guess I can relate to that. I'd feel kind of funny if I had to give my father a bath."

"Does your father live here in Sumter?"

"He lives in Nashville. But I don't see him all that much anymore. He and my mother got divorced back when I was a kid, and after he got married again, we started drifting apart."

"Where does your mother live?"

Beth continued her gentle strokes, now rinsing the soapy film from Miss Violet's fragile skin. "She died in a boating accident about five years ago somewhere near Australia. But I hadn't seen her since I was seventeen."

"Are you all by yourself?"

"No, I have a younger sister who lives in Knoxville with her husband, and a very handsome nephew who's almost a year old. I'll bring in some pictures tomorrow if you want to see."

"I do."

"He's a cutie-pie. And his Aunt Beth spoils him rotten every time she sees him, but I figure that's what we're here for, right?"

"I thought that's what grandparents were supposed to do," Miss Violet said with a chuckle.

"Did you spoil Audie when she was little?"

"I don't think we did, but we wanted to. She didn't get a lot of attention from her mama. It was hard for her to get used to having people hug her and tell her what a pretty girl she was."

"What happened to her mother?"

"Nobody rightly knows. She left home when she was sixteen with some man who was nearly forty. We didn't see her again till she showed up with Audie. Little girl was two years old and didn't even know how to chew her food."

"My goodness." Beth had no idea of Audie's precarious start, and felt a swell of compassion for her. She and Kelly also had tough times, but at least their physical needs had been met.

"Marla stayed with us for a week or two, then one morning she just up and left without saying goodbye. Left Audie with us. We didn't hear from her again until Audie was about ten. She called us from Las Vegas, wanting money. Lewis hung up on her."

Beth shook her head in disbelief. "I can't understand how a mother can just leave her child. Audie sure was lucky to have you and your husband."

"We worried so about raising her, on account of the way her mama turned out."

"I'd say you don't have to worry anymore. Audie turned out pretty well if you ask me. She seems like a really good person." Because of her work, Beth tended to form her opinions about people based on how they treated their elders. That made Audie aces in her book, even if she was a little on the wild side.

"Bless her heart, she sure has been good to me and her Grampaw."

"That's because she loves you very much. I can see it all over her face. And I can see the same thing in yours." Beth was startled to see a tear trickle down the old woman's face. "What is it?"

"Audie's not going to have anybody when I go."

"No, I'm sure you're wrong." Beth gently brushed Miss Violet's curly hair with her hand. "She told me she has friends who look out for her. And one of these days, I bet she'll meet somebody and fall in love, don't you think?"

"I hope so."

"Yeah, don't you worry, Miss Violet. Audie will meet the right person someday and be very happy."

Audie coaxed one of the calico kittens from its litter with a string. "See, they like to play with just about anything." She dangled the string over the box again and another one joined in the impromptu game. "Especially each other."

Doug Caldwell and his daughter smiled with delight. They had come to the shelter to get the six-year-old her very first pet.

"We just got these kittens in this morning. Four of them are adopted already. The little ones go in no time."

"We definitely want one, but I'll let Kathy pick it out."

"I always recommend getting two so they won't be lonely. It's better when they're really young if they can be with a brother or sister."

"I don't think we can handle two."

"Oh, two aren't any more trouble than one, Mr. Caldwell." Audie had the sales pitch down to an art. Hardly anyone left the shelter with only one cat. "I had three once and it took the same amount of time to feed them and clean the litter box. And it's fun to watch their little personalities develop because they'll be different as they get older."

"I don't know, Audie." Caldwell looked at her with obvious doubt.

"Look, you'll probably want another one eventually anyway. If you get both of them now, you save twenty dollars on the spaying or neutering and all the shots. It's forty-nine apiece if you get them separate, but only seventy-eight for two." She darted the string between the two kittens she thought should stay together. "Besides, you'll break their little hearts if you just take one." She knew the little girl wouldn't stand for that.

"Let's get both of them, Daddy."

"Are you going to take care of two?"

The girl nodded with excitement.

"All right. What do we have to do?" He reached for his wallet.

"I just need you to fill out some paperwork. I'll have somebody run them over to Dr. Martin first thing in the morning so they can be"—she paused to examine first one and then the other—"spayed. Almost all the calicos are girls. They'll stay the night there and get their shots on Friday. They should be ready to go around noon."

"Why can't we just take them with us now?"

"Sorry, but we don't allow animals out of here that aren't neutered or spayed, or that don't have their shots. We can't afford for somebody not to follow through. Next thing we know, you're standing there with another box of kittens."

41

Caldwell nodded and stooped to comfort his daughter, who was clearly disappointed. "I guess it'll be Friday, honey."

"It'll pass in no time, Kathy," Audie said, holding out a kitten for the little girl to pet. "Besides, you've got a lot of work to do to get ready. You have to pick out names for these little babies. Then you've got to get their litter box set up and go to the store and buy their food and pretty little bowls. And don't forget the toys. They like balls and little stuffed mice . . . and I bet they love you too!"

"Thanks, Audie. I appreciate it."

"Thank you, Mr. Caldwell. I'm happy to see them going to a good home."

Audie smiled as she watched them walk out. The only remainders from the new arrivals were one kitten and the mama cat, not even a year old herself. She was confident she could get them out the door in a package deal too, but that was going to be trickier.

"I wish I could get you to give lessons, Audie."

She turned and grinned at her boss. There were many things she liked about her job, but being appreciated by Oscar Shaw was at the top of her list. Their work at the shelter was heart wrenching sometimes, and he never took any of his staff for granted.

"The two-for-one's a piece of cake, especially if the kid comes in."

"Have you thought any more about that outreach job?"

Audie shrugged. "A little."

"It won't matter if we don't get the endowment, but I believe we will. And if we do, you're only going to have a week or two to make up your mind."

"I told you, Oscar. I have a hard time seeing myself like that . . . dressing up, kissing people's asses all day. It's just not who I am."

"I think it is, Audie. You may not realize this, but you've already got the ass kissing down to an art. That's why you're so good at getting these animals out the door. I want you to do it on a bigger scale. If they make us a no-kill shelter, we're going to have a lot of these critters on our hands. We have to have people out there on the ground to educate the community and find more families willing to take them in."

"I like what I'm doing now." One of the things Audie liked best about working at the shelter was the casual atmosphere. And she didn't have to deal with bullshit when it came to the animals.

"I know. But somebody like you can do a lot more to help these animals than a backroom technician. This is an opportunity to make what you're doing here more than just a job. Right now, you're making what . . . eighteen thousand a year?"

Audie nodded.

"I know money's not all that important to everybody, but do you realize that the outreach job is going to pay almost thirty thousand?" He looked at her pointedly as he dug his keys from his pocket. Then he turned out the lights and held the door for her to walk out first. "Where else is somebody without a college degree going to make that much money in Sumter?"

"I know."

"Keep thinking about it. You might not get but one chance at this."

Audie slung her backpack over her shoulder and waved goodnight, her head reeling from the numbers Oscar had dropped. He was right on every single point, but she still hated feeling like she was being pushed into something, especially since he was a hell of a lot more confident about how she would do in that job than she was. The last thing she wanted was to take the promotion and fall on her ass.

What she really needed was somebody to talk it all out with—the pros, the cons, the unknowns. She already knew what Dennis would say. To him, the best jobs were the ones you walked away from at five o'clock. She could do that as a vet tech, but probably not in outreach. Jobs like that practically never stopped.

She also had a good idea how Joel would feel about it. Work wasn't about money to him. It was about making the world a better place, and that's what he did as a physician. So if Oscar was right that she could be more effective in the outreach job, that's what he would advise her to do.

The real problem was that Audie wasn't ready for such a big change right now. There was so much going on with Grammaw that she needed to be able to leave her work behind at quitting time. But she didn't want to be stuck in a low-paying job forever, so she was afraid to let this big chance pass her by.

She opened the door to her SUV and tossed her backpack across the front seat, where it scattered the library books she had picked up this morning for her Grammaw. The image of Beth Hester popped into her head, and she suddenly got a great idea about who she could talk things over with.

Beth scraped her plate into the sink and rinsed it thoroughly before placing it inside the dishwasher. Crumbs and garbage attracted ants, and it didn't take long for them to take over the kitchen. She had spotted two or three over the weekend and had to set aside her test preparations to give the kitchen a good scrubbing.

Ginger had called earlier in the evening to say she was just about ready for the U-Haul, now that she and Mallory had seen each other three nights in a row, including a sleepover last night. Beth was happy for her friend, but she wasn't really interested in the level of detail Ginger wanted to share.

All evening, Beth had thought about calling Audie. The story Miss Violet had told about how the girl's mother had just dumped her with her grandparents really touched her heart. There was a whole lot more to Audie Pippin than she ever would have guessed. She still had her brash side—youthful and perhaps a bit reckless—but there was no way a person could survive a rough start like that and not have a lot of inner strength.

Beth pulled the scrap of paper from her pocket and looked at the number, which she had already committed to memory. It wasn't critical that she talk to Audie, but she had a perfectly legitimate reason. Several reasons, in fact.

She dialed the number and waited through four rings. She was about to hang up when she heard the phone pick up.

"Not tonight, Tinkerbell! I've got a headache."

Tinkerbell? "Uh, hello?"

After several seconds of silence, a meek voice answered, "Hello."

"Is this Audie?"

"Yes."

"It's Beth. Beth Hester, from the nursing home."

"What's happened?" Audie practically shouted.

Beth's heart suddenly pounded with panic. It hadn't even occurred to her that a sudden call from her might be frightening. "Nothing! Sorry, nothing's wrong. Your grandmother's fine."

"God, you scared me half to death."

"I'm so sorry. I didn't mean to."

"It's okay. I probably didn't need those ten extra years anyway."

Beth hadn't embarrassed herself this badly in a long time. Phoning Audie had been a mistake. "I really am sorry. I just wanted to tell you that I was able to order the chair today like I said, so you won't have to bring in your checkbook tomorrow."

"Oh." More awkward silence for Beth to endure. "Thanks for letting me know."

"You're welcome." Calling Audie at home just to tell her about the chair order now seemed like a pretty flimsy justification for scaring her out of her wits. "I also wanted to let you know that your grandmother seems to be adjusting very well. I know people don't always like to discuss care in front of the patient, so I sometimes call the families after work. I hope this is okay."

In truth, she rarely called a patient's family at home. That job usually fell to Hazel or Clara, and she started to panic at the possibility that Audie would realize that.

"Sure . . . I don't mind at all."

Beth breathed a sigh of relief. Audie had calmed down and her own heart was getting back to its slow, steady pace. "You left today before I had a chance to tell you how well she was doing."

"Yeah, I don't think Grammaw really wants me around when she's getting a bath or something like that. I didn't want her to be embarrassed or anything."

"I can understand that. It's always kind of tough for people to handle when they first realize they need help with personal things. What's funny is that nine times out of ten, what bothers patients most is knowing how uncomfortable other people are when they see all the things they need."

"I didn't mean to make a big deal out of it. Was Grammaw upset that I left?"

"Not upset, really. But she seemed a little down about it, if you want to know the truth. I think she thought you were embarrassed and that made her feel bad because she can't help it." Beth hadn't meant to go off on this tangent, so she hadn't really thought through her next words. "Sometimes we just have to give the people we love permission to be sick and let them know it's okay."

"What are you saying?"

Beth noted Audie's defensive tone and scrambled in her head to get clear on what she wanted to say. The last thing she wanted was to make her feel bad about anything. Audie was like a breath of fresh air at the nursing home in the way she doted on her grandmother.

"I'm just saying that . . . it's kind of like what we were talking about last week. Your Grammaw's more worried about you than she is about herself. I think she needs to know that you accept her like this."

Beth got a sinking feeling as Audie went silent, no doubt wallowing again in her feelings that the whole situation was somehow her fault. Everything about this call was turning out wrong.

"Look, I didn't mean to make you feel bad. The best part of your grandmother's day is when you're there, and it's really great you're so faithful about your visits."

"I'm—it's not just being faithful," Audie sputtered, the frustration in her voice growing. "I don't come to see Grammaw because

I feel obligated. I come because I love her and I miss her being at home."

"I know, I know." Beth began to think she should just hang up already before she made things worse. "I think I probably should let you go. I didn't mean to scare you by calling you at home. I really just wanted to tell you about the chair and let you know that she's very well and a lot of that is thanks to you."

"Thanks . . . and I'll think about what you said."

"Okay . . . goodbye."

"Bye."

Beth pressed the button to disconnect the phone. Then she buried her face in her hands and groaned.

Chapter 5

Audie shifted beneath the sheets, her brain registering immediately that she wasn't in her own bed. She opened her eyes in the familiar room and sat up, searching for a clock. It was there, on the other side of Regan, but it was turned away.

She stretched across the slumbering form to check the time, unconcerned that she was squashing her bed partner. Seven forty-five. Time flies when you're having sex, she thought.

She dropped a loud smooch on Regan's naked shoulder, her playful signal that it was time to get up.

"Go back to sleep," the woman mumbled.

"Can't. Grammaw's moving to a new room today and I promised I'd help."

"Two more hours."

Audie fixed her lips on Regan's neck and pretended to suck, prompting the girl to scoot away and rub the skin furiously.

"God, you're mean!"

"I was giving you a passion mark. How can you call that mean?"

"Passion, my ass! You'll go to hell for lying. You were giving me a hickey to get me up." Despite her protests, she slowly rose in the bed.

Audie chuckled with mischief. Of all the women she knew from the Gallery, Regan was her favorite. She was sweet and sexy, and like Audie, wasn't looking for anything but a good time. "You're the one that made the deal with the devil. All-night sexual favors for taking me back to my car in the morning."

"I was drunk and horny. Those promises shouldn't count."

"Fine. I'll just take your car and leave it in the lot at the Gallery."

"How can somebody be so sweet at night and so ruthless in the morning?"

"I was drunk and horny too. At least you can go back to bed. You don't have to be at work until three."

"I suppose I should be counting my blessings that I didn't offer to help you move your Grammaw today." Regan stood up and stretched, allowing Audie to admire her body.

"It's not too late to do the right thing. Especially since I gave you everything you wanted last night." Audie swung her legs out of bed and tugged on her jeans.

"Nobody's that good, Audie. Not even you."

Audie clutched her chest as though taking a dagger. "I simply can't bear this anymore, Regan. You treat me like a plaything," she said, her voice dripping with overly dramatic sarcasm.

"You are a plaything."

"Oh, okay."

Beth steered Miss Violet's chair into the hallway and looked over her shoulder at the two young men who had come to execute the move. "You can leave that recliner, but there's a new one in the storage room that needs to be set up."

"You want the bed to go first, though. Right?"

"That's right. Then bring the nightstand and everything in the closet."

"What about this TV?"

Beth leaned over Miss Violet's shoulder. "Audie's picking that one up, isn't she?"

Miss Violet nodded. "And bringing me a new one."

"You can leave it," she said to the workmen. Beth pushed her charge into the sunroom, from where they had a view of the parking lot. There was no sign yet of Audie's bright yellow Xterra. Beth had seen it out there practically every day, but Audie seemed to be avoiding her since their ill-fated phone conversation of a couple of weeks ago.

The decision to call Audie at home that night was one she regretted, especially the part about giving Audie unwanted advice. Not only had she insulted someone who might have been a potential friend, she had damaged communications with the family of a patient. If things didn't smooth over soon, she was going to have to report the situation to Hazel.

"There's Audie now," Miss Violet said.

Beth looked out the window to see Audie struggling with a large box, apparently Miss Violet's new TV. "That looks heavy. I'll go lend her a hand."

She hurried out to the lot just in time to grab the door of the cargo hatch.

"Thanks," Audie grunted under the weight of the TV.

"Let me take one end."

"I think I can get it."

Beth couldn't tell if Audie was trying to push her away, or just trying to look tough, but when Audie started to struggle, she jumped in to help with the load. "I think your Grammaw's going to love this bigger one."

"Yeah, it was on sale for one twenty-nine. That's about two dollars a pound, just like hamburger."

Beth laughed, relieved at hearing Audie make a casual joke. "I can't believe you picked this up by yourself."

"Me neither." Audie balanced her end on her knee as she opened the glass door.

"Let's set it down here and I'll ask the movers to come get it when we're ready for it." Beth stood up straight and clutched her back. "They just took the bed down to the other room. I told them to leave the little TV where it was."

"Grammaw said somebody else could have it if they wanted it."

"That's nice of her. I bet Mr. Skelly would like having it in his room."

"I can carry it in there if you want."

"No, I'll get the movers to do it. Your grandmother's in the sunroom."

"I'll go say hi. I've got some more boxes in the car."

"Can I help?"

"Thanks, but I think I can manage." She started down the hallway toward the sunroom and stopped. "By the way . . . I thought about what you said . . . that part about letting Grammaw know it was okay for her to be sick."

"I'm sorry about that. I shouldn't have stuck my nose where it didn't belong."

"But you were right." Audie stepped closer again so she could lower her voice. "I guess I just thought if I kept acting like everything was okay, then it would be."

Beth could see how hard it was for her to talk about her grandmother's declining health. "Who am I to argue with the power of positive thinking? It sure is working on your grandmother. She's doing great here."

"I . . . you guys . . . I think she likes it here."

"I think she does too, but a big part of that is you coming by every day. When I bring her back from breakfast, it's like she can't wait to see you."

Audie's face lit up at first, but then she frowned. "Is she okay after I leave?"

"She's fine, Audie." Beth clutched Audie's shoulder and shook it gently. "Let us do the worrying, okay? We'll let you know if anything comes up."

Audie glanced at the hand on her shoulder. "Am I driving you crazy?"

Beth laughed, grateful for the change in mood, and dropped her hand. "No, but I'll let you know that too."

Audie grinned. "What are you doing here today? I thought you were supposed to be off until Wednesday."

"Glenda called in sick. She's going to trade me for next Saturday."

"Good deal. Hope you get to do something fun."

"So do I." More likely, her day off would involve house cleaning and errands. As Audie turned, Beth glimpsed for the first time part of a tattoo between the top of her low-slung jeans and the bottom of her T-shirt. Before she could make out what it was, Audie had sauntered down the hall.

Everything seemed back to normal between them again, like it had been a couple of weeks ago. Beth was immensely relieved to have their misunderstanding behind them, but she didn't understand why. All she knew was she wanted to be Audie Pippin's friend.

"I was wondering where you were," Violet said, giving Audie her best smile.

"I spent the night at Regan's. But I brought everything for your new room. Beth just helped me carry in the new TV."

"How's Regan?"

Grammaw knew most of her friends, but Audie had never talked much about her personal relationships, particularly with "special" friends like Regan. She had always been understanding and accepting when it came to Audie's sexual orientation, but that didn't mean Audie wanted to share details.

"She's good. She said to say hi. I heard you had a visitor yesterday afternoon."

"Dennis. Did he tell you he brought me flowers?"

"Yeah, and he said you hugged his neck. So then I hugged it too."

"He's a sweet boy."

Dennis was a perverted pothead, but her Grammaw did not need to know that. "Are you excited about your new room?"

"I can't wait."

"Oh, good! I found you both." Clara Cummings, the social worker, appeared in the doorway of the sunroom, a small stack of folders in her hand. "I hear they're getting your new room ready, Miss Violet."

"That's right."

"Maybe this would be a good time for us to talk and take care of some business."

Audie looked at her Grammaw and shrugged. "Sure."

"Why don't we go down to my office?"

Audie pushed the wheelchair down the hall, passing Beth again. This time, she flashed a wide smile. "Thanks again for your help."

"No problem," Beth said. "I'll come down later and check out the decorating."

They continued on to Clara's office, where she closed the door and took a seat behind her desk. Audie positioned the wheelchair in front of the desk and slumped into a chair by the window.

"Audie, your grandmother and I were talking the other day and she asked me some questions about finances that I thought the three of us should talk about together."

"Whatever . . . I can go get the checkbook if you want. It's in the car."

"No, we're okay about all that. We need to talk about some more serious things, starting with the house."

"The house?" Audie looked at her Grammaw and back at Clara.

"I'm advising your grandmother to sign her house over to you. You'll probably want an attorney to handle the transfer and register the new deed. I can recommend one."

"Why does she need to do that?"

"It's just part of planning ahead. It's always a good idea to go through these things when we're all feeling fine and getting along. That way, we have time to think things through and make the right decisions. And once they're made, we don't have to worry about them ever again."

"But what's the hurry?"

Violet took her granddaughter's hand. "Audie, it was my idea for us to talk about this. I just want to make sure you don't have to worry about your future."

"Miss Violet, I think you're being very smart to plan ahead like this," Clara said. "Audie, you have no idea how much heartache and chaos goes on when people don't answer these questions ahead of time."

Audie stood, wishing she hadn't sat near the window. She wanted to be by the door, where she could walk out without having to go through these questions.

"Sit down, hon. Your grandmother needs for you to deal with this. Up to now, she's been doing all the worrying by herself. Give her what she needs to let this go."

Audie sat back down, nervously wiggling her fingers to tamp down her agitation.

"I'm recommending the house transfer now so that you won't have to worry in the future about someone else trying to stake a claim."

"What?"

"She tells me that her daughter—your mother—might be out there somewhere. Now from what she says, you'll probably never see her again, but you'd be surprised how many people turn up when they sniff money."

"And she gets nothing from me!" Violet said, banging her good fist on the arm of the wheelchair for emphasis. "I want Audie to have everything."

"You'll need to spell that out in a will, Violet. The attorney can handle that for you, too." Clara pulled a business card from her desk drawer and passed it to Audie. "When you take over the house, you'll need to move all of the associated expenses into your name. That's also to keep people from making a claim against your grandmother."

Audie sighed.

"I have money in a CD, sweetheart. You can cash it in to pay for everything."

"I don't need money. I can pay the bills."

"I looked at the records, Audie. When the transfer goes through, they'll probably reassess the value of the house. Your tax bill might be a couple of thousand dollars next year. You have to plan for that."

"Whatever." Audie had sat through more than she cared to hear.

"It's a big deal to pay your taxes on time. If you don't, somebody can come along and take your house—and you won't get a dime for it."

"Audie can manage that." Grammaw took her hand and squeezed it tightly.

"I can see how much this is bothering you, Audie. Nothing we've talked about today means that we expect anything bad to happen. On the contrary, we're looking forward to having Miss Violet with us for a long time."

"I know."

"Then I need to ask you to bear with us so we can get through the rest of these decisions. Can you do that?"

Audie nodded, not even looking up.

"Okay." Clara pulled a form from the folder. "There's still the matter of this durable power of attorney. Your grandmother wants to give you the power to make all the decisions concerning her affairs, no matter what happens to her." She pushed the paper across the desk. "She's already signed it. It just needs your signature right where the arrow is."

Audie took the offered pen and scratched her name on the paper.

"Thank you. Now I know Beth Hester also mentioned to you the DNR form. This one doesn't have to be signed today, or any time, for that matter. But you two need to discuss what kind of action you want us to take in the event of cardiac or respiratory failure."

Audie swallowed hard. "Is there anything else?" Since she was still leaning forward, she could see the last form in the folder, labeled "Funeral Arrangements." She knew those were finalized back when Grampaw died, so there was nothing left to discuss.

"No, that's about it. Thanks for doing this, Audie."

"Yeah, at least it's over with."

"That's right. Just call that attorney and she'll get the paper-work going. There's really nothing else to it."

"Okay." Audie stood and grasped the handles on the wheel-chair, glad to finally be exiting the room, which had felt more like a torture chamber than an office. "I can't sign that DNR, Grammaw. Please don't ask me to."

Her keys and purse in hand, Beth stopped by Miss Violet's new room to admire the decorations. Audie had done a fantastic job hanging pictures and arranging knickknacks on the bookshelf she had brought from home. The new TV was now mounted on the wall, and Miss Violet watched comfortably from the adjustable recliner.

"This looks great, Miss Violet."

"It's like home, but without the dirty dishes."

"I told you you'd like it here."

"You just missed Audie."

"I bet she's tired. She worked hard today."

"It was a hard day for her all around, I think."

"I saw you both going in with Clara this morning. Was that tough?"

"It scares her to think about things."

"I'm sure it does, Miss Violet." Beth had seen that fear for herself when she followed Audie outside the first day. If there were some way to help out, even if it was just lending an ear, she would. But Audie seemed to have her own friends. "I'm leaving for the day. I just wanted to stop in and see your new home. You have a good night."

"I will."

Beth headed out through the front doors and squinted in the bright sunlight. As she put on her sunglasses, she spotted the familiar SUV still sitting on the lot. Audie had the cargo door open and was arranging the empty boxes. "Hey, need a hand with something?"

"Nah, just flattening these boxes. I thought I'd stop by the recycling center on the way home."

"I went by your Grammaw's room. You do good work."

"Thanks." Audie managed a feeble smile. "And thanks for moving her down there. It's nicer, and I bet it's quieter too."

"Anything's better than being across the hall from the laundry." Beth started for her car at the other end of the lot.

"Where are you off to?"

Startled by the question, she turned and lifted her sunglasses. "I was going to head home and do some reading for my class. What about you?"

"I thought I'd go get Buster and head out to Sumter Point. Want to come along?"

The invitation surprised her. It must have taken a lot for Audie to reach out like that, and the chance to lend support and friendship was exactly what Beth had wished for only moments ago. "Yeah, sure. I need to run home and change."

"Me too. Why don't we meet in the parking lot at the Point in half an hour?"

"See you then."

Chapter 6

Audie had no idea what Beth would be driving, but recognized her immediately when a blue Mazda Protégé pulled in next to her SUV. The car was several years old but appeared to be in good shape, its paint job still like new. "There she is, Buster. Be good."

Beth got out and clicked the lock on her car door. She was wearing sneakers, pressed white shorts and a sleeveless blue cotton shirt. Audie looked down at her own attire, sloppy by comparison—baggy khakis that hung just below her knees and a tank top.

"Been waiting long?"

"No, just a few minutes." Buster tugged on his leash to greet the new arrival. "Watch out for him. He likes to jump."

Beth approached slowly with her hand outstretched. "Hey there, Buster."

"He won't hurt you, but I don't want him to get your clothes dirty."

"It won't matter."

Audie hoped she was telling the truth, because as soon as Beth got close enough, the dog lunged upward, leaving dirty streaks down her front. "Buster, down!"

"It's okay," Beth assured, brushing her shirt and shorts in vain. "I should have warned you to wear old clothes."

"It's fine."

"He gets excited with new people . . . with all people, actually." She unhooked his leash and tossed a Frisbee across a grassy field.

"Nothing wrong with a friendly dog. Did you get him from the shelter?"

"Yeah, after Grampaw died." When Buster returned with the disk, Audie steered them toward the trail that ran alongside the Cumberland River. "Didn't I see you down at the shelter a few years ago?"

From the look on her face, Beth was thrown off-balance by the question. "You might have. I came in to pick out a dog."

"You were with somebody, I think. And you adopted a dog together."

Beth nodded. "A rat terrier."

"How's he doing?"

"It was a she. We called her Diva. I guess she's doing fine. I haven't seen her in a while."

"Your friend has her?"

Beth sighed. "If you mean the woman I came in with, yes. But she isn't a friend of mine anymore."

Beth's hostile tone seemed out of character, but it explained why she had said she spent her time at home alone, studying for exams. "An ex-friend, I guess."

"An ex, period." Beth sounded a little tentative at the admission. "You knew I was gay, didn't you?"

"I . . ." Audie bobbed her head all around, as if saying yes and no at the same time. "I thought maybe you were."

"In fact, you and I came to the same Fourth of July picnic right here in this park a few years ago."

Audie grinned. "I don't remember that one. Must have been a good party."

"We left early . . . Shelby and I. She got freaked out about being seen in public with a bunch of lesbians."

"Ah . . . paranoid."

"Among her other personality disorders." Beth shrugged. "She wasn't comfortable unless everyone around her was more miserable than she was."

"Hey, I just realized something. You're talking about Shelby Russell, aren't you?"

"Attorney-at-law, in case she didn't mention that part."

"I met her at a party once. I didn't really talk to her, but now I know why she looked so familiar."

"Because you saw her at the shelter?"

"I guess. I recognized you that day because I knew you were Kelly's sister. And I remembered you two getting the dog together, so I sort of assumed you were a couple." Audie tossed the Frisbee ahead for Buster. "I heard a story about her from one of my friends. He works at a finance company and he said she came in one day screaming that one of their Hispanic customers had just rammed her car. Dennis said they walked out to look at it. It was barely scratched, but she demanded they call the police. He said she was a real bitch, like she wasn't going to be satisfied unless this poor guy bought her a brand new car or got sent back to Mexico."

"Sounds like the Shelby I try to forget."

"Then you'll really like this part. When the police got there, they impounded her car because she had a bunch of outstanding parking tickets."

"Oh, that's rich."

"It's good to see assholes get what they deserve, isn't it?"

"Believe me, she deserves a lot worse than that." Beth laughed aloud. "But it's a good start."

"So how long were you two together?"

"About three years. We split up not long after we got Diva."

"How come she got to keep the dog?"

"It wasn't like we discussed it. I came home one day and found a For Sale sign in the yard. Diva was gone and so was Shelby and all her stuff."

"Ow! That's cold."

"It's pretty classic Shelby Russell. She always does it her way."

"I guess it's good to be rid of her then, huh?" Audie hadn't picked up on even a trace of sadness or disappointment.

"Absolutely! I don't even think I realized what a total control freak she was until she wasn't there anymore. All of a sudden, I had so many choices I didn't know what to do."

"So when are you coming in to get another dog?" She laughed as Beth rolled her eyes. "Hey, it's only fair. I patronize your business. You should patronize mine."

"I don't know about a dog. I think cats might be less trouble."

"Either one's good company. I'd have gone nuts at home by myself if I hadn't had Buster there."

The path grew narrow as it wound into the woods by the river, forcing Audie and Beth to walk closer together.

"Looks like I'm going to be a homeowner soon, at least for a little while."

"A little while?"

"Yeah, Grammaw said if I didn't want all the responsibility, I should sell it while the prices are up. Then I can get an apartment or something."

"I wouldn't do that if I were you. Sometimes I wish I had bought a house instead of a condo. I miss having a yard. And sharing a wall with people isn't very private."

"Yeah, that's the down side. I'm just not sure I want the hassle of taking care of everything. It's a lot more responsibility than I want to bite off right now, what with Grammaw sick and Oscar pushing me to take that new job I told you about."

"Oscar's your boss?"

"Yeah, he's the director at the shelter. Our board wants us to go to no-kill status, which means we keep every single animal that's fit to be somebody's pet until we find them a home. We all want to go that route, but we'll need to ramp up our programs to get people to adopt. Oscar wants me to take an outreach job, because I'm pretty good at talking people into taking animals home."

"I bet all your friends have a shelter pet, right?"

"No, I'm better than that. Most of my friends have two or three shelter pets."

"Uh-oh, something tells me I'm in trouble talking to you about this."

"I don't know about trouble, but you're at the top of my list when the next litter of kittens comes through the door." She gave Beth a satisfied grin. "And that will probably be tomorrow, so you might as well go home and get ready."

"You sure don't waste any time."

"Hey, you're the one that brought it up."

"So I did." Beth took the Frisbee from Audie's hand and gave it a feeble toss to Buster. "It sounds like you'd be good at a job like that. Are you going to take it?"

"I'm thinking about it. I could use the extra money if I keep the house and all. Like I said, I just wish everything wasn't happening all at the same time."

"You look like you're handling it all pretty well."

"My friends drag me out so I won't stay home and feel sorry for myself. You ever go the Gallery?"

"What's the Gallery?"

Audie couldn't believe her ears. "What kind of self-respecting lesbian doesn't know about the Gallery? It's a bar and dance club."

"Sorry, bars aren't my thing. I guess I didn't get the partying gene like some of us did." The mischievous smile she threw in at the last second saved her from Audie's usual defensive retort. "What do you like about it?"

"It's a fun atmosphere. Most of time, it's just a bunch of shameless guys looking to trick."

"If that was supposed to be a selling point, you lost me."

Audie chuckled. "Really, it's fun. They have drag shows and karaoke contests. And Friday is Ladies Night, which means more girls are there, but some of the guys dress in drag so they can get in for five bucks too." She saw the corners of Beth's mouth turn up. "Admit it. That sounds like fun."

Beth gave her what looked like a grudging nod. "Who do you usually go with?"

"Mostly my friend Dennis. Sometimes Joel and Dwayne."

"You don't have any . . . girl friends? I don't mean like . . . girl-friends. I mean . . . you know what I mean."

Beth's question caught her off-guard. She was surprisingly embarrassed, not wanting to admit the truth, that girlfriends to her were only fuck-buddies. "I know most of the girls there."

"But there's no one you're close to?"

"Some more than others. Nobody in particular." She knew she was being cryptic, but for some reason, confessing her sexual habits to Beth was as hard as talking to her Grammaw. Her usual strategy when things got too personal was to change the subject. "I really can't believe you've never even heard of the Gallery."

"Sometimes I feel like I've lived my whole life inside a bubble. I've never been much of a drinker, and at the risk of sounding like my parents, I'm not all that crazy about loud music either. You go in a place like that and you can't even talk to anybody."

"It does have a certain deleterious effect on conversation." For Audie, that was part of the appeal.

"Deleterious?" Beth scoffed. "Where did you get such a big word?"

Audie grinned. "I just threw that in to show off. You forget that Grammaw was a librarian. She made me learn a new word every week. I'm surprised she hasn't started on you too."

"I bet I could get you to take my nursing boards for me."

"That's next month, right?"

"October fifth. Two weeks from today."

"I'm sure you'll do great."

"If I don't, it won't be because I didn't put the time in. I feel like it's all I've done for the last year."

Buster suddenly took off, prompting Audie to sprint down the trail in pursuit. She cut through the woods at a turn in the trail, grabbing him by the collar before he snagged his prey, a furious brown squirrel. "No!"

"I bet he's a real prince around cats," Beth said.

"He's all right once he gets the introductions over with." Audie clipped the leash into place. "He just hadn't met that particular squirrel yet."

The trail's end was just ahead, a bluff overlooking the river. Already, several clusters of people were staking out their space to watch the sunset.

"Want to find a spot?" Audie hoped she would say yes, but she had caught Beth looking at her watch earlier.

"God, I can't remember the last time I stopped long enough to watch a sunset."

"Sounds like you're overdue then." She tugged Buster's leash and led the way to a grassy perch. "I try to come out here at least once a week. Sumter Point's one of my favorite places."

"It's beautiful. I was out here once with Shelby, but she wouldn't sit down because she was afraid of getting her pants dirty."

"She would have loved Buster." Audie scratched his head as he settled down. "It's prettier when there are a few clouds."

"I have a view off my balcony, but it's nothing like this. There's something pristine about a sunset where all you can see is water and trees."

"So if you like it so much, why you don't get out here more often?"

"I've just been busy with class. I'm supposed to be reading two chapters tonight for my class tomorrow night. I was going to do it today but I got called in."

They watched in silence as the sun disappeared behind the rolling hills. As it grew darker, the familiar, pungent odor of marijuana smoke drifted to where they sat. Without even realizing it, Audie closed her eyes and inhaled the scent.

"Is that what I think it is?" Beth asked.

"Mmmm . . . probably."

"People just . . . smoke that in public?"

"Not just anywhere. But you can't really see who it is."

Beth looked around the bluff with a scowl. "When you're a nurse, you don't think about people using drugs just to get high. Drugs are for saving lives and fighting pain."

Audie bit her tongue to keep from pointing out the virtues of marijuana. "I guess you haven't been around pot all that much."

"Maybe once or twice back in high school, but not since."

"Have you ever gotten high?"

Beth snorted. "You're kidding, right?"

Come to think of it, it was pretty farfetched to imagine Kelly Hester's big sister toking on a weed. "I just wondered."

"I never quite understood the appeal. Why would people want to do something that makes them feel out of control?"

"It's not out of control. It's . . ." Audie suddenly realized what she was admitting, but it was too late to stop now. "Sometimes it's nice to feel relaxed."

"I take it you smoke marijuana sometimes?"

Audie nodded, trying to appear casual. "Once in a while." Practically every night was more like it. In fact, if she had been here on her own, she would have searched out the source of that smell.

"Kelly had some trouble once back in high school, but I think she learned her lesson."

Audie recalled sharing a bong with Kelly and a couple of her friends at a party, but she knew better than to volunteer the memory. It was clear that Beth wasn't comfortable at all with the idea. Time to change the subject again. She stood and held out her hand to help Beth to her feet, gesturing at the pink sky. "Was it worth it?"

"Sure was. I need to make time for this."

"Like I said, I try to come at least once a week. You're welcome to join us whenever."

"Thanks. I might take you up on that." They started down the path toward the parking lot.

Audie was surprised to hear herself invite Beth along for future walks. This ritual was usually a quiet time for her to work out important decisions or just relax and enjoy the solitude. But she liked the idea of sharing this walk with Beth and getting to know her better. They connected pretty well, better in some ways than she and Dennis did. Of course, she was a different person with Beth than she was with Dennis. She doubted Beth would have much use for the partying and pot smoking she shared with some of her other friends. Beth was more like Joel and Dwayne, mature and responsible. But that didn't mean Joel and Dwayne weren't fun.

"What kind of class are you taking?"

"Geriatric care management. It's my last class and I thought it was going to be a breeze, but the woman who's teaching it buries us in work every week."

"You just go once a week?" She smiled to see Buster nuzzle Beth's hand for a pat, which she delivered.

"Seven to ten on Tuesdays. Can't you tell by the bags under my eyes on Wednesday morning?"

"I noticed those, but I figured you were up late doing something else . . . maybe something a little more fun." Audie enjoyed the blush that crept up Beth's neck.

"If that was a dig at me for commenting on your alcohol breath, it was pretty cheap." Beth poked her tongue in her cheek. "And way off base."

Audie threw her head back and laughed. "So no late nights fooling around and no drinking or loud music. What does that leave?"

"I go to movies sometimes," she said, sounding almost defensive. "But I guess I'm basically a homebody."

"Then that makes me an away-from-homebody."

"Are you out every night?"

"Not every night, but four or five nights a week. If I'm not at the Gallery, I'm usually at a friend's house or something. Or at somebody's party."

"It wears me out just to hear about it."

"You should come out with us one night. I guarantee you'd have fun."

They had reached the parking lot and Buster began tugging toward the Xterra.

"Thanks for asking me along on your walk."

It was hard not to notice that Beth had simply ignored her invitation, but she wasn't going to give up so easily. "I'm glad you came. Buster likes you, so you can come again whenever you like."

"I passed the Buster test, eh?"

"Don't knock it. Animals see things about people that the rest of us can't see." She opened the driver's door and the dog jumped inside, trying out every seat until he settled for shotgun. "I mean it about coming out with us. We don't do anything fancy, just a few drinks and laughs. And somebody always stays sober to drive home."

"Maybe after my boards."

"We'll celebrate."

"I'll definitely be ready to drink to that."

Beth stretched to grab the portable phone, which she always brought with her when she soaked in the tub. "Hello."

"My long lost friend!"

"Ginger! God, I was wondering if I was ever going to hear from you again."

"Yes, I've come up for air."

"I'm not sure I want to know what that means."

"It means I wish I'd met Mallory about ten years ago. I would never have given Tonya a second look."

"But then you would never have met me."

"I knew there had to be a cosmic master plan for all that suffering. Where were you all day?"

"I worked for Glenda. But she's working for me on Saturday."

"Good! You can have lunch with me. Mallory has to work eight to four."

"Where can we go that serves second bananas?"

"Funny, Beth. When you meet somebody and drop me like yesterday's horoscope, I'll be sure to pout too."

"Oh, stop. I'm not pouting. I just missed you is all."

"I've missed you too. What have you been up to?"

"Studying my tail off."

"See? You haven't even had time to miss me. But now it's time for you to take a break, woman."

"I'm having a break right now. I'm warm and naked . . . and wet." Beth rolled her eyes, not believing those words had come out of her mouth.

"I know you. That means you're in the tub. You need some real action."

"Like what?"

"Like come with Mallory and me on Friday night to Nashville. It's Ladies Night at a dance club called the Gallery."

What were the chances two people who didn't even know each other would make an invitation like that on the same day? Freaky. Or maybe it was that cosmic master plan. Either way, if she went to a place like the Gallery, she didn't want to go as a third wheel. "It so happens you're the second person today to invite me to the Gallery."

"Who was the first?"

"Audie Pippin. We took a walk out to Sumter Point today and talked about a bunch of stuff. She mentioned that she goes there a lot."

"Audie . . . the hot chick you called a baby dyke?"

"I did not call her a baby dyke. I said she still looked like a teenager, and she does. Besides, it wasn't like she was asking me out or anything like that. She just offered to have me come along with her and her friends."

"So are you going?"

"No." Beth almost laughed aloud at Ginger's dramatic sigh. "You know how much I hate bars."

"When have you ever been in one?"

"I went to that one with you in Atlanta."

"That was a pool hall. The Gallery is a dance club. And Ladies Night means you might even get lucky."

"Yeah, right! Audie says half the women are really drag queens. My luck I'd go home with one of them."

"You could always go with a date, you know. If you don't want to go with Audie, Mallory has a few friends who are—"

"Hold it, Ginger." Beth sat up in the tub, her relaxed mood crumbling. "I really am happy you've found something special with Mallory. You believe that, don't you?"

"Of course."

"Then believe this too, because I really mean it. I'm not the least bit interested in meeting anybody right now. I've got too much on my plate to worry about somebody else."

"So if that's the case, what's with you and Audie Pippin?"

"Nothing."

"But you're out strolling with her down by the river."

"Yes, but that was sort of spontaneous. We were walking out of the nursing home together and she said she was going and asked me if I wanted to go too." She pulled the plug on the tub and began to wipe the soap film from the sides as it drained.

"And then she asked you to come to the Gallery."

"Yes, but that doesn't mean—"

"You may not think it means anything, but it sounds to me like Audie might be interested."

For reasons she couldn't imagine, Beth broke into an embarrassed grin. "That's just . . . absurd. We're not even from the same planet."

"Why is it so absurd? If you were interested in someone, wouldn't you ask her to do things with you? What did you guys talk about?"

"We always talk about—" Beth started to say Audie's grandmother, but she realized they hadn't discussed Miss Violet at all today. "Today, we talked about dogs and houses and jobs . . . nothing too personal." But then she related the secondhand story about Shelby.

"If you two talked about Shelby, I'd call that personal."

"No, Shelby's name only came up because Audie asked about Diva. She works at the animal shelter, you know."

"What I know is that you're either not paying attention or you're holding out on your best friend."

"I am not holding out! There's nothing to hold out. Audie seems like a nice person and I'll admit she's hot to look at. But she's also a party animal and she probably thinks I'm an old maid."

"You're not that much older."

"It's not just our age, Ginger. Nine years isn't all that much. But we're at totally different places in our lives. I'm thinking about my next career move and she's thinking about her next drink."

"Would you go out with her if she asked you?"

"She would never ask me. I'm nowhere near her type." Beth shivered as she climbed out of the empty tub.

"Okay, you win. You've obviously got this all figured out."

"I don't have anything figured out." Beth was irritated at her friend's attitude, and couldn't keep the sharpness out of her voice. "But I know myself better than you do."

"Okay, I said. No need to make a federal case out of it. I just thought you might appreciate having a friend that cared about you."

Beth sighed. Ginger could be quite the drama queen. "I'm sorry. You know I appreciate you. I just felt like you weren't going to let it go, no matter what I said. If there was something there to tell, I would. There's nothing there. And that's fine by me, because I have enough to do right now."

"I'm sorry too. I know you're stressed and I didn't mean to add to it. I still want to have lunch with you on Saturday."

"Now that, my friend, is a date."

They said goodbye and Beth dabbed the few remaining drops of water from her skin. How could any sane person think somebody like Audie Pippin would find her interesting? They had virtually nothing in common, and Audie could have practically anyone she wanted . . . and she probably did, Beth figured. Besides, Audie seemed like the kind of person who wanted to keep her life simple—the house, the job—so why would she want to complicate things with a relationship?

Chapter 7

Beth entered Miss Violet's room with her medical chart, not bothering to mask her concern. "What's this I hear about you having trouble breathing?"

"Just a little," Violet answered, as though she hated to be a bother. She was dressed in her housecoat and sitting in the new recliner.

"When did it start?" The third shift charge nurse had made her notes at four thirty this morning, but Beth guessed that Miss Violet waited before calling for help.

"Last night, after supper."

"And you didn't tell anyone until four thirty this morning?" She took out her blood pressure cuff and wrapped it around Miss Violet's arm. "You can't wait that long. If there's something wrong, we want to fix it as soon as possible."

"Okay."

Beth recorded the vital signs in Miss Violet's chart. "I'm going to make a note for Francine to call Dr. Hill. He may want to see you."

"But I'm all right now."

"It's just a precaution. I can't let anything happen to my favorite patient." She squeezed Miss Violet's hand, recognizing the truth of her words. "I'll talk to Audie when she comes in and let her know what we plan to do. In the meantime, I think we ought to bring this chair forward a little so you can breathe better."

"Beth! Come quick! Mr. Skelly fell over in his breakfast." Wanda, an LPN like Beth, but with only two years on the job, looked frantically at Violet, then back at Beth.

"What?"

"I think he's . . ." She waved her hand to fill in the blank.

Beth got the message. "Go ahead and finish raising this up, Miss Violet. I'll come back and check on you. I promise."

Quickly, she followed Wanda to Mr. Skelly's room. "Where's Francine?"

"Carla said she was on a break. She had to run home real quick."

"How could she leave with Hazel at the county office?" Beth rushed into the room to find Mr. Skelly just as Wanda had described—his face in his oatmeal, and probably dead.

"She said she'd be right back."

Beth rolled her eyes in disbelief. Hazel and Francine were the only RNs on staff during the day. With both gone, there was no hierarchy to make decisions or to handle emergencies. Right this minute, Beth was the senior staffer just by virtue of having been there the longest.

Taking charge, she tilted Mr. Skelly back in his recliner and rolled the portable tray aside. A quick check of his pupils showed them to be unresponsive, and he had no pulse.

"Should I get his paperwork?"

"No, it isn't necessary." There was no Do Not Resuscitate order for Mr. Skelly—that she knew for sure. He wasn't ready to leave this earth, he had told her. He had even threatened Beth that he would come back to haunt her if he died on her shift. "Get the crash cart and have somebody call nine one one."

Wanda ran to do as she was told.

"Hang on, Mr. Skelly." She checked the old man's airway and unbuttoned his shirt. Then she wiped his chest with a towel in preparation for applying the pads.

Wanda returned, pushing the emergency cart. "Francine just got back. She's calling the family."

"She's the nurse, for Christ's sake! You go call the family and tell her to get her butt in here!" Beth was confident she could perform this procedure, but she wasn't the right person to be in charge of a critical situation.

She turned on the machine and affixed the pads to Mr. Skelly's chest. She was attaching the lines when Francine finally came in.

"His family says not to resuscitate."

"It's not their call," Beth said sharply. "He doesn't have a DNR. We have to do this."

Francine stepped forward and took over, albeit begrudgingly. "It's not like anybody would complain if we didn't."

After two unsuccessful jolts, the paramedics arrived and loaded Mr. Skelly into an ambulance, where he would be transported to the emergency room and likely declared dead. And by tonight, another family would be elated to learn that a bed was opening up.

"Beth, I . . ." Francine ran her hand through her hair, exasperated at the morning's events. "You were right about the DNR. I just . . . I was talking to his son last week and they were going to talk to the old man about it. I thought maybe they did already."

"He never would have agreed to it."

"Figures. He was too mean to die."

"I think he was just scared. But it doesn't matter, I guess."

"You know"—Francine nodded toward the double doors at the entry, where Hazel was pulling into her parking place near the entrance—"if Hazel finds out I wasn't here, I'll probably lose my job."

"You should lose your job, Francine. You knew she was gone,

and there was nobody here who was qualified to deal with emergencies like that."

"I know, but I was only gone for twenty minutes. I ran home and changed clothes because I got my period. I couldn't work like that all day."

Beth sighed. "You should have at least told me."

"I know. I made a mistake."

Francine was a decent nurse, not exceptional, but decent. Beth knew they could do a lot worse, but today was a classic example of why Francine shouldn't be given any more administrative duties. "I won't volunteer anything, but if Hazel asks me, I won't lie to her."

"That's all I can ask, Beth. I owe you one."

Audie opened the crate and reached inside with caution. The feral tomcat didn't care for his confines, nor did he appreciate being touched.

"Easy, boy." Deftly, she clutched the scruff of his neck and dragged his stiffened frame through the door. For a cat that had scraped his meals from dumpsters, he was gorgeous. He had the face and build of a small Siamese, but his coat was silky black. Audie guessed him to be about eight months old. "Now go play," she said with sarcasm, unable to imagine this one doing anything playful.

Audie yawned and rolled her neck to loosen up. For the first time in what seemed like a year, she had fallen asleep in front of the TV last night. It wasn't that the show was boring, or even that she was overly tired. It was that smooth, mellow, leg-numbing, consciousness-thieving bag of some of the finest stuff she had ever smoked.

Bless Dennis.

Though the couch had certainly seemed comfortable at the time, it was exacting its toll today. She had looked for Beth this morning to snag a couple of aspirin, but there was some kind of emergency going on and she hadn't even gotten to say hello.

Beth Hester. Audie had been thinking about her a lot lately, especially since that night Beth had called and gotten on her case about her attitude toward her Grammaw's condition. Until yesterday, she had been avoiding Beth at the nursing home, trying to get up the nerve to tell her she had been right. That realization came to her a few days after the call when she caught herself arguing with her Grammaw to do her physical therapy even when it hurt. Definitely time for a reality check.

The walk out to Sumter Point had been revealing, not only because Beth had talked so openly about herself, but also because Audie had practically hung on her every word. Beth wasn't like her other friends, the ones she knew from the Gallery or from parties in Sumter. Beth was more down to earth and not so full of herself. It could be fun to introduce her around a bit—though probably not to the wilder crowd.

The familiar tune of her cell phone interrupted her thoughts. Without even looking, she knew it would be Dennis, and that he expected to be congratulated for his acquisition.

"Good afternoon, Mr. Bell."

"It's about time you showed me some respect."

"For once, I agree."

"Nice, wasn't it?"

Audie leaned out the doorway and saw Oscar at his desk down the hall. Tim was out hosing down the dog runs, so she didn't have to worry about being overheard. "It rendered me incapable of movement or thought."

"No shit. So you want to go the Gallery tonight?"

She collected the litter pan and food bowls and set them aside so she could wipe out the black cat's crate. "I don't know. What's happening?"

"Nothing special. I saw somebody the other night and we didn't get a chance to talk. I was hoping he'd be there tonight."

"Since when do you need to talk to somebody?"

"Come on, Audie. You give me shit all the time for tricking. Now I'm trying to get to know somebody and you're still giving me shit."

"Whoa! I didn't know this was your future husband."

"You're such an asshole. When was the last time you talked about something other than whose turn it was to wear the strap-on?"

The idea of Dennis actually having an emotional relationship with somebody was a difficult concept to grasp. But there was no denying he had her number too.

"All right, I take your point. What time?"

"The usual. Out at nine, back by midnight."

"You mean out at nine, back by one thirty."

"Whatever. Gotta go with the flow. But it's your turn to drive."

"Fine, I'll pick you up." She lifted the feral cat and stroked his slender neck, careful to avoid his nips, which seemed more annoyed than playful. Eventually, he surrendered, turning his head so that she scratched him just right. "And wear that pink shirt. It makes you look sensitive."

"Suck me."

"Ewww!"

Beth was heading out the door for the day when Hazel blocked her path.

"Isn't there something you need to tell me about?" the director asked.

Beth got a sinking feeling in her gut that the news of the day had already reached her boss's desk. "Probably nothing you don't know by now."

Hazel chuckled and gestured toward her office. She followed Beth through the door and closed it. "I heard it all from Wanda. I haven't talked with Francine yet. She's going to get a reprimand in her file."

Beth nodded and sat down on the love seat. Hazel joined her and offered the candy dish. As usual, Beth couldn't resist taking a chocolate bar. "I think she'll be relieved with that. She thought she might lose her job."

"No, and she has you to thank for that."

"Because I covered for her?"

"Hell, no. I still would have fired her." Hazel kicked off her shoes and put her feet on the coffee table. "But I'm stuck with Francine until you graduate, so don't go screwing around and flunking your boards."

"Oh, great. Just what I need—more pressure."

"You need any time off to study?"

Beth shook her head quickly. "No, just work as usual. If I have too much time I'll start freaking out."

"You have a big advantage going in, you know that?"

No, Beth didn't know that at all. Everyone else in her nursing class was calm and collected and she was a nervous wreck. "How do you figure that?"

"Just think of all the regulations and procedures you come in contact with here. You know things because you use them every week, not because you read them in a book. When you come to a question you don't know the answer to, just close your eyes and see yourself doing it."

"I wish it was that easy."

"It is . . . or at least it will be for you. I worked as an LPN for four years before I took the boards. You wouldn't believe how much of the test was practical."

"I sure hope you're right. I just need to review a little bit every night, and not overdo it."

"Sounds like a good plan. So what's up with Violet Pippin?"

"I don't know. She said she had trouble breathing so I asked Francine to call Dr. Hill. He'll be by in the morning."

"Will you try to be there for that?"

"With Francine?"

"Instead of Francine. You can make the chart notes, and you're better with the patients . . . especially the ones that know what's going on."

"Miss Violet definitely knows what's going on."

"What about her granddaughter? She was quite the grouch, as I recall."

"To put it mildly. But Audie's better now. I found out that her grandfather got questionable care in an Alzheimer's facility in Nashville, so I don't blame her for being vigilant."

"She's happy with us then?"

"I think so. Miss Violet likes it here, and Audie seems to be satisfied."

"Good." Hazel stood and opened the office door. "Thanks again for being there today. You saved all our asses, you know."

Beth shrugged. "Except Mr. Skelly's."

"Those we can't always save."

"You're putting a hold on the Black Demon?" Oscar saw the note on the feral cat's crate.

"Yeah, a friend of mine was thinking about getting a cat. I think BD's a pretty good match."

"I hope she has plenty of Band-Aids."

"He's calmed down a little today. Watch this." Audie opened his crate and reached in to scratch his head. In an instant, he lunged at her finger and she pulled it back out. "See? No blood. He's ready to make somebody a nice pet."

Oscar tilted his head, clearly unimpressed.

"Really, I had him out earlier and he let me pet him. I think he's ready to come around."

"That's good news for him. His time's up on Friday."

"He'll be a lap cat by then."

"If you tame BD, you deserve a medal."

"I'll take a raise instead," Audie said, knowing already what Oscar would say.

"You'll get a raise when you take the outreach job."

"There is no outreach job."

"That's going to change real soon." Oscar looked around to make sure no one else was within earshot. "Roy Lee said they got the major gift they've been after and they invited the press to come to their October board meeting."

"That soon?"

"I saw the declaration myself."

"I guess this is really it, then."

"I won't be surprised if they start building on by the end of next month."

"How many more techs are they going to hire? One of Dennis's friends is looking for a job."

"Probably two new ones and somebody to replace you. Tell whoever it is to get in here and fill out an application. Your new job starts up in December."

Audie caught that "your job" part, but didn't bother to object this time. The more she thought about it, the more she realized it was an opportunity she couldn't afford to pass up. Somebody needed to move these animals, or the whole concept of a no-kill shelter would fall flat. With Oscar's support, she was growing more confident she could do it. And there was certainly nothing wrong with making more money.

Beth opened her eyes to check the clock. Ten after one, only fifteen minutes since her last peek.

All evening, she had sat through her class, her head miles away. She couldn't seem to quiet her thoughts.

It wasn't unusual for her to be distracted and lose sleep after a patient died, nor was it particularly troubling. She was glad that, after witnessing dozens of deaths at the nursing home, she was still moved by the profundity of the passing of a human being from this world. It saddened her that Mr. Skelly had been alone, both in his moment of death and in his final years of life. Perhaps her sorrow tonight was him keeping his vow to haunt her.

Violet Pippin was on her mind too, specifically, her problems with shortness of breath. The worst-case scenario was that she had suffered another small stroke, one that affected her lungs. At least Dr. Hill was coming in tomorrow morning. Maybe he would find just a simple respiratory ailment, something they could ease with medication.

It was normal for her to process a patient's death, but it wasn't like Beth to bring home problems like Miss Violet's. As a health care professional, she wanted to be concerned but detached, lest she lose the objectivity she needed to make sound decisions. In this case, her anxiety about Miss Violet's condition seemed as personal as it did professional. She had worried all evening about the fact that, in the commotion surrounding Mr. Skelly's death, she had missed telling Audie about the problem and how they were going to address it.

She had tried to call Audie several times, but never got through. This wasn't the sort of news one left on an answering machine, but Audie was probably going to be upset not to hear about it sooner. More than anything else, it was worry about her reaction that was keeping Beth awake tonight.

Audie looked over at Dennis and smiled. He was slumped in the front seat, too low for the safety restraints to do him any good. If they suddenly had an accident, the seat belt would probably rip his head off. He was out of it, the victim of his evil weed.

Audie had waved off the offer of a toke this time, knowing it would kick her ass and make it hard for her to drive. She had contented herself with deep breaths of the sweet aroma as Dennis had smoked the whole joint by himself, except the roach, which he left in her ashtray with a half dozen others.

She couldn't wait until tomorrow so she could bust his chops about his puppy love display at the Gallery. The object of his infatuation was David, a nice-looking architect who seemed equally enchanted. All night, the two of them had danced and talked, their smiles never broken.

The earth might stop turning on its axis if Dennis Bell ever actually fell in love. Or Audie Pippin, for that matter. Though she ragged on Dennis without mercy for his insatiable sexual appetite, she understood and identified with his aversion to serious relationships. It was hard to see the appeal of having the same person in your face day after day, and in your bed night after night.

Joel and Dwayne seemed to have a healthy relationship, but they were older than most of her friends, and theirs was the exception rather than the rule. From what she saw around her, the norm for relationships was more along the lines of what Beth had described with Shelby Russell. Two people hooked up. Then one turned into a gigantic human asshole and shit all over the other one. Where was the appeal in that?

"Wake up, Tinkerbell. You're home."

Dennis opened his eyes and looked about to get his bearings. "Already?"

"I've been driving around all night, dickhead. You have to be at work in two hours."

"Don't fuck with me, Audie. You know how I am when I'm fucked up."

"It's a quarter after one. If you go straight to bed, you might be conscious by seven thirty."

Dennis groaned and got out of the SUV. "Do you have anything to eat?"

"You're not really hungry. It's your brain playing a trick on your mouth. Just go to bed."

He nodded and shut the door. Audie waited at the curb until he disappeared through the door of his first-floor apartment. She had planned on smoking a joint once she got home, but she wouldn't need it tonight. Not that she ever really needed it. It was just a nice way to relax. But tonight, she was too tired to truly appreciate it. And that stuff was too good to waste by falling asleep.

Chapter 8

Audie crammed the last half of the powdered donut into her mouth and wiped her hand on her shirt, leaving a smudge of confectioners' sugar on her chest. Ever since Beth's comment about her Grammaw thinking she was skinny, she had been trying to eat better . . . or at least eat more. It was paying off, she thought. Her ribs were no longer visible, which was good. But she was getting a slight pooch in her stomach, which was bad.

If she were honest with herself, the real reason for the recent weight gain was the late-night munchies she got from smoking pot before bed. She was doing more of that now that Grammaw wasn't at home. If she didn't get a grip on it soon, she would be as big as a house.

With that in mind, she folded the top of the bag over to take the remaining donuts in to a certain nurse. Beth looked fit and healthy, so she could probably burn those extra calories off in no time. Audie had noticed the other day at the river that the muscles in Beth's legs and shoulders were well-defined, almost like an athlete's. Her own legs had long since lost the muscle tone she had when she played basketball. The only real exercise she got these days was through her work activities or playing Frisbee with Buster.

Audie smiled as she entered the building and heard a chorus of staffers down the hallway singing "Happy Birthday" to one of the residents in the sunroom. She continued in the other direction to her Grammaw's room.

"Sounds like you're missing somebody's birthday party down in the—"

She stopped short, her knees nearly buckling at the sight of the oxygen tank and hose that looped around her grandmother's head and into her nostrils.

"What is this? What's wrong?"

Beth rushed through the door. "I just saw your car. I tried to catch you—"

"What the hell is all this?"

"Audrey!" Violet gasped harshly.

"It's just to help her breathe," Beth explained calmly. "Dr. Hill came by this morning and checked her out. He believes she has a mild bronchial infection. He gave her a shot and prescribed antibiotics."

"But it's serious enough that she needs oxygen?"

"He just thought it would help her feel better."

Audie started to relax. "So she's okay . . . except for a little infection?"

"That's right." Beth started to back away. "Can I see you out here in the hall for a minute?"

"Sure." Audie followed her and leaned against the wall.

"I just wanted to tell you I was sorry for not talking to you sooner. We had so much going on here yesterday that you were gone before I knew it."

"Yesterday?" Audie could feel a swell of anger inside, but she tried to maintain her cool. "This happened yesterday and I'm just now finding out?"

Beth nodded casually, not grasping the seriousness of Audie's reaction. "It was reported on the overnight shift, and I had Francine put in a call to Dr. Hill yesterday afternoon."

"I can't believe you didn't tell me this! What the fuck were you thinking?"

"Audie, we had it under control."

"I don't give a shit what you had under control! You should have at least told me. I'm her only family, for God's sake." Audie could see the resentment building on Beth's face, but she didn't care. Beth had promised to take care of Grammaw and to keep her informed every step of the way. "What if something had happened?"

"There was a problem and we took care of it." Beth's voice was like jagged ice. "The reason you were not informed was because we had an emergency yesterday while you were here. One of our patients went into cardiac arrest and that usually takes precedence over family updates."

Audie started to interrupt but Beth held up her hand and continued in a clipped tone.

"I tried to call you at work yesterday but you were busy. I did not leave a message because I thought it was something we should talk about directly. Then I called you at home last evening, both before and after my class, and you did not answer. The best I could do under the circumstances was talk to you this morning."

No explanation was good enough for Audie as she imagined the possibilities of what might have happened. "I have a right to be informed about things. You're the ones that made me sign the goddamned power of attorney. I'm supposed to make the important decisions, not you."

"Should we have held off on calling the doctor until we got your official permission, or can you trust us to do our jobs?"

"If this is how you do your jobs, maybe Grammaw needs to be somewhere else."

"If you aren't satisfied with our care, then perhaps you should look into other arrangements."

Audie posed defiantly with her hands on hips as Beth spun and walked away.

"Come here." The raspy voice was her Grammaw's.

She returned to the room and knelt next to her grandmother, inspecting the workings of the tank and the tube. "I can't believe they didn't tell me about this."

"Audie, I'm ashamed of you. You weren't raised to speak to people like that."

"I'm sorry, Grammaw. It's just that sometimes you have to use rough language to get people's attention. They had no right to—"

"Be quiet and listen." She looked directly into Audie's eyes as she spoke. "I will not stand for you to talk to Beth that way, especially on my behalf. She treats me with care and respect and she deserves to be treated that way by you."

In her twenty-two years with her Grammaw, Audie had learned when it was best not to open her mouth. This was one of those times.

"I will not consent to be moved to another place, and if I ever hear you say that again, I'll tear up that power of attorney and sign it over to Clara Cummings. Do you understand me?"

"Yes, ma'am."

"I'm through talking to you today. Go on home, and don't come back until you've apologized to Beth."

Audie stormed out, her face burning with both anger and humiliation. She couldn't believe her grandmother was actually taking Beth's side. She was just trying to stay on top of things so something bad wouldn't happen like it had to Grampaw.

Beth helped Mr. Wortman from his wheelchair to the bath chair and secured him with the straps. When he was in position, she pressed the controls to submerge him into a whirlpool tub.

"Does the water feel good, Mr. Wortman?"

The elderly man was non-verbal, but nodded his head without making eye contact.

Satisfied he was comfortable, she busied herself with folding a basket of towels fresh from the dryer. It was mindless, allowing her too much time to dwell on her confrontation with Audie.

Beth had expected Audie to be upset, but nothing had prepared her for the vicious outburst. Clearly, she was mistaken to have assumed their budding friendship had earned her a modicum of trust. If Audie didn't trust her to care for Miss Violet, she probably didn't trust anyone. And reaching out to her to prove otherwise would only set up more unreasonable expectations.

She felt awful.

If Audie made good on her promise to move her grandmother, it would be even worse. Miss Violet was happy, and she was thriving here as best she could.

Beth knew she had screwed up this time. That's why she hadn't been able to sleep last night. No matter how personally insulting it had been to listen to Audie's diatribe, she needed to apologize for not following up. She also needed to get off her high horse and start behaving like the professional Hazel expected her to be. She should have gone to look for Audie as soon as the situation with Mr. Skelly had been settled. At the very least, she should have left a message at her work. That would have been better than this.

Anything would have been better than this.

Audie rapped her knuckles on her boss's door. "Hey, Oscar. Is it okay if I leave early, say . . . in about ten minutes?" It was only three o'clock.

Oscar dropped his pen and looked up. "You might as well. Your head hasn't been here all day."

"Sorry."

"Something up with your Grammaw?"

"Nothing all that serious, really. She just had a little trouble breathing."

"Well go on if you need to. Just make a note on your time card. And tell her I said to feel better soon, okay?"

"I will." She felt guilty leaving Oscar with a false impression. "Oscar, I . . ."

"What is it?"

"Just . . . I lost my temper out at the nursing home this morning and pissed off a few people, including Grammaw. The reason I need to leave early is to go make it right."

"Okay."

"And I need to take BD. I'll see that he's neutered and gets all his shots this week."

"I hope you're not using that demon as some kind of peace offering."

"Yeah, actually I am."

"You know somebody that likes bloody scratches and bite marks?"

Audie shrugged. "We'll see. If it doesn't work out, I'll keep BD myself."

Beth was shocked to see the yellow Xterra parked next to her car in the lot of the nursing home. As she approached, Audie got out and came around to the back.

"Audie, I'm sorry."

"No, I'm the one that's sorry. I'm an asshole. Even my own Grammaw thinks so."

"You are not. You're just worried about her and I don't blame you."

"No, she's right. I've been thinking about it all day." Audie's look was truly contrite. "The truth is, I haven't worried about her at all since she came here. I know she's getting the best care possible, and we owe that to you."

"No, it's not just me."

"But you're the one I trust. And I was way out of line with everything I said this morning. I guess I was just scared or something because I didn't expect it."

Beth walked closer and put her hand on Audie's shoulder. "I appreciate you coming back today to tell me. I've had an awful day thinking about it."

"Me too."

"But I have to apologize too. I should have kept trying to reach you or I should have left a message or something. You shouldn't have had to find out about it that way. I know it must have scared you half to death."

"I overreacted. I guess I—"

"That's enough. You're forgiven. I hope I am." Beth was thrilled to get a warm smile in response. "So how come you're not still at work?"

Audie drew a deep breath. "I had to make a delivery."

Beth was both surprised and intrigued when she felt Audie's firm hand press against the center of her back to guide her around to the passenger side of the Xterra.

"Remember that I told you I'd let you know when I got in a cat that I thought was right for you?"

"A cat?" Beth didn't remember actually saying yes . . . but she hadn't said no either.

Audie opened the car door and turned a blue plastic crate to the side so its contents could be seen—a small black cat with wide yellow eyes. "He was found in a dumpster behind the grocery store."

Beth leaned closer to peer into the crate. "This isn't a joke, is it? You really brought me a cat."

"It's not a joke. He needs somebody special to see past his wild side. There's a sweetheart in there, I promise you."

Beth fingered the edge of the crate, causing the cat to hiss. "I don't think he likes me."

"He's just afraid. Give him a little time."

"What's his name?"

"We call him BD, but you can name him whatever you like."

"What does BD stand for?"

Audie gave her a sheepish look. "Baby Doll?"

"Now why don't I believe you?" Beth peered back into the crate and started to smile. "I don't know what you've gotten me into, but no way am I taking BD home by myself. You're coming with me."

Audie grinned in return. "You've got yourself a deal. I need to stop off and pick up a litter box and some food."

Beth reached into her purse. "Let me give you some money."

"I'll get it. With all the business I send their way, they'll give me a discount."

"Do you know where Rock Creek is?"

Audie nodded.

"Building C. Upstairs on the left, number five."

"I'm thirty minutes behind you. First I have to go say hi to Grammaw . . . and tell her that I apologized and you're not mad at me anymore."

"Tell her I did the same."

As promised, Audie arrived at Rock Creek thirty minutes later. She tucked the large plastic bag of cat supplies under one arm and grabbed the crate with the other. BD hissed in response to being moved.

"Chill, BD. Your new mother's nice. You're going to end up fat and lazy, and probably sleeping in her bed. You could do a lot worse."

As she climbed the stairs, she heard the door above her open.

"Are you ready for your new baby?" she asked.

"Ready as I'll ever be." Beth led her into the condo and closed the door behind her.

Audie glanced around at the décor and a single word popped into her head: neat. Everything was in perfect order all through the kitchen, the dining area, the living room, even the porch, which she could see through the sliding glass door. She would have said comfortable, but it looked almost as though no one lived here.

"This is nice."

"Thank you. I've had it for a couple of years."

Her guy friends would replace the beige walls and carpets with vibrant colors, and toss out the traditional upholstered furniture for something made of modular cubes. None of it mattered to Audie. A sofa was to sit on, not to look at.

"Okay, where do you want his litter box?"

"In the guest bathroom, I suppose. I hate to subject my company to it, but I'd hate it worse in the master bath."

"Good thinking." She clipped the plastic parts together and handed it to Beth. "Put it where you want it and I'll fill it up."

When they were finished, they returned to the living room, where BD cowered in his crate.

"The first thing we should do is feed him so he associates being here with something he likes." She opened a small can and put it in the plastic bowl she had bought. "And his dining room will be where?"

"The kitchen floor."

"Ah, the best table in the house." She set the bowl down and started for the crate. "You ready to meet your new baby?" All along, she had noticed Beth sneaking peeks at BD.

Audie opened the crate and reached inside to pull the cat out. She held him close to her chest and stroked his neck as she talked softly. "He might feel more secure in the crate for a while, so don't be worried if he runs back inside. You can set it next to your bed if you want him to get used to being with you."

Beth reached out to gently scratch BD beneath his chin. "Is that purring I hear?"

"Barely."

"He's adorable. Do you think he'll let me hold him?"

"It's going to take him a little while, but I know he'll come around." She set him on the floor between them and rested a hand lightly on his back to keep him from running off. BD trembled, his eyes wide with fright.

Beth began to stroke his head. He was perfectly still, but Audie could see that he was far from relaxed. Suddenly he swiped at Beth's fingers.

"Ow! He scratched me."

Audie took Beth's hand in hers and turned it over, inspecting it for blood. "He didn't break the skin. That means he likes you." Still holding Beth's hand, she used it to stroke BD softly. "You can't let him reject you. Stay after him and he'll eventually give in. He just needs to be sure you won't hurt him."

"How old is he?"

"About eight months, I think. His teeth are clean." Audie was growing self-conscious about having her hand on Beth's while they both petted the cat but she liked the way it felt. "By the way, he needs to be neutered and get his shots this week, so if you want, I'll take him to the vet for you."

"Will he have to stay?"

"No, but he won't be very happy when he comes home."

"He doesn't seem very happy now."

"He will be. I promise. I wouldn't have brought him for you if I thought he wouldn't like you. And I know you're going to fall in love with him."

"Poor thing. I bet he really is a sweetheart."

"When he starts to trust you, you won't be able to get away from him. He'll be in your lap whenever you sit down, sprawled in the middle of your Sunday paper, and probably asleep on your pillow."

"But only if I spoil him."

"You won't be able to stop yourself."

"Does Buster sleep on your pillow?"

"No, he sleeps on a rug beside my bed. He likes to be close."

"So all I have to do is train BD to sleep in his crate."

Audie laughed. "Get serious. He's a cat. They train you, not the other way around."

"Something tells me I'm in trouble."

"I'll help you with anything you need. And if things don't work out, I'll even come get him. But I know they will. He's going to like it here, and he's going to be your boy real soon."

"I hope you're right."

She didn't want to let go of Beth's hand but this was getting ridiculous. "Let's show him where his food is." On their hands and knees, they steered him into the kitchen toward a bowl, where he tentatively began to nibble. "So how about it? You want me to take him to Dr. Martin's tomorrow morning? You can pick him up in the afternoon and he'll think you're his rescuer."

"Sure." Beth got up and walked to the kitchen drawer. "I take it you don't want to come by here at six thirty before I go to work."

Audie made a face. "Not particularly."

"So take this key. You can bring it to me when you come to the nursing home."

"Deal." Audie stood up and took the key. "I guess I'll get out of your hair."

"You can stay if you want. I have some leftover spinach quiche. I can throw together a salad."

"No, that's okay." Audie had never eaten quiche in her life. "You need some time alone to bond with BD. Thanks though."

"Maybe another time."

"You two have fun."

Beth walked her out while BD was still eating. "I'm glad you came back to the nursing home today."

"I am too. Thanks for making it easy."

"I really will take good care of your Grammaw."

"I know. I trust you."

"Okay, that was weird," Audie said aloud in the car. "You were getting off like you were in junior fucking high." She was nothing short of stunned by the sensations that had surged through her as she held Beth's hand. Something was wrong here, because she didn't think of Beth that way.

It wasn't that Beth wasn't worth a second look. She was. Nice body . . . pretty face. If a woman like her ever walked into the Gallery, Audie knew she would go out of her way to meet her. And if they hit it off on the dance floor, she would be more than willing to try out the horizontal version. She just didn't think of Beth that way.

Beth was older. Okay, so she wasn't that much older. And it wasn't really her age. It was that she acted so serious all the time, so settled. A woman like Beth wasn't ever going to walk into the Gallery looking to get laid. What she probably wanted was a relationship, a monogamous deal where you both came home for dinner and talked about your day. That was all fine and good for some people, but Audie wasn't one of those people. She liked excitement and adventure. And freedom. Besides . . . she didn't think of Beth that way.

Chapter 9

Beth turned the handle on the cylinder to close the air flow. "Dr. Hill said you should be better by today and probably wouldn't need this anymore."

"I am better," Miss Violet said, her voice significantly stronger than it had been the past two days.

Beth gently loosened the looped hose and cast it aside. Then she went about her morning routine of collecting vitals. "Your granddaughter is running late today. Did she tell you why?"

"She must be up to something."

"She brought me a present yesterday. See?" Beth held up her hand to show off a dark red scratch across the knuckles. "A cute little black cat that she said would be a sweetheart. She called him BD and implied that it stood for Baby Doll, but I think it stands for Black Devil."

"One of those wild ones from the shelter, I bet."

"That's right. And she was going to go by my condo and pick him up this morning. She's taking him to get neutered."

"You're lucky."

"How do you figure that?"

"She only brought you one."

Beth laughed. "Yeah, she said most of her friends had several. I guess I'm not that good a friend."

"Yes, you are. I can tell."

"Because she gives me wild animals?"

"You're the only one out here she talks to. And if you don't come by while she's here, she goes looking for you."

Beth was oddly pleased at this revelation. She liked seeing Audie every day, but had never noticed that Audie sought her out. To her, it seemed like the other way around. "I'll say this about her. If her idea of an olive branch is a carnivorous furball, I sure hope we don't have any more arguments like that one yesterday."

A familiar voice behind her made her smile. "If you're going to talk about me, the least you could do is say nice things in front of my own Grammaw."

"Sorry. I was just showing her my war wound." She held up her scratched hand. "And she thought you should do my dishes for a week while it heals."

Audie laughed. "I know my Grammaw better than that."

"So how did it go taking the Black Devil to the vet?"

"You figured that out, did you?"

Beth answered with only a smirk.

"Your little love muffin is getting his"—she mouthed the word "balls" silently—"snipped right this very minute."

"My poor baby."

"He'll be fine. And you'll be his hero when you pick him up and take him away from those bad people with the scissors."

"Where was he when you got there?"

"Hiding, of course. It took me forever to find him, but he was . . . under your . . . bed." Audie mumbled the last part.

"I'm surprised you were able to—" Oh, God. Beth could feel her face heat up like a flamethrower. If Audie had looked under her bed, she had to have seen—Oh, God.

"In fact, I had to get something to poke him with so he'd come out, so I grabbed your . . . coat hanger that was on the bed. I hope that was okay."

No matter how hard she tried, Beth could not force her eyes upward. Audie had found her vibrator. She turned to Miss Violet, still acutely aware of her deep blush. "I'm finished here. I'll be back to get you at lunchtime." Then she finally faced Audie. "And I'll pick up the devil's spawn after work."

To her horror, Audie followed her into the hall.

"Hey, for what it's worth?"

Beth braced herself for a remark that was sure to be humiliating.

"I have to keep mine in the drawer so Buster doesn't drag it around the house."

They stared at each other for a long moment before they both burst out laughing.

"I don't think I've ever been so embarrassed in my whole life."

"I wasn't even going to say anything. But then you asked about BD, and before I could stop myself, it was out."

"But then you enjoyed it. That little remark about the coat hanger?"

"Yeah, I wanted to see if you could reach that shade of the bricks on our front porch. You were this close." Audie held up her thumb and forefinger.

"Sorry I couldn't be more accommodating." Her misery wasn't over. After a blush as intense as that one, her neck and face would be splotched for the next half hour. "So how was BD? Did he go quietly?"

"He was fine. He'll be a little subdued tonight."

"And where will you be if I need emergency cat assistance?"

Audie dug her wallet from her backpack. "I'm glad you said that. I meant to give you this yesterday." She handed Beth a folded piece of paper. "It's my cell phone. You won't have to call all over the place looking for me anymore. I always have my phone with me."

"Okay." She tucked the number in her pocket. "Thanks."

"No, thank you." Audie's look was serious. "And I'll be home tonight if BD gives you any trouble."

"You should see him, Ginger. He's all black with huge yellow eyes. Audie said she thought from the shape of his face that he was part Siamese." Beth tucked the phone under her chin and got down on all fours to look under the couch. BD had vanished.

"I still can't believe you got a cat. You're going to be the classic lesbian old maid."

"I am not."

"I can see it now. No one hears from you for days and your neighbors start complaining about a bad smell. So they break down your door and all the mangy cats are eating out of your stomach."

"You're so disgusting." She opened the laundry alcove and stood on tiptoes to look behind the washer and dryer.

"So tell me again how you ended up with this cat."

"I'm not really sure how it happened, to tell you the truth. It was when Audie and I were talking about Diva and I said something like cats were less trouble. Next thing I know, she's handing me this little terror."

"Why didn't she get you a kitten?"

"I don't know. It was like she really wanted me to have this one. His time was almost up and no one else would have wanted a cat this wild."

"Are you sure you can tame it?"

"Maybe. If I can find it!"

"He's still hiding?"

"Yes. I guess I need to go. I'm going to have to tear this place apart."

"Good luck. Don't forget you're having lunch with me on Saturday."

"I won't. Talk to you soon."

Audie grinned as the door opened. "Miss him already, do you?"

"Not funny! I've looked everywhere."

"Obviously not." She stepped inside and followed Beth to the living room. "He's probably just hunkered down, sulking about the loss of his boyhood."

"I can't let him just hide out, Audie. He had surgery today. I have to make sure he's okay."

Audie pulled a small bag of cat treats from her backpack.

"He's not going to come out for something like that. I already put fresh tuna in his bowl."

"It's not to draw him out. It's to reward him when he comes." Audie walked into the kitchen. "I guess you looked in all the cabinets? Behind the refrigerator? In the refrigerator?"

Beth gave her a skeptical look and opened the refrigerator. "He's not here."

Together, they retraced the steps Beth had made three times already, from the closets to the cabinets to the furniture, even opening the sofa bed.

"And you're positive he didn't get outside?" They had turned the place upside down. There was nowhere else he could be.

"I haven't opened the door at all since I let him out of his crate."

"Not even the balcony?"

Beth shook her head. "No."

"And all of the windows are—" Her eyes landed on the one place they hadn't searched, and therefore, the only place BD could be. "Is your flue open?"

"My flue?"

Audie crawled over to the fireplace and peered upward. "He's going to bite the shit out of me."

"Do you see him?"

"No, but I'll bet you ten bucks he's stretched out on a shelf up there." Careful not to make any sudden moves, she reached her hand up inside the chimney. "Ow!"

98

"BD!"

"At least now I know which end is his head. No wonder he didn't like that." She reached up again and firmly grasped the nape of his neck, withdrawing him from his lair.

"Poor baby."

"Watch out, he's covered with soot."

"I don't care." Beth took him and cuddled him to her chest. "It's okay, BD. I know you hate Audie right now, but I won't let her hurt you anymore."

Audie rolled her eyes, but was secretly thrilled to see Beth making over the terrified animal. Without a doubt, she had bonded with the little fellow, and it was just a matter of time before he bonded with her.

"Think he'll want the tuna?"

"He may not have much of an appetite. Anesthesia sometimes has that effect."

Beth set BD in front of his bowl, where he immediately debunked Audie's claim.

"I appreciate you coming over. I was worried to death."

"I told you all you had to do was call." Audie surprised herself with her next statement. "And that offer's good for anything, not just cat stuff."

From the look on her face, Beth was definitely surprised. And why wouldn't she be, considering that just yesterday, Audie had cursed her out and threatened to move her Grammaw to another home?

"Thanks, Audie. I'll make the same deal with you."

In the few seconds of silence that passed, Audie sensed a dramatic shift in their relationship, from a casual friendship to something potentially deeper, and she felt a rush of warmth. If this had been Dennis or Joel, she would have reached out for a hug. With Beth, she held back, not quite trusting where they stood.

"Of course, making deals with somebody like you could be dangerous," Beth continued. "I see what you do with a simple 'I've thought about getting a cat.'"

"You'll thank me one of these days."

"But the scars will endure for always," she said with a dramatic sigh.

Audie chuckled. "I need to introduce you to some of my drama queen friends so they can see a real pro in action." She glanced at the books and papers that covered the dining room table. "I guess I should go so you can get back to your studying."

"I'm actually done for the night. I wish the test was this Monday instead of next. I'm ready to get it over with."

"So take a break. Let's go get something to eat." Audie looked at her watch. It was almost eight. She had come straight from the shelter and hadn't eaten anything since a ham and egg sandwich in the car on her way to work this morning.

"I already ate the rest of that quiche you crinkled your nose at yesterday, but I'll go with you."

"I did not crinkle my nose . . . much. There was a burger out there with my name on it."

"And what's calling you tonight?"

"I'm not sure yet. You want dessert?"

"I shouldn't."

"That's not what I asked."

"You're a bad influence."

"I've been hearing that all my life." Audie grinned and led the way down the stairs to her car, where she held the passenger door open for Beth. "Sorry for the mess. Buster's kind of a slob."

Beth collected the trash from the passenger seat and floorboard and passed it through the console. "I'll say. He just throws his fast food wrappers anywhere. Am I going to get something gross on my clothes if I sit here?"

Audie grimaced. "Gee, I hope not. If you want, I could take my shirt off and let you sit on it." She would have said the same thing to Dennis, but saying it to Beth made it come out sounding like a flirt.

"If you're going to do that, let's take my car so people who know me will see me riding around with a topless woman. It'll do wonders for my reputation."

"It would probably be good for mine too, being seen with better company than I usually keep." Audie turned toward her favorite diner. "You okay with Leon's?"

"Leon's has ten different pies every day. I can't believe I'm doing this."

"I'm a bad influence, remember?"

Ten minutes later, they were seated in a booth by the window, poring over the sticky plastic menus. A tired-looking waitress appeared to take their order.

"I'll have a piece of . . . apple—no—lemon pie."

"The apple's better," the waitress said in a flat voice.

"Okay, apple."

"You want that plain or hot with vanilla ice cream?"

Beth groaned before answering in a small voice. "Hot with ice cream."

"And I'll have a cheeseburger with onion rings instead of fries. No pickle. And a Coke."

"You want lettuce and tomato?"

"No, just ketchup."

The waitress collected the menus and disappeared.

"Audie, can I ask you a personal question?"

"Of course. I've seen your vibrator. We can talk about anything now." She was very pleased with herself to see the familiar blush return.

"You're never going to let me live that down, are you?"

"It's only been twelve hours. I should be allowed to get more mileage out of it than that."

"Fine."

"So what's your question?"

"Don't you ever eat vegetables?"

"Onion rings are a vegetable."

"Well, yeah . . . like apple pie is a fruit."

The waitress deposited Audie's Coke and a glass of water for Beth.

"Your Grammaw's right about you not taking care of yourself. Eating out at fast food restaurants all the time isn't good for you."

"Leon's isn't fast food."

"But you ordered a burger and onion rings."

"I know. But I hate to cook almost as much as I hate to go to the grocery."

"You need to start eating better. If you want, I can show you a few things that are good for you that are easy to make."

Audie recognized the kind gesture for what it was, but it triggered a memory of her Grammaw in the kitchen, something she probably would never see again. And with the memory came a sudden rush of tears.

"I'm so sorry! I didn't mean to upset you."

"It's okay, it's not your fault." Hastily, she wiped her eyes. "It just made me think about Grammaw running me out of her kitchen."

"I'm really sorry." Beth's hand crept across the table to Audie's. "I can't imagine how hard this is for you."

Audie took the hand and squeezed, trying to compose herself. "Everybody has hard times. I try not to think about stuff, but it comes anyway."

"Of course it does. Your whole life's been turned upside down." The waitress appeared with their food, but Beth didn't let go of Audie's hand. "And I'm here any time you want to talk."

"Thanks. I don't even know if there's anything left to say."

"Well, I know you're worried about what to do with the house. I've been through all of that and I can help."

It was true the house had been on her mind a lot. Every time she walked in, she vowed to sell it to rid herself of the empty feelings. But it was the only home she had ever known, and the other part of her wanted to hold all of its memories forever.

"Your ice cream's melting."

"It so happens I like it that way."

"Good thing, huh?" Audie squeezed her hand one more time and let go. "We'd better eat so you can get home. I bet BD's missing you."

Beth snorted. "As long as he isn't ordering things from the Home Shopping Channel."

For the second time in three nights, Beth lay awake long after turning out the light. Her mind was busy with the events of the day, especially the last few hours with Audie. Something was going on between them, but she didn't have a handle on it.

Everything was complicated by their circumstances. Were it not for Miss Violet, they might not have crossed paths at all, and even if they had, they probably wouldn't have been friends. Their lifestyles were so divergent. Audie was youthful and self-indulgent, while she thought of herself as mature and practical.

Beth hated to admit it, but she was probably reading way too much into Audie's overtures toward friendship. Audie was in a vulnerable place right now, and Beth was a solace, an ally for taking care of her Grammaw, nothing more. For Beth to pretend otherwise would only lead to disappointment, because the time would come that Audie's need for comfort and assurance would subside, and she would go back to her circle of younger, more interesting friends.

In the guest bath, BD was scraping in his litter box. The poor fellow was huddled in the corner of the dining room behind a potted plant when she got home, terrified and probably still hurting from his surgery.

Beth threw back the covers and got up to see how he was.

"Come here, you."

Even with the lights out, his dark form stood out against the beige carpet. He sat perfectly still, as though he were lost. She gently picked him up and carried him back to her bedroom.

"I can't believe I'm actually putting you in my bed."

She fluffed her pillows and leaned against the headboard. BD sat timidly by her side.

"Your whole world's been turned upside down too, just like Audie's. Hasn't it?"

As she stroked his back, he relaxed, gradually allowing his weight to come to rest on the bed. His feet remained tucked beneath him, just in case he needed to bolt.

"All of a sudden everything is different and you're afraid because you don't know what's happening. You just want everything back the way it used to be, don't you?"

He tipped his head toward her hand.

"You and Audie are a lot alike, you know that? You both act all wild and tough on the outside, like you don't want anybody to get too close."

She fingered the hollow behind his ear and he began to softly purr.

"But that's exactly what you want, isn't it? You want somebody close but then you don't know what you're supposed to do."

BD stretched out, finally giving in to her warm touch.

"All you know is that it feels good, right?"

Beth slumped lower in the bed, turning onto her side so that BD snuggled against her stomach.

"Audie was right. I'm falling in love with you already, BD. You know that?"

A heavy veil of sleep finally came and covered them both.

Audie squinted as she turned on the light in her Grammaw's bathroom. There had to be something in here for a stomachache.

Beth was right. She was going to kill herself if she didn't start eating better.

Of course, this particular malady probably had nothing to do with Leon's cheeseburger. The more likely culprit was the tortilla chips she had dipped in peanut butter after smoking a joint to settle down from the emotional roller coaster that dinner had turned into when she let herself wander off on a tangent to feel sorry for herself because Grammaw wasn't cooking anymore and then Beth held her hand again making her feel good all over and all she wanted to do was sit in the restaurant and hold hands all night so she could—

She shook her head wildly to clear it and located the plastic bottle of antacids. "Chew two."

It hurt to laugh.

"Chew two. Chew two. Chew two."

She clutched her abdomen as a cramp seized her.

"Why do I do this to myself?"

Chapter 10

"Margarita rocks, no salt," Audie said, squeezing between two groups of guys. "Hey, Mike. How's it going?"

"Not bad, Audie. You?"

"Good."

It was the same banter she shared with dozens of casual friends each time she came to the Gallery. Tonight's crowd was nice, about half ladies since it was Friday. There were a few new faces out there, women she hadn't met before. She would fix that.

"Here ya go."

"Thanks." She shoved a few bills across the counter. "Keep it."

She and Dennis usually worked it out so that he drove on Fridays, since it was Ladies Night, and tonight Joel and Dwayne had ridden along. Leaving her own car at home freed her up to have a few margaritas, which made dancing a lot more fun. She was always careful not to do anything stupid, like leave with someone she just met. But just in case she drank too much, Dennis and Joel both had permission to order her home.

Regan was at the club tonight, as was Deanna, another girl Audie sometimes hooked up with. Both were apparently alone, and thankfully, on opposite sides of the room. Either might be up for an overnight guest. All she had to do was work out a ride home to Sumter in the morning before work.

"Audie Pippin."

She reached out for a hug as soon as she spotted the familiar face. "Mallory. Good to see you." She and Mallory had shared a few sexual adventures, but didn't really connect otherwise. That was a couple of years ago, though, and Mallory was hot enough that Audie was certainly willing to give it another try.

"You still working at the animal shelter in Sumter?"

"Yeah, I haven't seen you around much."

"Nah, I've been working about a hundred hours a week. Credit card bills out the ass. That doesn't leave much free time."

"I'm glad you made it out tonight." She was about to ask for a dance when she noticed Mallory was holding a drink in each hand. "You here with somebody?"

"Yeah." Mallory's face brightened. "I met a woman a couple of months ago and she's already turning me into an old married lady."

There went that idea. "That's great news."

"Come on over, I'll introduce you. We're just hanging out with some friends in the corner."

There was no graceful way to decline, so she followed Mallory back to her table. It never hurt to meet new people, even if they were all attached. Experience had taught her that most pairings were only temporary.

Mallory made the introductions, saving her new girlfriend for last. "And this is Ginger."

"Pleased to meet you." Audie smiled and extended her hand, shocked at the brazen appraisal she was getting from this woman, right in front of her girlfriend. It was downright uncomfortable, but Mallory didn't seem to notice. Instead, she dragged up a chair and motioned for Audie to join them.

"We were all just talking about the first time we went to a gay bar."

"It was in Chicago in 1980," one of the women said. Audie wasn't even born then. "That place was a dive, nothing like this."

Ginger looked around the crowded room. "This is nice but I think I'd rather go to a place that was just women."

"A couple of women have tried to open clubs in Nashville that cater to lesbians. They just won't fly," Audie said.

"They might if they turned up the lights a little and turned down the music a lot."

"One of the places was like that. It had booths and tables, and a nice bar. But it sat empty three or four nights a week, and even when women came in, they didn't spend much money. Most of them would buy one drink and sip it all night."

Ginger shrugged as though it was Audie who didn't get it. "Not everybody needs to get smashed to have a good time."

"But you can't keep the doors open if people don't spend money. Liquor's got the highest markup, and the Gallery runs things all through the week, like contests and drag shows, just to draw a crowd."

That launched them into a discussion about how to attract women to a club, the diversity of the lesbian community, and the difficulty of marketing to a group that didn't share common avenues of communication.

"But I guarantee you this," Audie said. "If any of you have ideas for attracting women to the Gallery, Bruce will listen. He wants this place to be for everybody, not just the boys."

"Ideas like what?"

Mallory leaned into her girlfriend with an evil grin. "I'd show up to see you in a wet T-shirt contest."

"See?" Audie said, slapping her friend's hand with a high-five. "That's all there is to it. I'll go tell Bruce that you volunteer to spearhead a titillating event that's sure to pack the ladies in. What night would be good?"

"Wait a minute!" Ginger gamely laughed along. "Why bother with T-shirts? Let's just have a topless night."

"Now you're talking!" Regan joined them, smiling enthusiastically at what she had gleaned from the tail end of the conversation. "Hey, Mallory!"

Mallory got up to give her a hug and introduced her friends and Ginger. "You know Audie, right?"

"Very well," she answered, slipping an arm around Audie's waist so that her hand rested on her rear. "You gonna do this topless thing?"

"What do you think?"

"I'd certainly come." Audie didn't miss the double entendre.

Ginger cleared her throat. "Please tell me all of you are kidding."

"Don't you worry, sweetheart," Mallory cooed. "We'll have our own little topless night." Ginger was visibly relieved.

Regan tugged on Audie's hand. "Come dance with me."

"Excuse me, ladies." She drained her margarita. "I'd love to stay and chat but I just got a better offer."

Audie stayed on the dance floor the better part of the next hour, cutting out only to run back to the bar. She had all but decided to pursue more when Regan dashed off to the ladies' room. Audie took a brief hiatus of her own to chat with Dennis and Joel. The next thing she knew, Regan was out on the dance floor with her other prospect, Deanna. And before she had the chance to reclaim her spot, the two of them left together.

"You're losing your touch, Audie." Dennis never could resist tweaking her when she struck out.

"Tell me about it. If I'd known I'd be coming home with you guys, I wouldn't have had so much to drink."

"What's that got to do with anything?"

"I'm horny, stupid."

Joel laughed at her misery as he and Dwayne climbed into Dennis's backseat for the twenty-minute ride home. "Maybe that's fate trying to tell you it's time to quit screwing around."

Dennis found that amusing.

"What the fuck are you laughing at? Man, I knew this was going to happen."

"What?"

"You get religion all of a sudden and now everybody starts working on me. Why don't you and David go play house and leave me out of it?"

"We're not playing house, Audie." He sounded more annoyed than defensive. "I like David. I don't want to just trick with him."

"Good thing, since he's not giving you any."

"We both decided to get tested, if it's any of your business."

She turned in her seat to eye Joel, who badgered all the young men at the club to be responsible. She had given in too last year and let him draw blood at his office. "You must be very proud."

"Come on, Audie," Dennis whined. "Don't you ever wish you could be with somebody that cared about you, not just how you fucked?"

"I've worked hard to be a good fucker." She had probably had one too many margaritas to be having a truly serious conversation. Her mind drifted automatically to Beth Hester. Beth seemed to care about her, but had no apparent interest in how she fucked.

Dwayne was usually quiet, but even he couldn't resist piling on. "Even if you're God's gift to lesbians, wouldn't you like to share that with somebody you really cared about?"

Audie snorted. "You sound like my Grampaw before he found out I liked girls."

"Maybe you didn't give him enough credit," Joel teased. "It hasn't been that long since you had your heart broken by that woman with all the tattoos . . . what was her name?"

She folded her arms and slumped in the passenger seat. "Maxine, and she only had six. Besides, she didn't break my heart." Audie wanted a joint in the worst way, but she and Dennis never smoked around Joel.

"She was a low-life sack of shit," Dennis growled.

"Gosh, Dennis, tell us how you really feel."

"I would have kicked her ass if she'd gotten you hooked on coke. She was bad news."

Audie had to agree. Maxine was full of bad habits, but there was something about her that had been downright irresistible at the time. "I might have cared about Maxine, but she never cared about me."

"I'm not going to give you a hard time about what you do at the Gallery," Joel said. "There's nothing wrong with having fun if you use your head."

"Thank you." Audie didn't mean to sound sarcastic, but she didn't understand where these guys got off thinking she needed their permission.

Joel poked the back of her shoulder. "But it's a lot more fun when it's somebody you care about."

"You should have come with us," Ginger said, dipping her tortilla chip into a bowl of green chili salsa. "I nearly dropped my jaw when Mallory came back to the table with Audie Pippin. I had no idea they knew each other."

"I thought you said Mallory was from Bristol."

"She is, but they must have met at the club when she first moved here. I'd bet my left tit they hooked up."

Beth lunged for her soda as she nearly choked on a chip. "What makes you say that?"

"I don't know . . . just a feeling."

"You okay with it?"

"I guess. I don't have a right to complain about who she was with before. But it sure makes me wonder what she sees in somebody like me."

"That's ridiculous, Ginger. You have a lot to offer, and Mallory's smart enough to see that."

Ginger tipped her head. "Maybe, but I gotta tell you, Audie Pippin is hot. And she knows it too."

The fact that Audie was attractive was a given. But the rest didn't jibe with what Beth had seen. "She doesn't strike me as someone who really cares what others think about her."

"Maybe not consciously. But you can't give off the kind of signals she does without knowing it. You should have seen her last night, Beth. Her jeans were so tight you could practically see the outline of her pubic hair."

Beth had noticed that Audie wore her jeans very well, but she tried not to let Ginger's image into her brain. She didn't need to be walking around thinking about Audie's pubic hair. "That doesn't sound like the Audie I see every day. Of course, that may say more about me than it does about Audie."

"What's that supposed to mean?"

Beth shrugged. "Just that maybe she doesn't act that way around me because she doesn't see me that way."

"What way?"

"Well, like . . . I doubt she ever thinks of me as anything but a friend. She probably prefers girls who are a little more hip to a nurse who stays home and studies half her life. Hell, she probably wouldn't even be talking to me at all if I didn't take care of her grandmother. It's not like she flirts all that much."

"All that much? Do tell."

Beth leaned back to allow the waitress to deposit her plate. No way was she going to relate the vibrator story. "It's not flirting really. I told you, she asked me to come along with her to the Gallery, but it wasn't like she wanted me to be her date. My guess is that she prefers to play the field."

"That's what I figured too. But if you're ever looking just to get laid, I bet you could."

"You know me better than that."

"Yeah, I do. And you shouldn't be giving somebody like Audie Pippin the time of day. You deserve a lot better than that."

"Audie's not a bad person. She's just a free spirit." And frankly, Beth would love the chance to go out with Audie if she thought for a second Audie was really interested in her.

"I'll say. I think you'd be better off going out with somebody like Mallory's friend, Jan. She's a loan officer at First State."

"I believe we've already had this discussion, and the answer is I'm too busy."

112

"But your boards are . . . when?"

"A week from Monday. But I still have a class to finish and finals. And if all that works out, I may be starting a new job in December."

"You just keep putting your life on hold, Beth. You've always done that."

"I didn't with Shelby and look what it got me." She knew that would shut Ginger up, but she didn't expect to hear the hurt in her friend's voice.

"Fine, Beth. If you're happy like this, who am I to try to change that?"

"You're my friend, Ginger. I know that. This is not about Mallory's friend, or even all the stuff I have to do. I'm just stuck where I am right now."

"Shelby really did a number on you, didn't she?"

Beth set down her fork, no longer interested in her lunch. "This isn't all Shelby's fault. Hooking up with her was my mistake. I knew we weren't right for each other, but I didn't want to be by myself. I just . . ."

Ginger reached out and gave her a reassuring pat on the hand.

Beth was embarrassed to hear the shake in her voice. She should have gotten over this by now. "I'd been by myself for so long that I just thought life was going to pass me by if I didn't find somebody. So I settled for Shelby when I should have waited to find someone special."

"It's okay. I'm sorry I put pressure on you. You're right to wait for somebody special this time. I got lucky with Mallory, and it makes all the difference in the world. I was never this happy with Tonya."

"I'm really glad for you. But I'm not ready to meet anybody right now." She appreciated that her friend was willing to back off. But she wasn't about to share with her what she just realized—that as long as Audie Pippin was possibly in the picture, she wasn't about to get tied up with someone else.

⊱⊰

"Watch this!" Audie faked her throw twice before sending the flying disk low and straight across the lawn. Buster had to hustle, but he caught up with it just before it touched the ground.

"Good boy!" Violet slapped the palm of her good hand on the arm of the wheelchair.

From the shaded patio, a group of onlookers cheered as well, mostly visitors to the nursing home. Several were children, fresh from church for their weekly visit with an elderly relative. Audie and Buster kept them entertained.

"Here's one you haven't seen." She dangled the Frisbee in front of the dog as he waited obediently. "Okay, Buster . . . jump!" She flipped the disk in the air and he spun to catch it. Immediately, she took it from his mouth and did it again, five times in all without a miss.

"We're going to put you both in the circus!" The familiar voice belonged to Beth, who was wheeling Mr. Wortman to a spot in the shade.

"Grammaw tried to get me to run away but I kept coming back." Audie flung the Frisbee as far as she could to send Buster on his way. "How's BD?"

Beth walked closer so Miss Violet could hear. "He's terrible. He sleeps on my dining room table all day. And he knows he isn't supposed to, because he gets down when he hears me at the door."

"Then how do you know he was there?"

"There's a warm spot right in the middle of a pile of black hair."

"Sounds circumstantial to me."

"At least it isn't my kitchen counter."

"Grammaw, you want to go sit in the shade and talk with Beth awhile?"

"I can't stay out here," Beth said. "Two of our aides called in sick today, and we're down anyway because it's the weekend."

"Is there anything I can do to help?"

"That's a nice offer, but I think the county would frown on having one of our visitors distribute meds."

"I suppose you're right. Maybe I could just take blood or something."

Beth grinned at her silliness. "Actually, it would help if you could keep an eye on Mr. Wortman. I'll be back for him in about twenty minutes."

"Will do." Audie gave her a salute as she disappeared back inside. Then she positioned her grandmother's wheelchair on the patio next to a bench for visitors. "I'll be back in just a minute, Grammaw."

She jogged around to the parking lot and came back carrying Buster's water bowl, which she filled from the faucet on the side of the building.

"He likes coming out here and showing off."

"He's not the only one," her Grammaw said.

"What's that supposed to mean?"

"You know what it means, Audie. You like to show off for Beth."

"I—what—?" Nervously, she looked around to see if anyone was listening. "What are you talking about?"

Violet talked slowly, taking care to speak her words as plainly as possible. "I see how you act around Beth when you come out here."

"That's—I do not. I hate to be the one to break this to you, but I come out here to see you."

"I know that, Audie. But you can't tell me you don't look for her every minute you're here. I know you too well."

This was disturbing.

It was true that she always looked for Beth and tried to talk to her. That was because Beth was the only one out here she really trusted to take care of her Grammaw.

But they didn't talk about Grammaw every time. The last few days they had talked about BD . . . or Beth's board exams . . . or Audie's diet . . . or whether or not she should sell the house. And it was undeniable that she sometimes followed Beth out into the hall to give her a word of appreciation about something. Obviously, Grammaw had noticed.

This was disturbing.

"I like Beth," Audie argued. "She's really nice to you."

"The others are nice too."

"I'm sure they are. But Beth is different because she took in that cat. You know how important it is to me that people like animals."

"Audie, you're not fooling me."

This was disturbing.

"I think Beth's . . . pretty." It didn't kill her to say that. It was definitely true. "But don't go thinking there's anything going on."

She got up and shooed a fly from Mr. Wortman's hand. Then she came back to sit on the bench next to her Grammaw.

"Beth looks for you too," her grandmother said.

"What?"

"She comes to the room whenever you're there."

"That's because she's your nurse."

"Mmm-huh."

"I know you like Beth, Grammaw. So do I." Audie checked again to make sure no one was within earshot. "But I don't think she's interested in me like that."

Audie was surprised by the disappointment she felt at her own conclusion. She would like it if Beth were interested in her. Unlike most of the women she knew, Beth had her whole life under control. She had a career, a home . . . everything coming together just as she had planned. She had suffered through a bad relationship and probably knew all the mistakes to avoid. Audie didn't have a chance of attracting somebody like that. She didn't even have a plan for her life. The prospect of the new job terrified her, but not as much as decisions about the house. She fed her body nothing but junk. She rarely exercised. And she burned away her brain cells with margaritas and marijuana. Outside of her friendships with Dennis and Joel, the only relationships she knew lasted one night at a time.

Yes, it would be flattering as hell if somebody like Beth were interested in her.

Beth emerged from the building and slipped around to sit beside Audie, out of sight from the door. "Hide me."

Audie noted the satisfied smile on her Grammaw's face and gave her a warning look. "No problem. What did you do?"

"Nothing. I just need a minute to rest." Buster came over and laid his head in Beth's lap.

"It must be crazy in there."

"It is. Lunch starts in ten minutes and we just finished collecting the trays from breakfast. Our kitchen looks worse than the inside of your car."

"Hey!"

Beth ignored her objections. "Looks like you've worn Buster out."

"He just needs a little rest, then he's good to go again."

"I wish I could get BD to play. I got him a catnip mouse but he won't touch it."

"Really? Most cats can't resist those."

"Apparently, BD can."

"Are you sure he isn't playing with it when you aren't there?"

Beth frowned as she considered the question, and Audie discovered that the little crinkle above her nose was very cute. As soon as she realized that she was grinning stupidly, she looked away, embarrassed because her Grammaw had already noticed.

"Now that you mention it, I find it in a different place every time I come in."

"Then he's playing with it. He just doesn't know how to play with you. You need a toy that both of you can use at the same time." A very intimate image flashed through Audie's head, and it was all she could do to remember they were talking about a cat. "Like—like something with a string on it."

"I don't think I saw anything like that at the grocery."

"I'll pick up one from the pet store."

"Thanks. That'll be fun." Beth slapped her knees and stood up. "I guess I'd better get back in there. I'll take Mr. Wortman with me. Thanks for keeping an eye on him."

"No problem."

"Miss Violet, get Audie to bring you in for lunch in ten minutes, okay?"

Violet nodded her agreement. They watched her go and she turned to her granddaughter. "See? I told you."

Audie wasn't willing to accept her Grammaw's assessment. But now that the idea was planted in her head, she was certainly going to watch for it.

Chapter 11

"You looked like you were having a good time yesterday," Beth said as she pushed Miss Violet down the hall toward the dining room.

"I like Sundays because Audie stays longer."

"She's off today too, isn't she?"

"Yes, but she has a lot to do on Monday. She'll come by, though." Miss Violet reached up to pat Beth's hand. "Don't you worry."

"Wha—what do you mean don't worry? I wasn't worrying."

"I know, but you always look for her."

"I guess I do." She did look for Audie every day, but that was because Audie was a concerned and loving family member who counted on her for feedback about how her Grammaw was doing. Of course, Miss Violet was doing well, so naturally they talked of other things . . . like BD . . . her nurse's boards . . . Audie's diet . . . and what she should do about the house. And Beth admitted to herself that she sometimes asked Audie to follow her into the hall so she could give her a word of encouragement. Her initial impression—that Miss Violet's granddaughter was some kind of hellion—was wrong. She liked Audie, even more as she got to know her.

"I told her you always came to see me when she was there."

Beth felt herself start to blush. This conversation was getting out of hand. "I don't always do that. It just works out that way because she's usually there when I'm supposed to come in and take your vitals." Though she sometimes skipped over Miss Violet if Audie hadn't yet arrived.

They entered the dining room and started toward the table where Edith Platt was already eating.

"I told her wrong then," Miss Violet said. "I know she looks for you every day, so I thought maybe you looked for her too."

"Audie looks for me?"

"Mmm-huh." Miss Violet smiled at her breakfast companion. "Good morning, Edith. How are you today?"

Edith began the usual rundown of her maladies, effectively nipping the chat about Audie in the bud. But Beth had heard just enough to get her imagination going.

Embarrassing though it was, Beth was right. The Xterra was a pigsty on wheels.

Audie stretched her arm under the passenger seat and pulled out yet another wad of fast food wrappers. All told, she had enough trash from the car to start her own landfill.

She had no excuse for letting her vehicle get this nasty. It was the first car she had ever bought brand new, and she had always been proud of its sharp looks. But little by little, it had turned into a mud-covered trash heap. She was determined to bring it back to its classy state, a car anyone would be proud to ride in.

Audie tossed the vinyl floor mats into the power-wash bay and unraveled the clunky vacuum hose. With all four doors and the cargo hatch standing open, she deposited a handful of quarters in the machine and began the task of sucking up the debris, the usual dirt and leaves . . . french fries between the seat and console . . . sesame seeds from sandwich buns in the grooves of the seats . . . and in the ashtray, a half dozen—

"Damn it!"

But it was too late. In addition to being clean, the Xterra was now a drug-free zone.

Beth shifted on the couch, prompting BD to raise his head and check out his surroundings. Even after five days in his new home, he was still nervous about strange noises and sudden movements. But he had progressed from a hiding place under the furniture to a perch on the back of the couch, where he could warm himself under Beth's reading light as she studied.

Despite his reticence, Beth liked having BD around. At least he didn't bite her anymore when she tried to pet him, and though he maintained a watchful distance when she was reading or watching TV, he now slept next to her each night. There was definitely something comforting about having him close by.

Both were startled by a knock at the door. BD's response, which took less than two seconds, was to dash into the bedroom out of sight.

Beth had no idea who would be at her door at a quarter to nine, but she wasn't foolish enough to open it without turning on the light and looking through the peephole. And there, she got quite a shock.

Audie smiled and waved back at her. But that wasn't the shock.

"Wow! You look great." A major understatement. Audie was dressed in tight black pants that hung low enough to show off part of the tattoo that seemed to cover one of her hipbones. All that was visible above the leather belt was part of a leaf. It was impossible not to notice her nipples straining against a purple top that she wore like a second skin. It stopped just above her navel, which was pierced with a small gold hoop. But the biggest surprise was the beautiful reddish-brown hair that billowed around her shoulders. Up to now, Beth had never seen Audie without her ball cap. "Come on in." And stay all night.

"Thanks. I hope you don't mind me just showing up at your door. I would have called, but your number's not listed."

"It cuts down on telemarketers," Beth explained, bending over to grab her purse. She took out a pencil and ripped a sheet from a notepad by the phone. "But here, let me give it to you."

Audie stuffed it into her front pants pocket. "I'm on my way out to the Gallery tonight," she explained. "They've been having this amateur drag queen contest on Monday nights, and one of my friends is in the finals."

"Sounds like fun."

"If you want to come along, I'll wait."

"Oh, I can't." Beth pointed to her textbook on the floor by the couch. "I have to study. Besides, it's all I can do to get up in the morning after a class that lets out at ten. I'd be comatose if I went out to a club." She hated how old that made her sound. "If I didn't have to get up so early . . ."

"Yeah, there are definitely advantages to working eleven to seven." Audie held up a paper bag. "I brought a present for you and BD."

Beth looked inside to find a plastic fishing pole. At the end of the string was a fish stuffed with catnip.

"I promise you, he won't be able to resist this." Audie looked around. "So where's he hiding?"

"Judging from the tread marks on the carpet, I'd guess in my bedroom. I probably won't see him again until I turn out the light."

"Sorry about that."

"I think he'll be okay when he settles down and realizes that he's safe here."

"I think so too."

They stood in awkward silence until Beth remembered her manners. "You want something to drink? I may have a beer in the fridge."

"Thanks, but it's my night to drive. I'll get a soda or something at the club."

Beth was pleasantly surprised to learn of this arrangement. It was an interesting dimension to Audie's partying ways.

"Well, thanks for the toy. I'm sure BD's going to love it."

"You're welcome. Guess I'll be going." She started for the door.

Beth followed her and stood in the doorway, still practically mesmerized by her sexy appearance. "I'm really glad you stopped by. Maybe I'll come with you one of these days when I get finished with this school stuff."

"Yeah, I think you'd have a good time. I'll even try to get you home before you fall asleep."

Beth smiled. "It won't kill me to stay out one night."

"It's a date then." Audie flashed a bright smile and started down the stairs to her car.

The idea of having a date with Audie Pippin was enough to get Beth's imagination into overdrive. Of course, this probably wasn't that kind of date. Audie hadn't meant that at all. When you were young and hip like Audie—not to mention hot—you didn't date people who stayed at home and cleaned their kitchen for fun.

No, this wasn't a mark-it-on-your-calendar kind of date, but one she would look forward to just the same.

"Dwayne was funny as shit," Dennis slurred as he fell into the passenger seat.

"Yeah, too bad the judges didn't have a sense of humor. He should have won," Audie said. With one hand, she fished in the console for the joint Dennis had brought.

"Damn right." He buckled up for the ride home. "What did you and David talk about for so long?"

"Lots of things. I told him about the house and he said not to sell it. You got your lighter?"

Dennis dug in his pants pocket for a butane lighter. "He likes old houses."

"And we talked about how you used to be Joel's twinkie."

"I was not! I just lived there while I—"

"Whoa, shit!" Her rearview mirror had suddenly filled with flashing blue lights.

"What?"

Audie didn't answer. She was too busy trying to chew and swallow the joint she was about to light. "Are you holding anything else?" she mumbled.

Dennis shook his head numbly. "Just a popper."

"Shit. You better hope this is about a tail light." Possession of amyl nitrites was illegal, and maybe enough to land them both in jail. "Where is it?"

Dennis patted the breast pocket of his denim jacket. "Forget that. What about these?" He groped in the dark for the ashtray.

"They're gone." This afternoon's inadvertent cleansing now seemed like a sign from God. She pulled over to the shoulder of the road, squinting at the brightness of the flashing blue lights. As she rolled down her window, she mentally ticked off and dismissed all of the potential problems. Moments later, a flashlight blinded her. "Is there a problem, officer?"

He ignored her and shined the light into Dennis's face next, then all around the interior of the Xterra.

"License and registration."

Audie pulled her wallet from her hip pocket and her registration from her console. Out of the corner of her eye, she could see Dennis's knees bouncing with anxiety. As she handed over the documents, she asked again, "Did I do something wrong?"

And again, he ignored her as he read the information. Finally, he spoke. "Miss Pippin, I've been following you since you left a drinking establishment on Capital Drive. Have you had anything to drink this evening?"

"No, officer," she answered, letting out a small breath of relief. "I'm the designated driver tonight."

Clearly, he was unimpressed by her declaration. "I observed that you failed to come to a complete stop before executing a right turn onto Sumter Pike."

Audie recalled that the light on Sumter Pike turned green as she was braking, but she knew it was pointless to disagree. The officer was obviously disappointed that she wasn't drunk, and he wasn't going away empty-handed. Still, a bogus traffic ticket was better than a drug charge for one stupid popper.

"Remain in the car, please."

They watched him walk back to his vehicle, presumably to verify her license and registration and confirm she was not wanted in a dozen states.

"He's being a real asshole," Dennis said, his knees still shaking.

"He sure is. But we're going to kiss that asshole, aren't we?" As she ran her tongue over her teeth to free up the loose specks of marijuana, she made a mental note to always carry a bottle of water in the car.

"Hell, I'll give him a blowjob if it keeps us from getting arrested."

"You'd do that anyway."

In the side view mirror, Audie watched as a second car pulled in behind the first. That officer emerged from the vehicle with a German shepherd on a short leash.

"Shit. They're going to search us."

Dennis rolled down his window and dug the vial from his pocket.

"What are you doing?"

"Do you have any idea what they do to guys like me in jail?"

"You'd probably like it. Put that back in your pocket before somebody sees it."

The officers were approaching her side of the car in tandem. "Is that you, Audie?" The officer with the dog was addressing her.

"Matt! Is that Rocky?"

"Sure is."

She started to open the door but stopped. "Is it okay for me to get out?"

The first officer nodded and stepped back.

Audie hopped out and went straight for the shepherd. "He looks great. How's he doing?"

"He's spoiled rotten." Matt turned to the other officer. "Audie works at the animal shelter. I told her I was looking for a dog to train and she called me when Rocky came in."

They conferred for a moment in voices too low for Audie to hear.

"I'll let you take it from here then." He handed Matt Audie's documents and returned to his car.

Audie breathed a heavy sigh of relief and looked back at Dennis, who appeared to be mumbling a prayer in the front seat.

Matt handed her the driver's license and registration. "When Officer Mazil learned you hadn't been drinking, he became concerned that you might be in possession of some type of illegal substance. That's why he radioed for Rocky and me."

Audie looked at him somberly. She couldn't lie. Her only hope was that he wouldn't come right out and ask.

"I just explained to him that we were friends and I doubted you would ever be involved in something like that. He said he patrols this area regularly and . . ."

Despite the reassuring words coming from Matt's lips, Audie was reading another message loud and clear. Officer Mazil would be watching them. Matt was going to bat for her this time because of Rocky, but he was staking his reputation with the other officer that she wasn't going to do anything in the future to break the law.

"Thanks for understanding, Matt. We won't ever give you any trouble. I promise." She stooped again to scratch Rocky, then got back into the driver's seat. A few minutes later, they were back on the road to Sumter.

"I think we better go to church on Sunday," Dennis said.

"You heard Matt. We can't get in trouble again, and I bet this Officer Mazil is going to be watching. That means no more stuff in the car."

"Shit."

"It ain't worth going to jail, man. You'd have to take another blood test."

"Funny. I bet you'd be hot stuff in jail too."

126

"We'd probably be on our way there right now if it wasn't for Beth Hester."

"What the hell does she have to do with anything?"

"She told me my car was a mess so I cleaned it out. If I hadn't, that cop would've seen all that shit in the ashtray."

"What's Beth Hester doing in your car? Isn't she like . . . forty?"

"No, shithead! She's thirty-three. And she might come out with us to the Gallery one night."

"Isn't she like . . . ?" He covered a mock yawn. Audie knew it was a mock yawn because Dennis would never have covered a real one.

"You're such a dick. Ever since you met David, the shoe's on the other foot. Now you're giving me shit about going out with somebody for something other than sex."

"I never said you had to forget about sex. All I said was you had to have feelings for somebody other than just, 'That feels good. Give me another finger.'"

"Turd."

"So do you?"

"Do I what?"

"Do you have feelings for Beth Hester?"

Audie thought again about whether or not she really wanted to have this conversation with Dennis. Since he was drunk, he would give her more shit. But he would probably forget it all tomorrow.

"I like Beth. She's nice, and I think she looks good."

"For an old lady."

"She's not an old lady!"

"She acts like one."

"Just because she thinks killing your brain with tequila and pot is a big fucking waste of time doesn't mean she's an old lady." That was enough, Audie realized. She was getting pissed and Dennis was too drunk to know when to drop it. "Just forget I said anything."

"You can do better than her."

"And you're a fuckhead. Just drop it."

Audie crumbled up the last of the dried leaves into a folded rolling paper on her kitchen table. She had meant to give Dennis some money for more, but the encounter with Officer Mazil made that seem like a bad idea tonight. The whole incident had set her on edge.

On top of that was her exchange with Dennis. He could go fuck himself for all she cared. Going out with Beth to the Gallery wasn't all that big a deal until he made a federal case out of it. It was just dancing and drinking, for crying out loud.

She ran her tongue along the edge of the paper and sealed it. Then she scooped up the remaining seeds and stems and dropped them down the garbage disposal.

Beth had looked totally relaxed this evening in her T-shirt and sweatpants. When she had bent over to pick up her purse, it was hard not to notice the curve of her rear—without panty lines. Audie tried to imagine what her thong might have looked like, or if she had been wearing anything at all. Either was nice to think about. If she had hung out with Beth tonight, the whole scene with the cops would never have happened.

She still couldn't believe how lucky she was to be sitting at home in her kitchen instead of in a jail cell. She and Dennis had been drinking and smoking dope in the car for eight years and had never come that close to getting caught before. Tonight was a wake-up call. She wasn't going to waste it.

Chapter 12

" 'Morning, Wanda," Beth mumbled, stifling a yawn as she started down the hall to help bring the patients into the dining room for breakfast. That five-thirty alarm was murder on Wednesday morning.

"Hey, Beth. You awake yet?"

"I stayed after class last night to work with some people on a group project. I feel like I haven't even been to bed."

"You poor thing. You better get some coffee."

"I will."

For the next fifteen minutes, she guided her ambulatory patients down the hall and assisted those who were in wheelchairs. She always saved Miss Violet for last so she could spend a little extra time with her. She was surprised to find her sitting up in bed, but making no attempt to dress herself.

"Good morning, Miss Violet. Did you sleep well?"

The old woman didn't answer. She seemed to be confused.

"Miss Violet? Look at me please." Beth studied her face carefully, noting a slight droop in the left eye. She covered the right eye with her hand. "Can you see me?"

"Blurry." The word was barely mumbled.

Beth pressed the emergency call button and in seconds, Francine appeared.

"What is it?"

"I'm not sure. Miss Violet is having a little difficulty getting oriented, and she tells me the vision in her left eye is somewhat blurry." As much as she could, Beth downplayed the seriousness of the symptoms so as not to alarm her patient. "I thought we might want to have her checked out at the hospital."

"That's a good idea, Miss Violet. It's probably not serious, but it's best to be sure." As the charge nurse, Francine quickly began taking vitals.

Beth took Miss Violet's right hand and squeezed gently. "I'm going to call for an ambulance to take you, and then I'll call Audie and let her know."

Miss Violet's response was incomprehensible.

"Tell me again," Beth said, leaning close.

"She'll be scared."

"Yes, I know. But she'll want to be there at the hospital with you." Beth patted her hand and left, racing down the hall to the nurses' station. In moments, the ambulance was on the way from the hospital, which was less than half a mile away.

Nervously, she dialed the number for Audie's cell phone. After three rings, a sleepy voice answered.

"Hello."

"Audie, it's Beth."

"Hey . . . what is it?"

Beth wanted to make sure Audie was wide awake before she continued. "Your grandmother woke up a little confused with some blurry vision. We're sending her to the hospital to get checked out." She wanted to tell Audie not to worry, that it wasn't anything serious, but she didn't know that for sure.

"I'll be right there."

"No, don't come here. Go straight to the emergency room. She'll feel better if she sees you when she gets there."

"Will you come with her?"

"I can't. They won't let us do that. But I'll stay with her here until she leaves." Beth could hear Audie moving around.

"Tell her I love her." Audie's voice was shaky and scared.

"I will. And keep your phone with you, okay?"

"Okay."

Beth hung up and hurried back to Miss Violet's room. "They should be here any minute."

"Miss Violet's already feeling a little better," Francine said. "Isn't that right?"

"Yes," Violet answered clearly.

"It won't hurt to get you checked out, though." Beth heard the crew arrive and stepped into the hallway to wave them down. Then she returned and took Violet's hand again. "I called Audie. I think I woke her up."

Violet tried to smile.

"She's going to meet you at the hospital. And she wanted me to tell you that she loves you."

The attendants came in and took charge. In three minutes, Miss Violet was strapped to the gurney and on her way.

For what seemed like the twentieth time, Audie leaned over to confirm that her Grammaw was breathing normally. Dr. Hill said the oxygen tube was only a precaution, just like the IV bag of fluids. He also said he had upped the dosage of her blood thinner to ward off subsequent problems. For now, Grammaw was stable, comfortable and out of immediate danger.

Audie checked her watch and rummaged in her backpack for her cell phone. It was a quarter to four, which meant Beth would be getting home soon. She tiptoed to the door and looked back one last time, nearly colliding with Beth as she came through the door.

"Beth!" The sight of the familiar face flooded her with relief.

Beth must have sensed the emotion, because she held out her arms to offer a hug. "I was just going to call you," Audie said as she gave in to the embrace.

After a day like today, it felt good to be held. Beth had become one of the few people with whom Audie felt she could let down her guard when it came to her Grammaw.

"I came as soon as I got off work. How is she? Francine said Dr. Hill saw her."

Audie nodded. "He said it was something called TIAs."

"Transient ischemic attacks. That's what we all thought, but we weren't sure."

"He said it was like mini-strokes, but he didn't think there was any more permanent damage. And he gave her more Coumadin . . . I think that's what it's called."

"It's a blood thinner. It should improve her circulation." They walked down the hall to the visitor area and sat beside each other on the couch. "How are you holding up?"

"Okay, I guess. I don't like seeing her hooked up to all that stuff again."

"I'm sure that's really hard. But I don't think this is as serious as what happened to her last time she was here. Dr. Hill told Francine to expect her back at the nursing home tomorrow, so he must not be too worried."

"I know, but he said . . ." She put her fingers to her forehead to try to compose herself. The tears would come, but not until later when she was alone. "He said this was probably caused by the same thing that caused her stroke. So that means it could happen again, and who knows how bad it could be next time?"

Beth put her hand on Audie's thigh. "But he upped her medication. Maybe that will keep it from happening again."

"She went to sleep a little while ago."

"I'm not surprised. We've trained her to go down for her nap in the afternoon."

She recognized and appreciated Beth's attempt to lighten the mood. "So you guys can play poker?"

"Don't be silly. We watch the soaps."

Audie's stomach rumbled.

"I bet you haven't eaten all day."

"I haven't had time."

"We need to feed you before you fall over." Beth lowered her voice and leaned closer. "I don't recommend the hospital cafeteria."

Audie made a face. "I ate here once last time Grammaw was sick. Thought I was going to join her."

"I doubt it would kill you, but it wouldn't do much for your palate. Why don't we head out somewhere?"

"What if Grammaw wakes up and I'm not here?"

"Okay, you stay here and I'll go get you something. What sounds good?"

"I don't know . . . a cheeseburger and fries, I guess."

Beth frowned with disapproval. "You can't keep eating stuff like that."

"I was just trying to think of what was easy. I promise I'll eat whatever you bring." She reached for her wallet and pulled out a twenty, suddenly having second thoughts about what she had just said. "You won't bring me a salad or something like that, will you?"

"I know better than that," Beth answered with a wink. "And it's my treat. But remember, you promised to eat whatever I brought."

"And you remember that I've already had a hard day. Too many vegetables could push me over the edge."

"You gave us a little scare, Miss Violet. We don't like that." Beth leaned one hip onto the edge of the bed and held Violet's hand. Audie sat in the chair nearby, eating her barbecue dinner from a Styrofoam container.

"I'm sorry."

"Don't be sorry. Just don't do it again, okay? I've gotten used to having you around, and I miss you when you're not there."

"The food is better at the nursing home," Violet rasped. With

133

her right hand, she pushed aside the rolling tray. Most of her dinner had gone untouched.

"I'd offer you some of Audie's but I think she's eaten every bite."

"I have a little coleslaw left," Audie piped up.

"You eat it. It's good for you," Beth chided.

"I warned you about the vegetables."

"They won't kill you." She turned back to Violet. "I think that's the first one she's eaten since you went into the hospital."

"I told you she doesn't take care of herself."

"I'm trying to get her to eat better. What else should I work on?"

"Uh . . . hello, everybody! I'm sitting in the room." Audie looked incredulous, but neither her Grammaw nor Beth paid her any mind.

"She should be home in bed by a decent hour," Violet said.

"Eating better . . . home in bed. Anything else?"

"I want her to be happy."

By now, Audie had joined them at the edge of the bed, her good-natured smirk a sign that she was glad for these playful moments, especially after such a stressful day. "How am I supposed to be happy if I have to eat vegetables and go to bed early?"

Beth stood up and walked toward the window so Audie could have the space beside her grandmother. She felt lucky to witness a family moment like this, maybe even a little jealous. Her own family had always been distant. Only she and Kelly openly displayed affection, and even their relationship grew strained as Kelly got older and more rebellious.

"You should go home and feed Buster. You've been here all day," Violet said.

It was clear to Beth that Violet was tired from her ordeal, and Audie looked as though she needed a break too.

"I think that's a good idea, Audie. And it looks to me like your Grammaw could use some rest too. Is that right, Miss Violet?"

Violet nodded, her eyes closing for a couple of seconds.

"I guess we should go then." Audie leaned down and kissed her

Grammaw's forehead, a gesture so sweet it almost moved Beth to tears. "I'll be back tomorrow morning, okay?"

"Goodnight, sweetheart."

"Goodnight, Grammaw."

"Bye, Miss Violet."

"Thank you, Beth."

Audie shoved her hands in her hip pockets as they walked out into the hall. "I appreciate you coming by. That was nice."

"Your Grammaw's my favorite patient. I had to make sure she was okay."

"I think she likes imagining that you're taking care of me."

"What do you mean imagining? I just made her a bunch of promises. Now I have to follow you around at mealtimes and be at your house to tuck you in at ten thirty."

"I should warn you, there's only one thing that will get me in bed by ten thirty."

Beth was tempted to fan herself. "A half a bottle of tequila?"

"Okay, two things," Audie said, nudging Beth with her elbow.

"I'm coming up empty on the other."

Audie grinned. "Then my reputation isn't as bad as I thought."

"Well . . . I wouldn't say that."

"Oh yeah? What have you heard?"

Beth almost laughed at Audie's suspicious look. "Who says I heard anything? I've seen those eyes of yours after a night out. It takes more than tequila to do that."

"Like what?"

"Let's just say the tequila might have gotten you to bed by ten thirty, but it certainly didn't put you to sleep."

Audie smiled gently at the jibe. "So how many days do I have to show up with clear eyes to get you to forget the one time I didn't?"

Beth was taken aback by the sudden serious tone. It was almost as if Audie was hurt she had brought up that morning again. "You're right. I shouldn't have said that."

Audie shrugged. "It's all right. I haven't been a saint or anything, but I'm trying not to worry Grammaw, like you said."

"And you've done a great job. I really am sorry I brought that up again."

"It's okay. I needed somebody to tell me that back then."

"We all need to hear good things too. You should be very proud that your Grammaw has adjusted so well. I've told you before that I think it's because you're so faithful about coming every day, and because you don't worry her too much with how you're doing."

They walked out the front door of the hospital and turned toward the parking lot. Beth had intentionally parked near the familiar Xterra, thinking she might stay until Audie left and they could walk out together.

"Did you get something to eat?"

"I went for the Caesar salad with grilled chicken. It's in the car."

"Why don't you bring it over to the house? I'll show you a couple of ideas I got for fixing the place up."

"It's been a long day for you, Audie. Wouldn't you rather just go home and crash?"

Audie shrugged, a gesture that came off as almost shy. "I'm okay. I just . . . I thought we might hang out for a while . . . maybe talk."

Realization dawned suddenly for Beth, accompanied by a wave of compassion. Audie didn't want to be alone tonight after the day's emotional roller coaster. "I'd love to come over if you're sure. Does this mean you've decided to keep the house?"

"I think so, at least for now. My friend Dennis has a new boyfriend who's an architect." She clicked her key fob to unlock the SUV. "I talked with him the other night at the Gallery and he was telling me that a few renovations might make it worth a whole lot more if I do sell it, and nicer to live in if I don't."

"I love that kind of stuff. I can't wait to hear what he said. Lead the way." She climbed into her car and waited for Audie to back out. Then she followed her through the back streets to the quaint neighborhood two blocks off Sumter's downtown.

Beth was glad to get the invitation, and not just because she wanted to see the old house. It pleased her more that Audie was reaching out to her, and tonight didn't really have anything to do with Miss Violet or BD.

She followed Audie into the driveway and took a good look at the house, which was lit only by the streetlight. Buster appeared in the front window, barking his greeting. She had been here once or twice several years ago to drop Kelly off so she could practice basketball in the driveway with Audie and the other girls. The backboard still hung above the garage, but its net was gone and the rusted rim sagged.

"I take it you don't play anymore," she said, gesturing at the dilapidated basket as she got out of her car.

"Not in years. I guess that's the first thing that should go." Buster barked his welcome from inside the house. "I need to let him out. Watch out."

"I'll be okay." Beth was still wearing her light green nurse's uniform, which would go into the laundry basket as soon as she got home. She held her salad high as Buster greeted them with enthusiasm before running into the backyard.

"Come on in."

Beth walked into the kitchen from the side door and waited for Audie to turn on the lights.

"I should warn you there may be a few dishes in the sink."

From the hesitation in Audie's voice, Beth had expected to see pots and pans piled to the ceiling. Instead, the lights came on to reveal a few small plates, some silverware and several glasses sitting on the counter. That's when she remembered Audie didn't cook.

"Not too bad. If I leave anything out at my house, the ants take over."

"I drowned them all with bug spray already." She reached into the drawer and pulled out a fork. "Here you go. You can eat in the front room."

"Thanks. This is nice. I love the high ceilings."

"This is the first room David said to remodel."

"That's what I've always heard."

The kitchen was plain by modern standards, with solid green

Formica countertops and worn white appliances. The floral wallpaper was starting to peel in a few places, and the linoleum floor was scratched and stained.

"I always try to clean on Mondays, but Buster brings in a lot of dirt."

"It looks fine, Audie. I promise not to do a white-glove inspection, okay? I appreciate you showing me around."

Audie clapped her hands together. "Let's do the tour then. We call this the kitchen."

"Good thinking."

Audie grabbed two cans of soda and led the way, turning on lights as she went. The dining room was exactly as Beth had expected, with a dusty crystal chandelier above a mahogany dining suite that seated eight. The table was draped in a lace tablecloth that looked handmade.

"And through here is the living room, though no one ever lives in here."

It was decorated with modest antiques, including a beautiful Queen Anne davenport and wingback chair. Decorative ceramic lamps sat on tatted doilies around the room.

"This is where you were supposed to entertain all the men who came courting."

"Now you understand why we don't use it." Audie continued across the hall to what was obviously the family room. "This is where we actually live."

A well-worn sofa and recliner were positioned behind a coffee table. Both faced a gas log fireplace, and a large entertainment center sat in the corner.

"This looks comfortable."

"It is. I think I've spent half my life in this room."

"Look!" Beth was delighted by the collection of pictures on the mantle. "It's Audie Pippin when she was an innocent little girl."

Audie snorted. "I was never innocent."

Beth got closer and studied each one. "Where were your front teeth?"

"The tooth fairy got them."

"I remember you like this." She picked up a framed photo of Audie in her high school basketball uniform, kneeling with her hand on a ball. "I have this same picture of Kelly."

"There's a team photo here somewhere." She leaned over her grandmother's recliner and retrieved the picture from the lower shelf of the bookcase. "There's your little sister right there."

"Gosh, she's changed so much since then and you look exactly the same."

"Are you saying I still look like a kid?"

"With that ball cap and ponytail, yes. But not the way you looked when you stopped by my place the other night. That person was definitely not a kid."

"Speaking of going out, I'm going to hold you to what you said about coming out to the Gallery after your board exam. I think you'll have a good time." Audie cleared a space on the sofa and gestured for her to sit down.

"Is it okay to eat in here?"

"Of course. I told you, this is where we live."

"I've never really gotten into the bar scene."

"How come?"

Beth shrugged and opened her salad. "I didn't go out much back when I was your age because Kelly lived with me. I had to be home to cook and take care of the house. And I had to keep an eye on all the kids she hung out with too."

"You mean like me?"

"I didn't worry about you because I knew your Grammaw from the library."

Audie smirked. "Yeah, that got me a free pass with a lot of people. So why didn't you live with your parents?"

"My mom left us when I was fourteen and my dad married Helen, the woman they named hell after. I didn't get along with her, but it was even worse for Kelly because she was little and she still missed our mom. When I moved out, she begged me not to leave her. So I got a two-bedroom apartment and our dad made me her legal guardian."

"How old were you?"

139

"I was nineteen. Kelly was ten."

"That means you practically raised her."

"Pretty much." Beth picked up a chicken strip to eat with her fingers.

"I had no idea. I always wondered why I never saw her parents, but I didn't know she was living with you."

"She didn't tell many people. She wanted them to think she was like everyone else. You remember how important that was in high school."

"Not really. Being queer kind of burst that bubble."

"You knew back then?"

"I think I've always known. I told Grammaw when I was twelve that I didn't want a husband. I wanted a wife."

"What did she say?"

"She humored me, but she would ask me every now and then if I had changed my mind. I was still telling her no when I turned sixteen, so we had a serious talk about it. She told me that I had to be who I was, and that she'd love me no matter what."

"Wow. What a wonderful gift she gave you."

"I take it things weren't that easy for you."

"Not even close. I never talked to anybody when I was growing up. I just tried to muddle through. I figured one of these days I'd meet some guy and it wouldn't feel so uncomfortable. It wasn't until I got to Sumter Vo-Tech and hooked up with a women's group that I realized why everything was so out of whack."

"And Beth the Lesbian was born!"

"Yeah, but her growth was stunted by having to be home every night to take care of her sister."

"You never got to party at all, did you?"

"Not really. I went out a few times, but once Kelly was old enough to figure out the score, she got embarrassed about it."

"Is she cool now?"

"She's better. She didn't like Shelby much, but she swore that didn't have anything to do with her being a woman."

"And everything to do with her being an asshole?"

"Shelby had that effect on everybody." Beth ran her fork through the last piece of lettuce and swabbed it around to soak up the dressing.

"Except you?"

"No, she was always pretty selfish. I thought I could change her. I learned a big lesson on that one."

"My friend Joel's a pediatrician and he says people's personalities are formed when they are babies. You can teach them and train them, but underneath it all, they never really change."

"Do you believe that?"

Audie shrugged. "Maybe at some sort of basic level, like how we approach new things, or whether we're shy or outgoing."

"Have you always been quiet and reserved, reluctant to voice how you really feel?" The bewildered expression on Audie's face was priceless.

"I can't believe you said that with a straight face." Audie took the empty dish from Beth's lap. "Let me show you the rest of the house while I deliberate on a witty retort."

"Deliberate? Another big word for Audie."

Beth followed her back into the kitchen, where Audie opened the back door to let Buster in. The usual commotion followed before Audie firmly commanded him to settle down.

"You're good with animals. I'm sure you'll be great at the outreach job, but I bet the dogs and cats are going to miss you."

"Speaking of animals, how's BD treating you?"

"He hasn't drawn blood in a couple of days."

"You're home free, then." Audie pushed open a door off the kitchen. "This is Grammaw's room. She has her own bathroom."

The room was small but neat. Obviously, Buster wasn't allowed in here. They walked through another door back into the hallway.

"My room's upstairs." Buster led the way. "It's a little messy."

That was a serious understatement. The double bed was wrecked and clothes were scattered everywhere. Telltale sandwich wrappers were wadded up near a trashcan, obviously errant shots.

"Now whatever you do, don't go telling Grammaw about

141

seeing my bedroom this way. We don't want her to have another stroke." She turned and started back down the stairs.

Beth chuckled. "What do you think your Grammaw would say if she knew you were showing me your bedroom?"

"She'd probably think my standards have improved."

Beth stopped abruptly. Now that they were away from the hospital, Audie had let down her guard. But she wasn't being serious about anything this evening, so Beth knew better than to take a remark like that at face value. Still, it was interesting to hear how she compared to Audie's usual companions. "Was that actually a compliment?"

"Why yes, I believe it was. It must have slipped out."

"I knew it had to be an accident."

Beth was astounded when they reached the bottom of the stairs and Audie draped an arm around her shoulder. She couldn't resist wrapping her own around the trim waist. "Not only that, but you've just made history, Nurse Hester."

"Is that the first time you've complimented anyone?"

Audie chucked her with a hip. "No, but it's the first time I've ever shown a woman my bedroom."

"You're kidding!"

"Nope. It's kind of hard to bring women home with your Grammaw sleeping right below you."

"Ah, yes. I'm familiar with that principle. Having a little sister in the next room also has a deleterious effect on one's social life."

"You used my big word!"

"I know." Beth looked down and scuffed her foot as though embarrassed. "Your Grammaw would be so proud."

"See what I mean about raising my standards?"

Beth was pretty sure Audie was only teasing. But she liked having that arm around her, and she definitely liked the context of their playful banter. More and more, it seemed, she wasn't just Miss Violet's nurse.

Chapter 13

The sun was brilliant, its beams aglow in angular columns where they burst through the trees to slice the wooded trail. Ending the day at Sumter Point had become their circadian ritual, a chance to celebrate another glorious day at nature's theatre.

Audie reached out and took Beth's soft, warm hand as they strolled down the path. Never before had she known a magic like this, a tingling in her fingers where their hands touched.

Buster licked her hand again, imploring her to wake up and answer her cell phone.

Audie couldn't remember a time when she was this—

"Wha—?" She opened one eye and tugged her crumpled jacket closer, finding the phone in the front pocket. "Hello?"

"Audie, it's Beth. Nothing's wrong."

"What?" Audie swung her legs out from under the covers and sat up, getting her first clear look at the clock. Six-fucking-thirty on Monday morning! "What is it?"

"My car won't start."

"You need a ride to work or something?"

"No, I need a ride all the way to Tennessee State. Today's my test. If I'm late, they won't even let me take it. They don't offer it again until the spring and that means I won't be able to take the new job in December like Hazel wants me to and I'll have to go through all this cramming again and—"

"Whoa! I'll come get you. Just let me grab a quick shower."

"There's no time. I have to be there at eight and it'll be rush hour by the time we get into Nashville. That's why I was going so early."

"Okay, I'll be right over. Let me find a clean shirt at least."

"I really appreciate this." Beth knew she had said that already about six times, but she couldn't control her nervous energy. Racing to get there under the wire was the worst possible scenario for staying calm enough to take this stupid test.

But at least she had someone to call, someone she was certain would come to her rescue. Ginger would probably have taken her too, but Ginger was staying with Mallory most nights and Beth wasn't even sure she could find a number to reach her. Besides, if Mallory was the jealous type, she might not like her girlfriend doing a favor of this magnitude.

Beth had no doubts about Audie, though. Their friendship seemed to grow more solid with each passing day. In fact, Audie was invading her thoughts more often as they got to know each other—though, technically speaking, thinking about someone while using one's vibrator was called something else.

"We have plenty of time. Did you have a good breakfast?"

Audie's question brought her back to the here and now—not a bad idea, since she was about to take the most important test of her life. "I was going to eat when I got there. I thought it would help me relax, but now I won't have time."

Audie took a sudden turn into downtown Sumter.

"Where are you going?"

"You need something to eat." She pulled up in front of a coffee house and got out. "Stay here and take deep breaths. I'll be back in three minutes."

What part of anxious about being late didn't Audie understand? Beth tried to calm herself. The last thing she needed in her tumultuous stomach was food. This was her own fault for not having a better backup plan.

Audie returned in no time with a brown bag and a tall cup with a lid on it. "Here you go." Before Beth could even check out the contents, they were underway again.

"That was fast."

"You don't have to eat it all. I just wanted to make sure to get something you'd like."

Knowing Audie's eating habits, she was afraid to look inside the bag. Probably donuts or sugary coffeecakes. Her headache would start about halfway through the morning section of the test. But to her delighted surprise, she extracted a bran muffin with nuts, a cup of fresh fruit and a container of nonfat yogurt.

"Why didn't you turn around back there? Shouldn't we be going out the Sumter Pike?"

"Nah, it'll be too busy. This way's faster."

"Audie, this isn't the most direct route. I mapped it out on my computer and even timed it on Saturday to make sure I could do it."

"Trust me, this will be quicker. Back before we started using the designated driver, Dennis and I used to drive home this way from the Gallery because all the cops were on the Pike."

"But isn't this two-lane? What if we get behind a tractor?"

"There are six passing lanes between here and Four Forty and where it comes out is a reverse commute. We won't have to fight the traffic. What time do you have to be there?"

"Eight sharp."

"I'll have you there by a quarter till." She reached over and patted Beth's thigh. "Now relax and enjoy your breakfast."

Beth stared at the hand that still rested on her leg, amazed at how reassured she suddenly felt. And Audie was right that she needed to eat something before going in. They wouldn't get a lunch break until twelve thirty, and there was no way she could concentrate with her stomach making embarrassing noises. She opened the yogurt first. "I was wrong about you, Audie. All this time, I thought you didn't know what healthy food was."

Audie grinned at her. "I just picked three things I wouldn't want to eat."

"I should have known."

"How's BD doing?"

"He's great. He likes to get on the windowsill in the dining room where he's eye-level with the trees outside. That way, the birds and squirrels can sit out there and taunt him. He's so funny when he makes that cackling noise."

"They're probably still pissed at him for eating their relatives."

"I can't believe how much he's calmed down in just a couple of weeks."

"That's because of you. Whatever you're doing with him, he likes."

"Well, he should. He sleeps in my bed and practically eats off my plate. And the last couple of days, he's waited for me to get out of the shower so he could jump in and lick the water."

"Then he's way past happy. He'll be rotten soon. Is he sitting in your lap?"

"Not yet, but he leans against me so I'll pet him."

"Then he wants you to touch him. I bet if you didn't reach out to him, he'd move over into your lap."

They talked more about BD and how to bring him out, and before Beth realized it, they were pulling onto the campus at Tennessee State. It was twenty minutes to eight.

"I can't believe how fast we got here."

"I always keep my promises. Now where's your building?"

Beth directed her through the maze of one-way streets, past the barricaded lots to the fine arts building. "It's up there on the third floor."

Audie peered through the windshield. "So what's the schedule?"

"We should finish up about four, I think."

"What about lunch?"

"It's supposed to be from twelve thirty to two. I brought a—damn it!"

"You left it in your car."

"Shit."

Audie pointed to a bench that faced an adjacent courtyard. "I'll see you right there at twelve thirty."

"You don't have to do that."

"It's no big deal. But first, I'm going back home to get that shower you wouldn't let me take. Then I'll go by and see Grammaw."

Beth gaped at her in disbelief. "I really appreciate all you're doing. This could have been such a disaster."

"But it wasn't. Now relax and go in there and show them what you know."

Beth opened her door and got out, looking back one last time. "Thank you, Audie."

"Just remember one thing." Audie leaned across the console and said in her most serious voice, "You have to eat whatever I bring you."

Audie tipped her sunglasses onto her head as she entered the small shop and waited a few moments for her pupils to adjust to the dim light. For some reason, people didn't want to shop for sex toys under a fluorescent glare. Go figure.

"Hello."

She turned toward the voice, locating the shopkeeper, a balding man of about forty, atop a ladder near the back of the store. "Hey there."

"If you don't see what you want, we probably don't have it."

"Fair enough."

Little had changed in the year or two since her last visit to the

147

store, where most of the patrons were men. That was clear because their toys, books and videos dominated the shelves. The meager women's section was to the left, just inside the front door. Audie took in the offering of books with a sigh. There were only a few, and they were practically the same ones that had been there the last time she was here. But she hadn't come to look at books today. Instead, she was interested in a card, something fun to congratulate Beth for getting the test behind her. She went straight for the rack near the register.

"What kind of card says good job?" she mumbled to herself as she spun the display. The images that leapt out were couples, either in erotic or otherwise romantic poses. That's not what Audie had in mind. Beth was cute and sexy, but they didn't have that sort of relationship. She was looking for something more—

A picture of two women holding hands stopped her short. For the first time in her hectic day, Audie thought of the dream she was having when the phone rang this morning. She and Beth were walking together along the path to Sumter Point, holding hands.

Or maybe it was someone else holding hands with Beth, and Audie was just watching them together. She frowned as she tried to recall the details, the most vivid of which was how soft Beth's hand had been. So it was definitely her, not someone else.

That was confusing because Audie wasn't much of a hand holder. In fact, she couldn't recall holding hands with anyone other than Maxine, and that was usually for balance as she tried to walk around in a cocaine-induced haze. Hand holding was something lovers did.

Audie shook her head to clear her thoughts, turning her attention again to the cards. She needed something that said friends.

Why was she dreaming about Beth like that?

"Finding what you need?"

"Yeah, sure . . . right here." She picked up a card that pictured two women laughing. It was perfect. If there was one thing she liked about Beth, it was her easy laugh.

She tossed the card onto the glass counter, noticing it also served as a display case for a variety of personal accessories and sex toys. More than half the case was taken up by an assortment of silver cock rings and bondage tools, bringing to mind the time she accidentally opened Dennis's dresser drawer in search of a roach clip. It had taken her years to bury that image and now it was roaring back.

"The woman that works here on the weekends says this one's good." The shopkeeper opened the case from behind and drew out a lime-colored, V-shaped dildo with two heads. The shaft was spindled and made from flexible silicone. "It's called a Dual-Do . . . like a dual dildo. Get it?"

She was definitely intrigued, especially when she saw the battery compartment nestled at the curve. Closer examination revealed vibrating tines embedded in both ends of the shaft. This toy would be fun to share.

And no matter how hard she tried, she couldn't help but envision Beth on the other end.

Beth broke into a grin when she spotted the booted feet hanging out of the driver's window of the yellow SUV. She hated to think how things might have gone if Audie had not been there to save the day. Not only had she gotten out of bed at the crack of dawn to drive her to Nashville, she had given up practically her whole day in order to help things go smoothly with her test.

True to her word, she had returned midday to bring lunch—a veggie burger, of all things. She had even eaten one herself, and with tomato, no less. They laughed and made small talk about junk food, anything to keep Beth's mind off the pressures of her test. And now it was all over and Audie was here to drive her home.

So much for her notions about Audie being wild and irresponsible. Not even Ginger would have come through for her the way Audie had today. Beth needed to find a special way to say thanks.

"You're out early," Audie said as she hopped from the vehicle. Apparently, she had been keeping watch in the rearview mirror.

"I finished. The last part was all scenarios where you have to pick what you would do if this or that happened. I just imagined I was at work."

"I bet you got them all right." Audie held the door for Beth to climb into the passenger seat.

"It's what Hazel told me to do. She said just to let my experience take over. She was right."

Audie got in on her side and started the engine. "So all you have to do now is finish your class and you're home free."

"Yeah, but I'll spend the next two weeks chewing my nails off while I wait for my scores."

"But you feel good about how you did."

"Yeah, but not as good as I'll feel when I find out I passed."

"Is it too soon to celebrate?"

"I don't think I'm ready for that yet, but I wouldn't mind taking a walk or something to unwind a little. You want to go down to Sumter Point?"

For reasons Beth couldn't fathom, Audie's jaw dropped and her face suddenly went red as she looked away. "I . . . if . . . sure, if that's what you want."

She couldn't imagine why Audie would blush at such a simple invitation. "We don't have to. I've already used up your whole day off. You can just drop me at home."

"I don't mind, really. I just . . ." The flush had left her face, but her voice was unsteady.

That's when it occurred to Beth that Audie might have other plans for the night, maybe even a date. "You know, I should probably get home to BD instead. I have a couple of chapters I have to read for class tomorrow night."

"Are you sure? We can go for a walk if you want."

"It's okay, really. I don't know what I was thinking. It's been a long day. And I have to see about getting my car fixed tomorrow."

"I can help with that if you want. A friend of mine is—"

"I can't ask you to do that." Beth waved her hand in the air, reluctant to take continued advantage of Audie's generosity. "You've done more than enough."

Audie took the exit that would take them once again along the back roads to Sumter. They rode along in awkward silence, though how it got that way was a mystery. If Audie had a date, why didn't she just say so?

An excited Buster met Audie at the door, leaping straight up on all fours.

"I can't believe I'm such an asshole, Buster." She grabbed his leash and held the door for him to run out.

Why hadn't she just answered yes instead of swallowing her tongue and choking on it? She really had wanted to go, even if it meant shoving her hands in her pockets so she wouldn't get freaked out by seeing her dream come to life.

Something was going on with Beth. Grammaw had seen it, and now Audie could too. It was as if she was back in high school, nursing a crush on her art teacher. Except her silly daydreams about kissing Miss Wilson senseless were replaced by visions of sweat-soaked thighs slapping together as she and Beth Hester did the nasty with a lime green Dual-Do.

Audie dropped Buster's leash and plopped herself on the top step of the porch, burying her head in her hands. There she remained until the crunch of gravel announced a car in her driveway.

"Hiya, Tinkerbell. What brings you out of your cave?"

"I was hoping you could tell me," Dennis said, dropping beside her to sit on the step. "I've called you about nine times today and you never answered."

Audie pulled her cell phone from the breast pocket of her denim jacket. It was off.

"Oops."

"Everything all right?"

"Yeah, why wouldn't it be?"

Dennis shrugged. "It's your day off. Usually you call me. I just thought you might be pissed about something."

"I've been busy. What am I supposed to be pissed about?"

"I don't know. You were mad at me last time we talked. I don't remember what it was about because I was drunk. So when you didn't pick up my call, I figured it must have been bad."

"You shithead." She threw a gentle elbow into his side.

Dennis gave her a lopsided grin. "I know we're still friends if you call me shithead."

"If I ever got that mad at you, I'd tell you about it . . . while I was kicking your pansy ass."

"Well since you're not mad at me, how about you drive us to the Gallery tonight? They're having a Muscle Man contest."

"Be still my throbbing clit."

"Ew!"

Audie checked her watch. It was only seven. That would give her time to make a call or two. "Pick you up at nine?"

"Perfect." Dennis hopped up and started for his car.

"But I'm pulling out of that lot at midnight, with or without you."

"Right," he answered over his shoulder.

"And no weed."

That stopped him short and he turned around. "What?"

"That cop's going to be looking for us. I promised Matt he wasn't going to find anything ever again. No poppers either."

"Not ever?"

"You heard me. I gave him my word."

"But getting high's half the fun."

"So get high at home before we go. We just can't have it in the car."

"Great! First Joel and Dwayne, now you. Pretty soon I won't have any irresponsible friends left."

Still on a high from taking her test, Beth awakened earlier than usual for her day off. "What is that, BD?"

The cat poised for attack as he followed the ripple of her hand beneath the blanket. His hips twitched in anticipation of pouncing on the mysterious prey.

152

"You'd better get it."

He did, leaping across the bed to pierce her blanket—and her finger—with his razor-sharp claws.

"Ow!" Quickly she drew her hand out to find a small scratch, the skin barely broken. "I'm going to have to get Audie to teach you to play without claws."

She threw the covers back, and BD bounded from the bed and through the doorway, ready for his breakfast.

"I can't believe how well you've trained me already. I should still be asleep."

He wove between her legs as she filled his bowl. But the instant she set it on the floor, the doorbell rang and he darted back into the bedroom.

Beth couldn't believe her eyes to see Audie on her doorstep at such an early hour. For a second, she considered grabbing her robe, but dismissed her modesty and answered the door when the bell rang again. She hoped nothing was wrong.

Audie greeted her with a broad smile. "Hi, did I get you up?"

"No, the Black Devil beat you to it. What's up?"

Audie was dressed in her usual attire for a workday, jeans and a T-shirt, with the ever-present black baseball cap. She gestured with her thumb over her shoulder. "My friend Teri's here to fix your car, but she needs your keys."

"Audie! I said you didn't have to do that."

"I know. But she's a friend of mine and I know she won't rip you off."

Beth handed her the car keys.

"Stay here. I'll be right back."

Beth watched from her landing as the two women popped open her hood to look inside. They exchanged a few words before Audie started back up the steps.

"Teri says your battery's corroded. She has one on her truck that'll work, and she'll swap it out for sixty-five bucks."

"Is that all? It would have cost me that much just to tow it to the garage. Tell her to go ahead."

Audie gave her friend the signal and turned back to Beth,

pulling a card from her back pocket as they walked into the condo. "I forgot to give you this yesterday."

"What is it?"

"Open it and see."

Beth peeled open the envelope and pulled out the card, smiling to see the image of two women sharing a laugh. "Is this supposed to be you trying to talk me into taking another cat?"

"No, I think we're discussing what we keep under our beds."

Beth couldn't resist smacking Audie gently on the arm with the card. Then she opened it to read the congratulatory inscription. "Aw, that's so sweet. Thank you." She held out her arms and Audie stepped into a hug.

"I really am proud of you."

"That means a lot to me." Beth broke the embrace quickly, suddenly modest about her thin pajamas. "I wish you didn't have to work today. We could go do something to celebrate."

"I think we should celebrate at the Gallery on Friday night. You said you'd go when you finished with your test."

"I can't go this Friday. I have to be at work at seven o'clock on Saturday. What would your Grammaw say if I walked in with bloodshot eyes?"

"She's already used to that from living with me."

"Yeah, but you weren't giving her medicine."

"You got me there. But what about next Friday when you're off? I'll get Dennis to drive so we can both have a good time."

"You're serious."

"No, I'm Outrageous. Serious doesn't go to clubs. She went once and made everyone so miserable they asked her not to come back."

Beth laughed. "All right, I'll come next Friday. But you have to promise not to let me drink too much and make a fool of myself."

"No promises, except that you'll have a good time and I'll get you home safe and sound," Audie said, shaking her finger at Beth as she walked back out the front door. "I'll tell Teri to come up and knock when she's finished. I'm going out to see Grammaw."

"Tell her I said hi. I'll see both of you out there tomorrow morning."

She leaned in the doorway to watch Audie leave, delighted by the surprise visit and sweet card. Whatever confusion she had felt yesterday about Audie's strange reaction was effectively erased. Their friendship seemed as solid as ever, and unless she was mistaken, they now had what some people might consider a date. Beth only wished she knew if Audie was one of those people.

Chapter 14

Audie had been to the nursing home enough times to recognize an emergency when she saw one. This time, the nurses and aides, including Beth, were gathered two doors down from her grand-mother's room. Wanda waited at the side door to direct the incoming ambulance crew.

"Looks like something's going on down the hall, Grammaw." Audie pushed the door so it was partially closed, shielding her grandmother from the somber activity.

"Can you see who it is?"

Audie nodded grimly, knowing her grandmother would be upset to hear the news. "I think it's Miss Platt."

"I was afraid of that. She hasn't been to breakfast all week," she said.

Audie went to her side. "I'm sorry, Grammaw. I know she's your friend."

"We all have to be ready when our time comes, I guess."

Audie squeezed the frail hand, mentally pushing away a sense of dread. She would never be ready for that to happen to her Grammaw.

"Joel's going to try to come by on Sunday to see you." She usually didn't tell her grandmother about upcoming visits in case they didn't pan out, but she was desperate to change the subject.

"I haven't seen Dennis in I don't know how long."

"That's because Dennis is in love with somebody he met at the Gallery. I hardly see him anymore either." Audie enjoyed the way this news lit up her grandmother's face. She should have told her about it sooner. "Maybe he'll bring David by to meet you."

"I'd like that."

"I'll ask him tonight."

"You're going out with your friends?"

Audie smiled, knowing her grandmother approved of this part of her life, or any part that meant she was having fun. "You know I always go out dancing on Friday night."

"You ought to ask Beth if—" Before she could finish, the ambulance crew noisily rushed through the hallway.

The two of them sat quietly, solemnly waiting for a sign that the commotion had ended. Audie checked her watch. She had to be at work in twenty minutes, but she didn't want to go into the hallway in the midst of all the activity with Miss Platt.

"I'm not afraid of it, Audie . . . of dying, that is. I know I'll see your Grampaw when I get there and it will all be okay."

Audie was taken aback by the sudden statement and waited several seconds before she spoke. "I need you here with me," she said softly, trying in vain to control her cracking voice.

"I'm an old woman, sweetie. It happens to all of us."

"You're not that old. Some of these people here are almost a hundred. You should get to live longer." Tears began to spill freely from her cheeks.

"If it's meant to be, it will be. I just want you to know that I'm at peace with whatever happens, so I don't want you to worry about me. You hear?"

Audie wiped her cheeks with her jacket sleeve and nodded. Subdued voices outside the door told her things were finished with Miss Platt and she stood to leave. After talk of her grandmother dying, she couldn't get out of there fast enough. "I have to go to work."

"You be sweet, Audie."

"I will, Grammaw." She leaned over and kissed her grandmother's forehead and walked quickly out into the hall toward the exit. With her eyes puffy and red, she didn't want anyone to see her, especially Beth. Beth would try to comfort her, which would probably cause her to lose it altogether. The sooner she put this subject out of her mind, the better.

Audie managed to miss seeing anyone in the hall, but Beth didn't miss seeing her.

"Hey, Miss Violet. I just saw Audie leave and she looked upset. Is everything all right?"

"She doesn't like it when I talk about leaving her."

"Are you thinking about going somewhere? Because I'm not going to like that either." Beth tried to sound cheery, but the events of the morning had left her drained.

"What's happened to Edith?"

Beth shook her head sadly. "Her heart just gave out. I'm sorry."

"Did her son get here?"

"He came last night. He was with her this morning when she passed."

Miss Violet sighed heavily. "I'm glad. She wanted him with her."

"It's always good when the family comes. It's hard on everybody when it happens, but I think later they're glad they were there." Beth reached behind Miss Violet to fluff her pillow.

"It's going to be hard on Audie when I leave her."

"I know. She loves you very much." She pulled out her blood pressure cuff and positioned her stethoscope. "But she has a lot of friends who care about her. I know they'll see her through hard times. You shouldn't worry about her."

"Are you still going to be her friend even when she stops coming out here every day?"

The question surprised her coming from Miss Violet, though Beth had asked herself the very same thing on many occasions. "Of course I will. We've been spending some of our free time together getting to know each other. Did she tell you she helped me with my test the other day?"

"Yes, she told me."

"Your granddaughter is a very sweet person and I like her a lot. She's definitely someone I want for a friend."

"She likes you too, Beth," Miss Violet said, her voice now hoarse from talking more than usual. "I think she . . . I guess I ought not say more than that. Audie can talk for herself."

From her seat on the riser Audie had a clear view of the bar and dance floor as the club started to fill. Joel and Dwayne were dancing already, taking advantage of the open space on the floor so they could execute the elaborate routines they practiced at home.

Now on her second margarita, Audie was just starting to relax. Regan had arrived fifteen minutes earlier and started her social rounds—the same ones Audie usually made to see who might be available for company later on. Regan wouldn't venture to this side of the room, since the boys clustered here on Ladies Night.

Audie wasn't interested in going home with anyone tonight. After leaving the nursing home this morning, she had merely gone through the motions at work, her head filled with depressing thoughts about all sorts of things—death, loneliness, emptiness. She would have canceled on her friends tonight were it not for the comfort she always got from Joel's mature friendship.

Beth had become that kind of friend too, but Audie didn't want to lean on her. For reasons she didn't fully understand, she wanted to be strong for Beth. Everything she had been doing lately—accepting the new job, keeping the house, even cutting back on how much pot she smoked—proved that she was becoming more mature and responsible. Beth could tell Grammaw and she wouldn't worry.

But it wasn't just Grammaw she wanted to convince. She wanted Beth's respect and admiration too, and that's what had her so confused and flustered. She clutched the hair around her temples and leaned forward in frustration just as Joel and Dwayne returned to the table.

"What's up, babe?" Joel asked, his hand gently rubbing her back.

"I think I'm losing my mind."

Dwayne leaned over and shouted above the music. "That's nothing. Dennis is in the bathroom with Alan Edwards losing his soul."

"That shithead! What the fuck does he think he's doing?"

"I don't know. I guess things fell apart with David."

"If they haven't, they're about to." Audie nodded in the direction of the door, where David was craning his neck to look around. An unsuspecting friend pointed him toward the restroom.

"Shouldn't somebody go in there and head him off?"

"Dennis is making his own choices," Joel answered. "He knew David was coming tonight."

"But his choice is going to get somebody hurt."

Joel nodded in resignation. "Yeah, and Dennis is the one who's going to have to live it down. It's his reputation on the line. If he ever wants a real relationship, he'll have to work harder to earn somebody's trust."

They watched helplessly as David angrily stormed from the restroom and out the front door of the club. Moments later, a smirking Dennis arrived at their table.

"You fuckhead!" Audie couldn't contain her disgust.

"What's it to you? You're the one that laughed at me for caring about somebody."

"I never laughed at you! I just didn't think you were grown up enough to care about somebody else's feelings, and apparently I was right."

"I didn't know you and David were best friends," he shot back. "Besides, I don't need lessons in relationships from a slut like you."

Audie lunged across the table, instinctively wanting to smack that smug look off his face. Dennis stepped backward out of her reach, but his foot slipped off the edge of the riser and he tumbled onto the dance floor.

In no time, the bouncers were at their table directing all four of them to pack it in for the night. When they reached the lot, Audie stuck with Joel and Dwayne, leaving Dennis to drive home on his own.

Joel put his arm around her shoulder. "Let it go, Audie. He didn't mean it."

"Then why'd he say it?"

"You guys talk to each other like that all the time. It just comes out different when one of you is angry."

"He can go fuck himself."

Dwayne chuckled. "When word gets around about tonight, that's probably all he'll be fucking for a while."

"Serves him right." She squeezed into the back seat of the compact car, swinging her legs sideways so she would have more room.

Joel eyed her in his rearview mirror. "Why does it bother you so much that Dennis is tricking again?"

"I don't care where he puts his dick. But David's a nice guy and he doesn't deserve to be treated like shit." But that wasn't all that bothered her. "What happened to all that bullshit about caring about somebody?"

"I guess he wasn't ready," Joel said.

"He needs to grow up and realize there's more to life than just fucking."

"You're preaching to the choir, you know." Joel's face sported something between a grin and a knowing smirk.

"Don't give me any shit, Joel. I'm not in the mood."

❧

161

" . . . Mallory went over and asked Bruce about it and he said it wasn't a big deal, they just needed to go out and cool off."

"So you didn't even see who started it?" Beth asked. She and Ginger were crammed in a small dressing room, where she was trying to find something nice to wear next Friday when she went out with Audie to the Gallery.

"No, nobody saw anything until the one guy fell and the bouncers threw them all out."

"I wonder what it was about."

"Why don't you ask Audie? And then tell me so I can tell everybody else."

"Mmmm . . . She doesn't talk to me much about things like that . . . probably because I made her feel like going out to the Gallery was beneath me or something."

Beth twisted from side to side with a questioning look. The brown leather miniskirt clung to her hips and showed off plenty of her thighs. She had never worn such a provocative piece in her life.

"That's the one," Ginger said, beaming her approval. With a whisper she added, "You are going to get so laid."

"Stop it!" Beth could feel her face get red. "Audie doesn't think about me like that. She just wants me to meet her friends and show me what she does for fun."

"Do you seriously think Audie Pippin wouldn't go for you? I've seen her in action. She's hot for anything that moves."

"Thanks for the ringing endorsement," Beth said with a groan. She pulled off her shirt and hung it neatly on the hook.

"I didn't mean it like that." Ginger handed her the sparkly white top she thought would go well with the skirt. "I just meant she could have pretty much anyone she wants, but you're the one she asked to come with her."

"Yeah, with her and Dennis Bell."

"He's the one that ended up on the floor. Mallory says he's usually fun to be around."

"Right, and he's her best friend. Why didn't you take me on

your first date with Mallory?" Beth tugged the hem of the spandex top in a vain attempt to have it meet the waistband of the skirt. "This is too little."

"It's supposed to fit like that. Show a little skin."

Beth remembered Audie's outfit the night she stopped by on her way to the Gallery. Her bare midriff had sported a very sexy belly ring. "I don't think I have the figure for it."

"Don't be ridiculous. You look great. Except you'll need to wear a thong with that skirt or you'll have lines."

"A thong? With this?" Beth gestured at the hemline. "Why don't I just go naked?"

"Naked works too."

Beth huffed and pushed the curtain aside, stepping into the hallway to ponder her appearance in a three-way mirror. It was definitely a hot look, one that seemed ridiculous if Ginger was wrong. "What's Audie going to think if I show up looking like a hooker?"

"You don't look like a hooker, Beth. You look like half the women at the Gallery. But if you're more comfortable in wool slacks and a pastel sweater set, that's what you ought to wear," Ginger said, not bothering to hide her sarcasm. "Just don't expect to get laid."

"Did it ever occur to you that I might not want to just get laid? Some people want relationships with a little more depth." Despite her protests, she had been fantasizing about Audie so much that she wasn't sure she even cared anymore whether there were strings attached or not. If it turned out to be only a sexual fling—which it probably would—at least she would have the satisfaction of knowing she could interest Audie that way.

"Look, I know you haven't asked for my opinion, but you're my best friend so I get to tell it to you anyway. Right?"

Beth rolled her eyes and nodded.

"If you're wanting more out of Audie Pippin than a quick fuck, you're wasting your time. Mallory says she just hooks up and moves on. She might come back later or she might not. It's all a game to her. And I hate to admit it, but Mallory says she knows from experience."

Beth felt her stomach roll over. She could have done without knowing that Audie had once slept with Ginger's girlfriend. But it wasn't fair to judge her for how she had acted with other women. "That isn't the Audie Pippin I know."

"Maybe not, Beth, but that's who she is. I've seen it for myself. The way she moves from one table to another at the Gallery, how she dances with her hands all over somebody. She's sexy as hell, but she's not somebody you ought to get hung up on if you're looking for more than just a night or two. You deserve better than that."

Beth sighed and slumped onto the bench. "You know what's ironic, Ginger? I believe Audie actually cares about me. But I bet the thought of us having sex has never even entered her mind. She doesn't give off anything like that around me."

"Maybe it's because she respects you too much to treat you like she treats everybody else. That makes you lucky."

"You say that like she's a terrible person. She's not."

"I'm sure she's nice. But she better not treat my best friend like shit either."

"We haven't even been out yet, Ginger. At least promise you'll hold off on kicking her ass until she's done something to deserve it."

Ginger grinned. "Fair enough. But I guarantee if you show up on Friday night in that, she's going to hit on you big-time."

Beth looked back at the mirror one last time. "I guess I'm going to need some shoes too."

"Let's go, Buster!" Audie picked up the Frisbee and headed out the kitchen door with the excited dog on her heels. It was probably too cool for her Grammaw to sit outside, but she could watch them play from her window.

For most of the weekend, she stewed about the incident on

Friday night, so much that both her Grammaw and Beth had commented on her quiet mood. And as she headed outside, she was none too pleased to see Dennis pull into her driveway, blocking her exit. She tossed the Frisbee into the backyard for Buster and dropped to a seat on the top step of the porch.

Dennis got out of his car and walked toward her, meekly shoving his hands into his pockets. Though he sported a weak smile, his tentative gait gave away his apprehension.

"I called David to apologize. All things considered, I'd say he took it pretty well."

Audie didn't answer. Dennis was going to have to crawl back to her and even that wouldn't make up for what he had done to David.

"He said he thought we should have a little space, so that I could fuck myself until my dick fell off."

As usual, he was making light of his actions, trying to get a pass. But Audie wasn't buying it this time.

"Look, Audie. It just happened. You know I've always been hot for Alan, but he never gave me the time of day. We went into the john and did a line of coke and the next thing I knew, I was in his ass."

"Can we not talk about your dick for a change?"

Dennis sighed and slumped against the Xterra. "I didn't come over to talk about Alan or David. I came to say I was sorry for what I said to you. I know we've kidded around before and I honestly didn't think you'd get so mad."

"You didn't say it like you were kidding."

"I know. I was feeling defensive about being such a fuckhead so I took it out on you. In case you haven't noticed, I'm not the most mature guy in the world."

She couldn't argue with that.

"But you're my best friend and I fucked with that. That's what I'm really sorry about. I couldn't stand it if we weren't friends anymore."

His reasoning made more sense than she wanted to give him

credit for. Even Joel and Dwayne had noticed their propensity for vicious teasing. Besides, it wasn't as if he had called her something that wasn't basically true. She had done her share of sleeping around. "You think they'll let any of us back in the Gallery?"

Dennis nodded. "Joel made me call Bruce yesterday and apologize. He said it wasn't that big a deal. He just didn't want other people to think it was okay to be shoving each other around."

"I never touched you. You fell."

Dennis rolled his eyes. "I was afraid you were going to kick my pansy ass like you said."

"You're lucky I didn't."

"We're all lucky we didn't end up in jail."

Audie looked out over the backyard and tossed the Frisbee again to Buster. "I'm going to bring somebody next Friday . . . somebody I like."

"You mean a girlfriend?"

"No, just somebody I like. I want to dance with her and have a good time, and I want you to be nice to her."

"Does this mean I can't talk about my dick?"

"That's exactly what it means."

"Can I make fun of your pussy?"

Audie swung her foot out to kick him but he jumped aside. They really had gotten crude with each other over the years.

"Is it anybody I know?"

"Beth Hester." She looked away again, not caring to see his reaction.

"Beth Hester? You mean the—"

"Don't say it."

"I was going to say the cute woman that works out at the nursing home."

"Sure you were."

"You seeing her?"

"I might be. We're going out, but we never actually said it was a date or anything. I don't know what she wants, but I like being with her. Either way, I don't want you being your usual jerk-off self around her. She's not like that."

166

"I'll be good. You want me to drive? That way, you both can have a good time."

"You know, that's another thing. When it's your night to drive, you're not supposed to be blowing coke up your nose."

"Yeah, I know. I fucked up all the way around."

"I'll say. I'm going to drive us both. Beth's never been before and she may not like it."

"What's not to like?"

Audie shrugged. "She's not much for partying. And she goes to work at the ass-crack of dawn so she might get tired early."

"Maybe I can ride with Joel and Dwayne."

"Or maybe you should call David again."

"Probably. But if I have to crawl back there on my knees, it needs to be because I really want to and not because my friends all shamed me."

"You don't really want to?"

"He kept putting me off. I got tired of waiting."

"Putting you off? You mean all this time you've been seeing him you weren't getting laid?"

"It's like he wanted to be married first. I liked him a lot, but I'm not ready for that."

"Maybe he just wanted to be sure you weren't the type to fuck around on him."

"Guess I flunked that test. I'll talk to him again one of these days. I think he's got issues of his own, but maybe we can at least be friends."

Audie looked away pensively and, in a voice just barely above a whisper, said, "It's hard to put your emotions out there with somebody."

"Tell me about it. Tricking really is a lot easier."

"Maybe . . . it just isn't worth much at the end of the day."

Chapter 15

Audie couldn't remember a time when she had been this nervous. A quick call late in the afternoon confirmed she and Beth were still on for tonight, but on for what was still anyone's guess. Somehow, she had never found the right words to clear that up without creating a situation that might have embarrassed both of them. She hoped Beth thought of this as a date, because that's what she wanted it to be. Beth liked her—that much she knew—but she had never given any sign that she wanted more than friendship. All fine and good, except friendship wasn't enough for Audie anymore. She thought about Beth all the time, allowing herself to get carried away with what it would be like to run her tongue over those pretty lips and bury her face in the soft, warm skin of her thighs.

At least, she presumed those thighs would be soft and warm. That's how they were in her fantasies.

Beth Hester was under her skin more than anyone she had ever met, even Maxine, with whom she had been totally obsessed. But she had more to offer Beth than she had Maxine. And Beth had better things to offer in return.

The Xterra was squeaky clean, and Audie had on her best—and tightest—jeans with a form-fitting black shirt. She had her hair down, and for some reason that made her self-conscious. She practically felt like a different person.

She pulled into the space next to Beth's Mazda and peered up toward the condo, where a light was on in the kitchen. If this was a date, she should go up and ring the doorbell. But if it was two friends getting together to go out, a couple of toots on the horn would suffice. A full thirty seconds passed before she decided to get out and go to the door.

By the time she reached the landing on the stairs, Beth had come out of her condo and started down. With one look, Audie decided she wanted this to be a date.

"Wow."

"Hey," Beth answered with a shy smile. If the look on her face was any indication, she was as nervous about this as Audie.

"You look great," she said, her eyes running up and down to capture everything. What she looked was hot as hell and Audie couldn't wait to get her out on the dance floor. Determined now to treat Beth as her date, she rushed to open the passenger door and waited while Beth got situated before closing it. Then she hurried around to the other side and got in.

"I had no idea what to wear," Beth said.

"You guessed perfectly." She looked over as the interior light was fading and got an eyeful of thigh. Soft and warm—she was sure of it. And that was about the sexiest skirt she had ever seen.

"Thanks. I had help from a friend of mine. She's been to the Gallery a few times on Ladies Night and she gave me an idea of what people were wearing."

No one was wearing that, or at least they weren't wearing it as well as Beth. Audie would have noticed. "Who's your friend? Anyone I know?"

"Ginger Biggs."

"You mean Mallory Coffin's friend?"

"That's her."

"I didn't know you knew them." That meant Beth probably knew she and Mallory had fooled around with each other a while back, she thought dismally.

"Shelby the Asshole ran off with Ginger's girlfriend, Tonya, and she and I were left wondering what the hell happened. We ended up being best friends. I don't really know Mallory, though."

Audie was glad to hear that. Still, her history with Mallory was probably something that would come out eventually.

"They're supposed to be there tonight."

Audie tried to smile, but her head was already working on how she was going to handle running into the half-dozen women she had hooked up with, especially Regan, whose hands would be all over her as soon as she got there.

"I thought your friend Dennis was going to drive."

"He's going to ride with Joel and Dwayne. I can't wait for you to meet them. They're great guys."

"Joel's the doctor that comes to see your Grammaw, isn't he?"

The small talk was good for Audie's nerves, especially the mention of her grandmother. She felt herself relax as they drifted into casual conversation.

Beth propped her small purse against her leg, dreadfully self-conscious about how far her skirt had ridden up when she climbed into the car. Audie approved of her outfit—she made that more than clear—but that did little to diminish her discomfort about feeling so exposed.

Other than that, things were going pretty well. Audie had seemed nervous at first too, and Beth found that oddly comforting. Going out together like this definitely marked a change in their friendship, even if it wasn't clear what that change was.

"Here we are." Audie drove past the club and around the corner to an already-crowded parking lot. "Looks like a packed house."

"Are Fridays always this busy?"

"Nah, word probably got out that you were coming."

"Very funny." By the time she got her door open, Audie had already hurried around.

"You might want to leave your purse under the front seat. Just take your ID."

"I don't have any pockets."

"I'll carry it for you." Audie unbuttoned her shirt pocket and held out her hand.

Beth handed over her driver's license and started to collect a few bills.

"You won't need any money. I invited you, remember?"

"So you did."

Audie held the driver's license up to the streetlamp as they walked toward the club. "Elizabeth Jane Hester. We have the same middle name."

"I know, Audrey Jane. I remember the first time your Grammaw called you that. It was when you cursed at me."

Audie chuckled. "Yeah, that's when Grammaw thought you were all sweet and innocent. But don't worry, I set her straight."

"Hey, I only use bad words when I talk about Shelby. That shouldn't count."

"I wonder why I never see her out on Ladies Night."

"Because she's a social misfit. Let's hope she keeps that streak alive tonight."

They reached the front door to the club, which was already vibrating with the beat of the bass.

"Five bucks, ladies. And let's see some ID."

Audie held out both cards and passed the doorman a ten. Once inside, she stopped and scanned the room.

"Ginger's over there," Audie said, leaning close enough to make the hair on the back of Beth's neck stand up. She was pointing to a group of tables near the dance floor. Then she turned toward a small cluster of tables on the riser at the back of the club. "My friends usually sit back there, but we can go wherever you like."

171

"Why don't we—"

"What?"

Beth used her fingers to pull Audie's long hair back and leaned into her so that her lips almost touched her ear. "Why don't we sit with your friends for a while? We can go say hi to Ginger later."

Audie nodded and started through the crowd, stopping to reach behind her for Beth's hand. "So we don't get separated."

Beth didn't care if it was to keep her from picking pockets. She liked having Audie lead her through the club in front of everyone.

"Everybody, this is my friend, Beth Hester."

Beth gave a small wave to the three young men at the table.

"This is Joel."

"I've seen you out at the nursing home," Beth shouted over the music, taking his offered hand. She was tempted to tell him that half the nurses at the home swooned whenever he came around. He was definitely handsome.

"And this is his wife, Miss Dwayne."

Beth laughed and stuck out her hand. Joel's partner was wearing a strapless evening gown, rhinestone jewelry and a horrible blond wig that contrasted sharply with his black moustache and chest hair.

"Don't laugh, sweetie. I got in for five bucks."

"And this is my best friend on the planet, Dennis Bell."

Dennis glanced at Audie and grinned, as though being called Audie's best friend meant the world to him. Then he held out his hand to Beth. "Hi. You're Kelly's sister. I used to see you at the high school."

"That's right. I thought you looked familiar."

"How's Kelly?"

"She's doing great. Married with a one-year-old. She lives in Knoxville."

"Tell her I said hi."

"I will." Beth felt immediately at home among Audie's friends and took one of the open seats at their table.

Audie bent over her shoulder. "You want something to drink?"

"What's good?"

"I usually have half a dozen margaritas, but I'm only having one tonight since I'm driving."

"Maybe I'll have the other five." Beth hoped Audie knew she was kidding. She would be mopping up the floor after two.

"That I have to see."

"I'll go," Dennis offered, jumping to his feet. Beth was grateful, not wanting to be left alone at a table with virtual strangers.

"Is it always this loud in here?" she shouted toward Audie, who sat down and cupped her ear playfully as though not hearing the question.

"It won't seem loud when we're dancing. Your friends are out on the floor."

Sure enough, Ginger and Mallory were moving wildly to the music, just like all the other couples out there. Beth had never danced like that, but she had practiced lots of moves in the mirror. The last thing she wanted was to embarrass herself when she and Audie went onto the floor.

"Here you go." Dennis deposited two margaritas on the table and returned to his seat.

Beth held up her stemmed glass to Audie's. "Cheers."

"Cheers." Audie clinked them together and took a big swallow, watching Beth as she tasted her drink. "And congratulations again for finishing your test."

"Thanks. Mmm, that's good. I bet it kicks my butt." Beth took several gulps, finding the tart beverage quite refreshing.

"It will if you drink it down like that. You've been up a long time today."

"I cheated and drank coffee when I got home."

"Then you should have lots of energy," Audie answered, setting both drinks on the table as she stood.

Beth took her cue and stood too, nervously following Audie through the crowd to join the throng. Twisting and sliding, they stopped in the center of the floor, where Audie turned and began to dance. To Beth's relief, her style was low-key compared to the others, but she looked a thousand times sexier, swinging her hips in a sensuous rhythm.

Little by little, she loosened up, trying as best she could to mimic Audie's casual moves. She found herself staring at Audie's crotch, her imagination on overload as she recalled Ginger's remark about being able to see the outline of her pubic hair through her tight jeans.

"Want to go see your friends?"

The question came out of nowhere and snapped her back to the present. She had no idea how long she had been watching Audie's hips, but Audie had to have seen her. Beth fanned herself and blurted out a lame excuse for her growing blush. "It's warm in here."

Audie guided her to where her friends were gathered. Ginger was the first one on her feet, holding out her arms for a welcoming hug.

"Well?" she asked, careful not to let anyone hear.

Beth gave her a weak smile and a shrug. She knew what Ginger was asking, but the answer wasn't quite clear to her yet.

Ginger tugged her back. "At least tell me she liked your outfit."

"Oh, she definitely liked my outfit."

As they talked, Audie was making her rounds of the table, greeting Mallory and the others. Beth spotted a skinny blonde headed their way . . . Audie's way, to be precise.

"Hey, beautiful," the woman said, her voice dripping with invitation as she slid her hand over Audie's rear.

"Regan, hi." Audie twisted and stepped back so they weren't touching.

"Come dance with me."

"I, uh . . ."

Beth looked from one woman to the other and back, holding her breath as she waited for Audie's reaction.

"I'm here with somebody." She held out her arm and Beth quickly stepped into it, folding it around her waist. "This is Beth."

"Hey!" Regan's eyes traveled from Beth's head to her feet, and her face broke into a lascivious grin, giving Beth the distinct impression she was being invited to dump Audie and come along with her. "Interesting."

What the hell did "interesting" mean?

Before she could ask that aloud, Audie squeezed her waist. "Are you ready for another drink?"

Beth shifted ever so slightly, just enough to make it clear that she was no longer including Regan in their conversation. "No, what I'm ready for is another dance."

Audie concentrated on the sway of Beth's hips as the music pulsated, appreciating for herself what Regan had checked out. Beth had a great figure for a leather miniskirt, and her spandex top showed off every dip and curve.

Audie didn't usually dance with someone like this, four feet apart, unless it was one of those rare moments of boredom when she took to the floor with Dennis. She preferred to be closer . . . much closer. She liked having her hands all over her partner, pressing against her in a grind that heated both their bodies. It was foreplay for whatever else the night would bring.

So why wasn't she dancing that way with Beth?

Beth was the sexiest woman in the room as far as Audie was concerned. Audie knew practically all the regulars at the Gallery, and there wasn't a single woman here she didn't like. But none of them interested her like Beth.

The song faded, only to be replaced by another, this one with a slow, sultry beat. Audie took a deep breath and sidled closer, putting both hands on Beth's waist. "Stay with me?"

Beth was back-to-back with another dancer and had nowhere to go even if she wanted to. "I'll try."

Audie looked directly into her eyes as they bobbed two beats to one side, then two to the other. She wanted to erase the image of her with Regan, the one that painted her as a party girl only looking for a good time. "I liked saying you were here with me."

"I liked hearing it."

An array of unspoken emotions passed between them. Audie knew their friendship was changing right this instant and that Beth was feeling it too. She pressed her hip into Beth's and slid behind her, never breaking contact. From there, she dropped her hands to Beth's hipbones and pulled her close. Had this been someone else, she might have hooked her thumbs inside the skirt's waistband, but for now she was content simply to feel Beth's body against hers.

They kept their rhythm, but Audie subtly changed the double beat to each side to one long beat that lingered. Beth relaxed against her at the slower cadence.

"This is nice," Audie murmured, feeling a rush of tenderness that she had never felt when she danced with a woman like this. For the first time, her dance-floor caress seemed almost too intimate for a Gallery audience. But she didn't want to stop. She slid one hand up to Beth's waist, where she could feel the warm skin of her stomach between the top and the skirt. Her other hand began to roam the curves of Beth's hip, from her side to her thigh and back.

Beth responded by covering the hand on her waist with both hands and dropping her head to rest against Audie's shoulder. Unable to resist the bare skin, Audie planted a soft kiss on the long muscle of her neck. She easily could have gotten carried away after the first touch, but the music abruptly shifted to a rapid techno-beat.

She tightened her grip on Beth's waist, not at all interested in staying out on the floor now that the mood was broken. "Are you ready for that drink now?"

"Let's go outside."

Audie's heart skipped a beat. "Is something wrong?"

Beth took her hand and pulled her toward the door and out, not slowing down until they reached the doorway of an adjacent storefront. The awning shielded them from the streetlight and the prying eyes of patrons going in and out of the club.

"What's wrong?" Audie was beginning to think she had just made a huge mistake.

"Nothing. I just didn't want our first kiss to be in front of the whole world."

Audie barely had a chance to draw a breath before Beth's open mouth covered hers. But her response was instantaneous. She took Beth's head in her hands and held her in place, asserting her own lips and tongue in hungry exploration. It wasn't just a kiss to her—she was trying to say something, trying to tell her about these feelings she had.

She felt Beth's cool hands slide underneath her shirt against the bare skin of her back and she answered in kind, stroking the leather-clad backside from waistband to hem. Their kisses intensified and before she realized it, she had slipped her fingers underneath the skirt to caress soft, bare cheeks. Beth's hips ground against her until she thought her knees might buckle.

"I knew you'd be a good kisser," Audie panted when their lips finally broke apart.

"We should have done that sooner."

"Now you tell me. You've been driving me crazy all night." She hugged Beth close and kissed her again. "You think we should go back inside before we get arrested?"

"The way I'm feeling right now, I think we'd get arrested in there too. Maybe we should go back to my place."

Chapter 16

If anyone had ever told her she would be making out in public with a woman whose hands were all over her naked ass, Beth would have laughed them off the face of the earth.

All the way home, Audie's hand rested on her thigh, and she had never been so turned on in her life. She was sure Audie could hear her heart pounding as they pulled into her condo complex. She had no doubt about what they would do upstairs and she was ready for it. It didn't matter if there were strings attached or not. All she wanted was to feel Audie all over her tonight.

"I thought we'd never get here." Audie killed the engine and leaned across the clunky console, pulling her into an embrace. "Now where were we?"

"I distinctly remember your mouth was on mine," Beth answered, parting her lips as she fell into Audie's arms. They kissed again, less hurried than their first one on the sidewalk. Audie's soft tongue gently rimmed her lips and teeth, teasing her own tongue to reciprocate. As their breaths grew deeper, Audie's hand wandered to the inside of her thigh, barely inches from the lace thong that shielded her growing arousal. "Maybe we should take this upstairs," Beth sputtered.

Audie chuckled. "But I cleaned my car just for you."

"Sorry, but I have a five-minute limit when it comes to making out over a gearshift. We're pushing that now."

"Then maybe we should go upstairs and find some more limits to push."

Even in the dim light, Beth discerned a smug, playful look. Audie was keeping things light, but Beth didn't care. She wasn't going to kid herself that this was about anything but a good time. She glanced down at the door handle and back. "So do I have to get my own door this time?"

Audie practically flew out her door and around to Beth's side. She extended her elbow, which Beth took with her hand, and led the way up the stairs.

"You realize when I open this door that that beast you gave me is going to demand all of my attention. I hope you can handle being second."

"I could always coax him into a closet and shut the door."

As predicted, they were greeted by BD, who merely insisted on a scoop of fresh food. Beth served it up in the kitchen as Audie looked on from the doorway.

"He looks happy . . . and occupied," Audie said.

"You don't look very occupied." But she looked very sexy, Beth thought. She was going to have to find a way to convince Audie to wear her hair down more often.

"I have some ideas for things we could do to stay busy."

"I hope they involve more kissing." Beth leaned into her, placing both palms just above her breasts. Audie met her with another kiss, wrapping her arms around Beth's waist.

"Lots of kissing . . . in lots of places."

Beth shuddered hard as she envisioned Audie's lips traveling across her breasts.

Audie released her grip and leaned back so they were face to face. For the first time all night, her confidence seemed to waver. "Did I say something wrong?"

Beth felt the beginnings of a blush. "Definitely not." She pulled Audie's face back to hers and they kissed again, slow and luxurious, as if kissing was all there was. Beth loved this sweet connection, but she was bursting for more, and she didn't care if it happened right here on the kitchen floor.

As if reading her mind, Audie's hands returned to her rear and gently worked the miniskirt up so that her fingers were caressing bare skin. "Does this look as beautiful as it feels?"

"You'll have to answer that one yourself . . . but we might be more comfortable in the bedroom."

"I like bedrooms. Bedrooms are good."

She flipped off the kitchen light and took Audie's hand to lead her into the bedroom. A trickle of light seeped in through the blinds on the sliding glass door. "Do you want the lamp?"

"I don't know how else I'm going to compare the look and feel."

Her hand shaking slightly, Beth clicked the bedside lamp on low and turned once again to face Audie. "Will I get a sticker when you're finished that says 'Inspected by Number Twenty-Three'?"

"I'll give you anything you want," Audie answered, grasping the hem of the spandex top and slowly pushing it upward.

Beth raised her arms to allow it to be removed. Like everything else she wore, her bra was new, a white satin underwire with lace trim around the tops of her breasts.

Audie brushed the lace with her fingertips. "This is pretty," she whispered.

Beth felt her breasts rise in anticipation of being touched, but the tickling sensation traveled to her shoulders instead. With a gentle nudge, Audie turned her to face the bed.

"Lie down for me, just like this."

Beth pulled the covers back and crawled onto the sheet face down, ever conscious that her short skirt and thong left little to the imagination. She shuddered again to feel Audie ease herself onto the bed alongside her, her warm hands gliding across her back and down to her thigh.

"You've been torturing me all night with this loincloth, you know . . . especially when I discovered what was underneath it." She fingered the thong. "Please tell me this matches your bra."

"It does." Audie's hand was completely under her skirt now, stroking the curves of her rear. Her hips began to writhe, and she pressed into the mattress with need. She felt Audie shift her position slightly and the zipper on her skirt was lowered. Bit by bit, the leather slid down her legs, leaving her in only her thong and bra.

"You're beautiful, Beth." As her hands roamed the naked flesh, her lips trailed from Beth's spine to her shoulder.

"I want to feel your skin next to mine."

The air felt cool as Audie pulled away, but Beth heated up inside as she waited to feel Audie's body next to hers. She began to roll over but a hand stopped her.

"Stay like this for me."

Beth lay back down, listening to the sounds of clothes being removed. When Audie returned to her, the sleek sensation of the naked body on top nearly took her breath away.

"Is this what you wanted?"

"Exactly." She reached a hand behind her and stroked Audie's hip. "But who's torturing whom now?"

"I want to take my time with you," Audie murmured, her hair falling across Beth's back. "But I promise to give you everything you need. Will you let me do that?"

Beth nodded and relaxed as her bra was unhooked and pushed off her arms. She lifted slightly and pulled it aside, dropping it carelessly on the floor beside the bed. Audie massaged her back with a featherlight touch, stroking the sides of her breasts as her fingers wandered. It was exquisite, but Beth was already looking past the backrub, her breath hitching each time Audie's fingers wandered below the thong.

"Why don't we take this lovely thing off too?" Inch by inch, the thong was lowered and she heard Audie draw a deep breath through her nostrils. "I'm never giving this back."

She quivered as Audie's long hair tickled her calves, her knees and her thighs. When Audie's lips touched her backside, she instinctively raised her hips. She had no idea that part of her body would be so sensitive, but Audie seemed to know.

"I'm an ass woman, in case you haven't figured that out," Audie said, kneading both cheeks as she kissed the pliable skin. "And yours makes me very glad of that."

"You . . . I'm so . . . it . . ." Beth couldn't seem to form a complete thought.

"I'm going to touch you now."

She shook as Audie's fingers glided through her wet flesh, collecting her essence, which she then used to paint the length of her cleft until it was slick. Beth responded by bending a knee to spread her legs, not caring that she was fully exposed.

"That's lovely." She painted one more swipe. "I have to feel you inside."

Beth moaned as Audie entered her vagina, and every four seconds thereafter, in the same rhythm as curled fingers slid in and out against her wall. The accompanying sensation of Audie's tongue lapping the moisture from her cleft was more than her body could stand. Her clitoris, which had been screaming for a touch, didn't seem to exist anymore. An orgasm was roaring forth from somewhere deep inside, and she held her breath to prolong its impact.

"Oh, God." Finally, she gasped deeply as she pulsed around the fingers that slid in and out. With her eyes closed tightly in concentration, she waited until the tremors waned. "That was . . . oh, God . . . I can't even talk."

Audie gently pulled out and whispered into Beth's ear. "You don't have to talk. Just relax and let it flow through you." She pulled up the blankets to cover them and snuggled her body close, tucking one arm underneath so that it rested between Beth's breasts. "We're just getting started."

Still face down, Beth could smell herself faintly on Audie's hand and lips. She focused on the feel of the warm skin on hers, trying to discern where her own body connected with Audie's breasts, hips, and—

"I want to see your tattoo," she said, using both hands to push herself up. "I've been dying to know what it is."

Audie chuckled and rolled onto her back as Beth sat up and threw back the covers. The sight nearly stole her breath—not the tattoo, but the smooth-shaven pubis. So much for Ginger's claim about being able to see pubic hair through Audie's jeans. "Wow."

"Do you like it?" Audie stretched the skin to show off a red apple hanging from a tree branch.

"I love it." Beth forced her eyes onto the tattoo. "It's an apple."

"Not just any apple," Audie said, reaching up to caress one of Beth's breasts.

"It's a pippin."

"That's right. But we'll be kicked out of Eden if you take a bite," she added playfully, leaning forward to close her lips around a nipple.

Beth gasped as her nipple reacted. "I'll take my chances." She bent down and wrapped one arm around Audie's waist, the other underneath her thigh. Her lips landed in the middle of the red circle of the tattoo, which she sucked and nibbled before dropping to her ultimate goal, the shaven folds.

"Let me help you with that." Audie swung her leg across Beth's body, forcing her onto her back. Then she scooted forward and lowered her center onto Beth's waiting mouth.

Beth relished the sensation of the smooth skin against her face, licking all around the slippery lips. She was determined to make it last as long as possible, but each time her tongue crossed the rock-like clitoris, Audie moaned and jerked. She couldn't resist the urge to hear her cry out again and again.

"I'm going to come, Beth. Don't stop . . . don't stop . . . oh, yes . . . coming . . ."

Beth gripped Audie's hips, trying to no avail to keep her from pulling away. But Audie seemed desperate to move and collapsed in a heap next to her on the bed.

"I can't hold myself up when I come that hard," she gasped.

"You don't always have to be on top, you know," Beth answered, rolling over and burying her face in Audie's sweaty neck. Then she had an alarming thought. "Or do you?"

Audie laughed and squeezed her shoulders, seemingly content to rest for now. "No, I don't. But I can be selfish about what I want and watching you do that to me was high on my list."

"How long is your list?"

"Oh, it's very long."

"What happens when we get to the end of the list?"

"That's the beauty of it. The list never ends, because you never cross anything off. That would be like saying 'I don't want to do that again.'" She kissed the top of Beth's head. "And I want to do everything again."

Beth rested her hand on Audie's breast and began to tease the nipple, smiling when she felt it grow stiff.

Audie captured her fingers and held them tight. "Are you going to tell Grammaw that you kept your promise and had me in bed by ten thirty?"

"I don't think I'll be sharing any details about tonight with your grandmother."

"Aw, I didn't know you were shy. Does this mean I can't hang your thong from my rearview mirror?"

Beth groaned and wriggled her hand free, snaking it down to cup the soft skin around Audie's sex. "This was a delightful surprise, by the way."

"Glad you approve. You can't keep your hands off me, can you?"

Beth propped up on her elbow so she could look into Audie's eyes. She had never had any patience for games, and that included holding back her feelings, even if it meant saying too much too soon. "No, I can't. I've wanted to be with you like this." She was relieved to feel Audie's arm tighten around her shoulder.

"Why didn't you say something?"

"Because I wasn't sure until tonight that you even thought of me this way."

"That's because I'm not very good at talking about things . . . and I didn't think you ever thought of me this way either."

"I hate to break this to you, Audie, but everybody probably thinks about you this way."

Audie's face changed to show a hint of irritation.

"It's not a bad thing, trust me." Beth tipped her chin upward so they were looking at each other. "And it's not all you are, either. But I bet most people don't get to see the side of you that I do."

"Which is?"

"Which is a sweet, sensitive young woman who loves her Grammaw very much . . . and who jumps out of bed at six thirty and gives up her whole day off because a friend of hers is freaking out." She planted a soft kiss on the tip of Audie's nose. "And you also happen to be very beautiful and very sexy."

Audie pulled her in for a timid kiss. "I always feel good when I'm with you."

"You make me feel that way too."

The next kiss grew in intensity and Audie's hands began to wander again across Beth's naked skin, settling on her nipples. "Did I happen to mention that I'm also a breast woman?"

Audie gently wriggled her tingling arm from underneath Beth's shoulder. Apparently, neither of them had moved a muscle all night. Of course, that tends to happen when you go to sleep exhausted, she reminded herself with a smile. Beth had worn her out, and if the dead weight beside her was any indication, the sentiment was mutual.

Beth had her number right from the beginning, putting an end to any notions she might have had about being in control of their adventures. Audie rarely let herself get topped, ever since Maxine had drilled it into her head that good sex was about power. Maxine was crazy. Good sex happened when you cared about somebody. Of course, it didn't hurt that Beth knew her way around a clitoris. And around . . . and around.

Audie studied the peaceful form beside her, fighting the urge to wake her with a kiss on her ear. If this were anyone else, she probably would have tiptoed out the door by now. There was never a good reason before to hang around after a night of sex, but that really wasn't what last night was about.

So what was different this time?

The answer came easily. Everything.

Last night hadn't been just a night of pleasure seeking, like it was when she was with Regan or Deanna . . . though she had certainly found plenty of pleasure with Beth. But they had shared much more than sex, talking into the night about their friendship and how their feelings had grown.

If Audie had ever been in love before, she hadn't known it. But nothing had ever felt like this. She probably should have been scared or panicked to realize that, but all she felt was happy, especially with Beth here beside her.

So maybe that's why everything had been different last night. Could it be she had just made love for the first time in her life?

"Hey." Beth squirmed closer and wrapped an arm around her waist, burying her face in Audie's breasts.

"Good morning, beautiful." She leaned forward and kissed the ear that had been tempting her, noticing BD's position on Beth's outstretched thighs. "Are you aware there's a pussy between your legs?" The cat sat up and scratched behind his ear. He had spent part of the night on Audie's pillow, but it was clear his true loyalties were with his new mistress. "And your clock is flashing, which means the power went off last night and it's probably time for me to be at work."

"Are you always this chatty in the morning?" Beth groaned.

"Always. And cheerful . . . especially after a night like last night." Audie stretched for her watch on the bedside table. Eight

186

thirty. "I hate to break this to you but I have to go. There's a border collie on Second Street who really wishes I'd come home and let him out to pee."

Beth pinned her in place by looking directly into her eyes, her expression serious. "I woke up last night and watched you sleep."

"Do I snore?"

"No. You looked so . . . I just wanted to hold you and be close. I liked you being here."

"I liked being here too," she answered, lofting her eyebrows twice in a lascivious gesture. But Beth wasn't amused, and Audie began to suspect there was more to what she was saying than her simple words. "Is everything okay?"

"Yeah, I just . . . I should probably shut up until my brain wakes up or I'll say something stupid."

"No, you shouldn't. You should tell me what you're thinking or I'm going to worry that something's wrong."

"Nothing's wrong, Audie, really. Last night was wonderful."

"I thought so too. But I hear a 'but' in there."

By this time, Beth wasn't meeting her eye, focusing instead on a couple of small moles near her breast, tracing her finger from one to the other and back. "You remember I told you last night that being with you was something I've wanted?"

"Yes, and in case you didn't hear me, I told you the same thing."

"I know." Beth momentarily looked at her but then went back to her finger play. "And I'm really happy about finally being together like that. It's just that . . ."

"What is it? Tell me what's wrong."

"I don't know what you're looking for from me and that's got me a little worried."

Audie swallowed nervously, thinking she might be on the receiving end of a brush-off.

Beth showed mercy and continued. "I wouldn't change a thing about last night, no matter what. But I don't want to do this again if it's just for fun. You mean more to me than that . . . and sex means more to me than that. If we're going to work our way through that list of yours, I want it to be because we care about each other, not just because it feels good."

Audie relaxed as a wave of relief washed over her. "I do care about you. How can I prove that?" She gasped as a hand beneath the covers cupped her sex.

"If we're going to share ourselves this way, I need for this part of you to be just for me."

Now it was clear. This was about her blasé attitude regarding casual sex, one she knew Beth didn't share—and one she was pretty sure she no longer held. What was ironic was that she had come to the conclusion on her own only moments ago. "Then you're in luck, because it just so happens that I don't want to share that with anyone else."

Beth let out a contented sigh. "That's all I needed to hear."

Audie pulled her close as she struggled to sit up in bed. "Then I'm"—she punctuated her words with a kiss—"glad we got"—another kiss—"that settled."

Beth pushed herself up and ran a hand through her hair.

Audie smiled appreciatively at the sight of her body, now in all its glory in the light of day. "You're very pretty, you know," she said, sighing deeply.

"Sure you don't want to call in sick?"

"I do, but I can't." Audie didn't think Oscar would buy hormonal overload as a legitimate illness. "We just hired two new vet techs and I have to train them. And Saturday's our busiest day."

"You're so responsible."

Audie snorted. "That's not something I hear a lot."

"It should be. But take it from me. You don't want it to be all they say about you."

"There's probably no danger of that."

"Seriously, look at how you've stepped up in the last few weeks. You're about to take on a new job with a lot of responsibilities, and you're managing the house all on your own. It's a lot to do."

Audie was mildly uncomfortable with the praise. "I'm not doing anything that other people don't have to do all the time too."

"I know. But you haven't let it take away your fun like I did. I always thought I could do one or the other, but you've made me see that I can do both."

Audie sure enjoyed the sexy side of Beth she had seen last night at the Gallery, but what appealed to her most was her serious side, something she never saw in women like Regan or Deanna. "Do you always talk about such heavy shit first thing in the morning?"

Beth laughed. "Only when you wake up chatty and cheerful."

"Sounds like we need to make a deal or something."

"I'm for anything that means we wake up together."

"Then why don't we try this again tonight?"

"I think I can be persuaded."

"Good." Audie swung her legs out of bed on the other side. "But for now, I need to hurry home before Buster makes me pay."

Beth tossed her dust cloth and grinned broadly as the phone rang again. Audie had already called her four times today just to talk. Most of what they said was silly, but Beth didn't care. She had never been this giddy about a woman in her whole life and it felt great. "Hello, there."

"Hello, yourself."

"Ginger!"

"So where did you disappear to last night? One minute you and Audie were getting all steamy on the dance floor and the next thing I know you're gone."

"We, uh . . . came home a little early." Beth knew she would be hearing from Ginger.

"So? I want to know everything. Did things get steamier? Did you get laid?"

Beth sank onto the couch and threw her feet up on the coffee table. "I can't believe you."

"Oh, come on, Beth. I tell you everything."

"Including things I don't want to know." She counted off a few silent seconds, just in case Ginger might change the subject or give up on her quest for knowledge. No such luck. "Okay, yes. Things got steamier."

"And you got laid?"

"Yes. God, I can't believe how bad I'm blushing and you're not even here. But I am not going to tell you everything."

"Just tell me this. Was I right about Audie, or do you actually think there's more to it than just sex?"

"I think you were wrong . . ." If the four phone calls were any indication, Audie was as excited about their new direction as she was. "But time will tell."

"I wouldn't mind being wrong, Beth. I hope Audie's as good for you as Mallory is for me. It's nice being with somebody who doesn't live life under any sort of pretense."

"You mean like our ex-assholes?"

"Exactly. I never have to worry what Mallory's thinking or planning. If it's on her mind, she says it."

"Yeah, I think Audie's like that."

"And I don't know about you, but I like having somebody tap my adventurous side in the bedroom. I'm betting Audie does that for you just like Mallory does for me."

"You're making me blush again." A click on the receiver indicated another call. "Ginger, you know I love you, but I have another call and I'm thinking it's Audie."

"That's okay. But plan on meeting me for Chinese on Tuesday because you're telling me everything, got it?" She hung up before Beth could reply.

Chapter 17

Audie sauntered toward her Grammaw's room, craning her neck each time she passed a doorway in hopes of catching a glimpse of Beth. They had been all but inseparable since the weekend until last night, when Beth went to class and Audie stayed home with a lonesome Buster.

"Hi, Grammaw," she said, tossing her coat onto the bed.

"Good morning, sweetheart." As she did most mornings after breakfast, Violet sat in her recliner working the crossword puzzle from the newspaper.

"You need any help with those big words?" Audie teased. "Better yet, maybe you ought to put that way and give me your undivided attention."

Violet set her pencil down and looked at Audie with a twinkle in her eye. "What in the world are you up to, Audrey Jane?"

Audie smiled, unable to contain her look of mischief. She was bursting to tell her Grammaw about Beth, but she had wanted to wait until today when Beth came back to work. "I have some news for you that you might like."

"I knew there was something. You've been full of piss and vinegar all week."

"I thought you might be interested in knowing that I have a girlfriend." The astonished look on her grandmother's face was priceless.

"Is it . . . someone I know?"

"You're going to meet her in a few minutes. She's coming by just to see you." Astonishment turned to bewilderment, and unless Audie was mistaken, maybe even disappointment.

"Well, do I look all right?" Violet brushed her lap to straighten her housecoat.

"You look great, Grammaw."

Audie broke into an enormous grin as Beth came in, a grin that grew even larger when it was enthusiastically returned.

"Good morning, Miss Violet. How are you today?"

"All right, I guess."

Beth seemed to notice the uneasiness and immediately looked at Audie for a clue. "Is this woman giving you trouble? I can have her thrown out."

"She says her new girlfriend is coming to meet me."

"Her new girlfriend?" Beth's eyes went wide.

"That's right," Audie said with a smirk. "I told her my new girlfriend would be by soon."

Beth pulled her stethoscope and blood pressure cuff from her pocket. "I think I'll stick around for that. But maybe I should get your vitals now in case you don't like her."

"I think Grammaw will like her just fine. Everybody likes her."

"Everybody? That's a little hard to believe," Beth said, holding up one finger to silence the conversation as she took her reading.

Audie waited until she stripped the cuff from her grandmother's arm. "Yes, and she's very pretty. The only—"

"Pretty is one of those subjective things, though. Someone else might think she's a dog."

Violet's head snapped up in obvious shock.

"She's no dog, believe me. What I was going to say before I was so rudely interrupted"—Audie paused to glare at Beth—"is that her only problem is her tendency to be argumentative, especially when you try to compliment her."

"Argumentative, huh? I beg to differ," Beth answered, now wearing a smirk.

Audie studied her Grammaw's brightening expression as realization dawned. She took Beth's hand and squeezed it. "So meet my new girlfriend, Grammaw. What do you think?"

"I knew it!"

"You did not."

"I sure did. I've been watching you both, the way you always watch for each other." Violet's eyes sparkled with happy tears.

"I guess she finally noticed me, Grammaw."

"Don't believe that. I noticed her the day she chewed out that ambulance crew for pushing you around too fast."

"She was pretty hard to miss that day, wasn't she?" Violet asked.

Audie turned and picked up her coat. "I guess you two will gossip about me now because I have to go to work." Audie leaned over and kissed her grandmother's forehead. "I'm glad you're happy, Grammaw."

"I am."

"Excuse me just a minute, Miss Violet. I'll be right back." Beth followed Audie into the hall and lowered her voice. "So I'm your girlfriend, am I?"

Audie grinned, feeling more than a little cocky. "I'd like you to be."

"I haven't been anyone's girlfriend for a long time."

"Well, I've never even had a girlfriend before, so there."

"I see." Beth waited silently as Wanda walked by them on the way to the sunroom. "I think I'd like being your girlfriend, Audie."

Audie leaned close and whispered, "Good. What I'd like is to give you a big kiss . . . right on your—"

"And maybe you'll come over and do that tonight?" Beth

stepped away as Hazel walked out of her office and started down the hallway.

"After work. See you then."

Audie nodded a greeting to Hazel as she exited, wondering what the director would think if she knew that Nurse Hester was now her official girlfriend.

"I can't believe how much I missed you last night," Beth said, leaning naked against the headboard as she watched Audie undress. "I was tempted to drag you into the supply closet at work and have my way with you."

"You should have. We could have supplied each other with all sorts of things." Audie stepped out of her jeans and left them crumpled on the floor. "Is that one of your fantasies? To do me in the supply closet?"

"Maybe." One of her fantasies was coming true now, as Audie stood naked at the foot of the bed shaking her hair from the pony-tail tie. What she hadn't envisioned was the bright red and yellow apple in the midst of all that creamy white skin.

"Did I ever tell you I had a dream about us once? We were walking on the path toward Sumter Point holding hands."

"That's pretty hot."

"Smart aleck. What was freaky was that I had that dream the night before your test, and when you got back in the car that afternoon, you said you wanted to go walking down there."

"So that's what happened. I wondered why you started acting so weird."

"I wasn't acting weird."

"Yes, you were."

"Anyway, we should do that sometime. Then you'll be the woman who makes my dreams come true." Audie stretched across the foot of the bed, propping her head in her hand.

"What are you doing down there?"

"Looking at you."

"Oh, yeah? What do you see?"

"Someone very beautiful."

Beth stretched her leg so her toes could brush against Audie's nipple. Audie answered by grasping her foot and kissing the instep.

"I bet you could see me better if you got closer."

"But when we're close, sight gets sacrificed for the other senses." Her words came slowly, and with a hypnotic effect. "We touch, we smell, we taste. We hear each other's moans and cries . . . but we close our eyes to focus on those sensations. I want to watch you. I want to see you throb when you come."

"You better look fast, then. I could almost come just listening to you talk like that."

"Where's your vibrator?"

"My vibrator?"

"I know it isn't under the bed because I peeked when you were in the bathroom."

Beth leaned over and opened the bedside table. Before drawing out the sleek, white toy, she looked once more at Audie just to make certain she was serious. She was.

"You want to know what I do with this?" She held the rubber tip to her nose and sniffed, delighting in the smile that appeared on Audie's face. Then she settled back against the pillows. "I usually start out on low . . . and I . . . define my perimeter." With the toy whirring softly, she trailed the tip around the edge of her pubic hair, stopping well short of contact with her clitoris.

"Your lips are shining already."

Beth continued her outline, drawing only slightly closer to her need on each circuit. She was determined to make the experience last as long as she could, especially when she saw that Audie had begun stroking her own slippery slit.

With her free hand, Beth teased her nipple to a peak. "I usually imagine"—she paused to draw a deep breath—"that it's you doing this." She darted the vibrating head over her clitoris, which caused a sudden contraction in the muscles around her vagina.

"That looked like it felt good."

"It did." Beth did it again, allowing the head to linger near the spot that begged for her attention. She didn't want to come yet, but Audie's hand was moving faster and her eyes had taken on a smoky haze. Unable to resist, she bore down on a sensitive point just below her clitoris. "I'm gonna come."

"I'm watching you."

With those words, Beth had the presence of mind to spread her legs wide as the steady contractions began.

"God, that's beautiful." Audie's hand stopped. "That's what I'm going to see from now on whenever I close my eyes."

Beth backed the buzzing head off her clitoris to draw out her orgasm, then collapsed, dropping the vibrator silently at her side. She could do three, sometimes four in a row like this, but that hardly seemed fair, since Audie hadn't yet come even once.

Audie nudged Beth's knees together and crawled up her body to straddle her hips. "How do you feel about sharing your toys?" She picked up the vibrator and flicked the switch, gently wedging it between them so that it touched both of them.

Beth watched mesmerized as Audie glided forward and back, her long hair swaying with every move. Their contact increased rhythmically as they rocked until finally Audie froze, her mouth open and her eyes shut tight. Beth held her breath as another orgasm erupted from within, matching her first in intensity and duration.

Two sets of hands tangled as they fought for the on-off switch. It really was possible to get too much of a good thing.

"God, that was good," Audie sighed, sinking into place alongside Beth. "I need more kisses."

Beth met the searching lips in a tender kiss that left her breathless. "I'm starting to think you weren't kidding about having a list," she gasped. "You're just one surprise after another."

"I can't get enough of you." As if proving her point, her fingers wandered to the curly patch of hair and she began to tease the damp folds. In no time, she was probing for entry, and when Beth raised a knee, she slipped two fingers inside and held them still. "I love being inside you. I want to be connected to you . . . and show you how I feel."

"How do you feel, Audie?"

"I want to know all there is to know about you—things no one else gets to see."

"I've never shared these things with anyone else, not like this."

Audie pushed a little deeper inside and kissed the corners of Beth's mouth. "What do those feelings sound like to you?"

She rested her fingers on Audie's lips. "I don't want to put any words in your mouth."

"Then let me say them." She looked Beth directly in the eye, and in a voice barely audible, uttered a simple phrase that shook them both. "I love you."

"Audie." Beth took her face and pulled it close, packing all the tenderness she could into a kiss. She knew she was being given a gift, probably a gift Audie had never given anyone. Their passion escalated, and Audie's gentle strokes brought her to yet another climax.

"I love you," Audie said again, falling onto her back. "And I love saying that."

"I love hearing it." Beth curled into the crook of her arm to sleep. "You make me feel so beautiful."

"You are." Audie stretched and turned out the bedside lamp.

"Come back here before BD gets between us."

They snuggled close and in a matter of minutes were on the verge of slumber. Audie shifted one last time and said, "If I wake up in the night, I'll probably go on home to Buster, okay?"

"Okay, but I don't like it when you leave."

"You can always stay at my house."

Before Beth could answer, the phone rang. "Who in the world calls me this late?" She plucked the phone from its stand. "Hello?"

"Beth? It's Norma."

"What is it?" She sat up and swung her legs over the edge of the bed. If the second shift charge nurse was calling at this hour, it was most certainly urgent.

"I was hoping you had another number for Audie Pippin. I've called her at home, but there's no answer."

Her heart began to pound. "What's wrong, Norma?"

"Dr. Causby says you're going to be just fine, sweetie," Grammaw said, brushing Audie's hair off her forehead. "You've got the flu, just like Grampaw."

"I don't feel so good."

"I know. I bet staying home from school for a few days will make you feel better, don't you think?"

Audie didn't care much about missing school. She was sore all over and her throat and sides hurt from throwing up. All things being equal, she would rather feel better and be at school with her friends.

"Sit up, honey. Drink some of this juice for me."

"Is Grampaw in bed too?"

"He sure is. He said he'd take you fishing down at the river when you both got well."

"How come you don't ever get sick, Grammaw?"

"I have to stay well so I can take care of my family. What would I do without my little Audie . . . my little Audie . . . Audie—"

"Audrey? Audrey Pippin?"

Audie shook herself awake and sat up, disoriented to find herself on a couch in the hospital's waiting room. Beth was curled up beside her, resting her head in her lap.

"I'm Audrey Pippin."

"Your grandmother's awake, hon. You want to go in and see her?"

"Yeah." She rubbed her face with both hands to clear her head. "Let's go, Beth."

"Maybe you should go in alone, Audie. It's you she'll want to see."

"No, I want you to come too." Audie knew her Grammaw would take comfort in seeing them together.

"Just for a few minutes, okay?" the nurse cautioned.

Audie nodded and pushed open the door. Her stomach dropped when she saw the array of equipment positioned around the bed—monitors, IV tubes, the oxygen mask. No matter how many times this happened, it was a sight she would never get used to. As she walked closer to the bed, she saw that her Grammaw's left eye was closed.

"Hi, Grammaw. I brought Beth." She brushed her knuckles against a wrinkled hand, which was bound with tape holding the IV in place. A lump formed in her throat as she fought back tears. "You scared us again."

Violet tried to smile, the only sign a slight upturn of her lips on the right side.

"They said Dr. Hill would come see you first thing in the morning, about seven o'clock. We'll come back and visit while he's here so we can hear what he has to say. Is that all right?"

A feeble nod and blink of her right eye was all Violet could manage.

"You get some rest, Grammaw. I love you."

Audie waited until she closed the door behind her to let her sob escape.

"Shhh . . . come sit down again," Beth said, her voice soft and low.

"I can't believe her heart stopped this time. She almost died."

"But she didn't. Thank goodness Norma found her right after it happened."

"Why does this keep happening to her? I thought the medicine was supposed to fix it."

"I don't know, Audie. That's something you should ask Dr. Hill." Beth led her back to the couch. "He won't be here for another couple of hours. You should lie down here and get some sleep. I have to go home and get ready for work."

"I wish you could stay."

"Me too, but I can't. Wanda's out this week and they'll be short-handed. But I'll be back after work."

"You're going to be so tired. You don't have to come back."

"I'll be okay. I want to come back."

"I should go let Buster out."

"Give me your house key. I'll do it."

Audie pulled the key off her ring.

"I'll leave this in the mailbox, okay? Now lie down and go to sleep. I'll make sure they know to wake you up when Dr. Hill gets here." She planted a quick kiss on Audie's lips and was gone.

Audie barely remembered closing her eyes before a nurse was shaking her shoulder. "Dr. Hill's just about done with your grandmother."

She was on her feet immediately and returning to the room, where she met the doctor on his way out. "How is she?"

His grim expression gave away his diagnosis. "Let's go sit, shall we?"

Audie followed him anxiously back to the waiting area.

"Your grandmother's had another severe stroke. This one has left her totally paralyzed on her left side. Do you understand what I'm saying?"

Audie nodded. "But she still . . . can function, right?"

"Yes, but it's going to be a struggle. It will be more difficult for her to breathe and to swallow."

"But they can mash up her food, though. I see lots of people out at the nursing home who eat like that."

"Yes, I'll move her to a pureed diet. But I want you to understand what we're facing here, Audie." He rubbed his chin thoughtfully and sighed, obviously distressed at having to deliver the news. "We expect very little improvement in her present condition. But more important, this could happen again, and each time, it will be more and more devastating."

"Can't you give her more medicine?"

"Well, we could. But it's a delicate balancing act. We thin the blood so that little pieces of sludge don't get stuck and stop the flow. But sometimes, damaged blood vessels can rupture, and if the blood is too thin, the patient will hemorrhage. Right now, we're about as close to that line as we can be."

"But it may not happen again?" As always, she needed a ray of hope.

"It may not, and even if it does, it may be a long time from now. Your grandmother's in very good health otherwise, and that works in her favor."

"Then let's just try to keep it that way."

Chapter 18

Beth turned her back to Francine and lowered her voice, knowing there was really no way to keep her phone conversation private in the nurses' station. "I'll come to the hospital as soon as I get off work, I promise." Over her shoulder, she saw Hazel go into her office. "Bye."

"How's Miss Violet?" Francine asked when she hung up.

"Audie says she's stable for now. We'll probably get some orders from Dr. Hill for a pureed diet."

"Med change?"

"I doubt it."

Francine nodded. "Any idea when they'll move her back?"

"Too soon to tell."

Hazel stuck her head out of her office door and said sternly, "Beth, may I see you in here, please?"

Beth swallowed hard and looked at Francine for reinforcement. She had little doubt that Norma would eventually tell Hazel about finding Audie at her place, but she couldn't believe it would happen so soon. "That didn't sound good, did it?"

Francine shrugged. "She's probably just worried about Miss Violet."

Like a march to the gallows, Beth's gait was apprehensive. It didn't help at all that Hazel closed the door as soon as she entered.

"Have a seat." She slid the candy dish across her desk, but for once, Beth declined, her stomach in knots. "I just got off the phone with Dr. Hill. He gave me the full report on Miss Violet."

"We almost lost her."

"We were lucky. Norma said she was making her last round before shift change."

"What do you think will happen now?"

"Dr. Hill believes she'll be able to come back on Tuesday. She's going to need a lot more hands-on care."

"I know."

Hazel smiled wryly. "I know you know."

That was the confirmation she expected. Norma had indeed relayed the news about finding Audie at her house. "If this is about last night—"

"Relax, Beth. I've got no problem with you and Audie Pippin. You're not the first nurse here who's gotten involved with a patient's family member."

Beth shook her head in disbelief. "It's really scary how you find out every little thing, Hazel."

"I told you, it's my job. Besides, Norma called me at home last night, and I was the one who suggested she get in touch with you to see where Audie was."

"So if you don't have a problem with it, why am I in here?"

"I thought it might be a good idea just to touch on the rules, which I'm sure you already know."

"I'll keep this away from work, if that's what you mean."

"I know you will, but it's more than that. You also have to remember that Miss Violet is your patient, and your obligation is to provide what's best for her, even if it isn't best for Audie."

"Of course I'll do that. But whatever is best for Miss Violet is best for Audie too."

"I know that seems obvious. I just want to emphasize it because you never know what will come up." Hazel helped herself to a piece of chocolate. "One of these days we'll have to sneak out of here and grab some lunch or something. It would be nice to talk about things other than work for a change. I can't keep up with what everyone is doing."

"I'd like that, Hazel."

"Oh, I almost forgot." She drew an envelope from a stack of papers on her desk and handed it to Beth. "I got this in the mail this morning. Your copy is probably in your mailbox at home by now."

Beth looked at the return address and began to shake. It was from the testing service.

"Go ahead, open it."

She turned the envelope over and inserted her fingertip beneath the slit, tearing it gently.

"Just rip the damn thing open so we can see what it says!"

She did, pulling out a letter and a stub with numbers. Hastily, she scanned both papers looking for her score. "I passed! Eighty-eighth percentile." She looked at Hazel with wide eyes then back at the paper just to be sure she had read it right. "It says my scores are being sent to the state."

"Which means you'll get your certification in a few weeks." Hazel seemed as happy with the news as Beth. "Which also means I'm going to put in for your transfer to charge nurse immediately."

"Immediately?"

"It'll take a while to process. But I'll talk to Francine today. I want you to start taking over her paperwork now."

"That bad, huh?"

"You have no idea."

"Does it hurt anywhere, Grammaw?"

Violet grimaced ever so slightly.

"I know you don't like being stuck to the bed like this, but they said you needed to get your medicine through here." She touched the IV tube that ran into her grandmother's hand. "And the mask will help you breathe better until you're stronger."

Audie pulled the stiff recliner closer to the bed. "Can you see me if I sit down here?"

"Mmmm," Violet mumbled through the mask.

"I called Oscar and told him you were back in the hospital and that I wanted the day off. You know what he said?" She was accustomed to the one-sided conversations. It was always this way when her Grammaw used a respirator. "He told me to take off the whole rest of the week. I've got ninety-one hours vacation time that I have to use this year, or I'll lose them. I figure I can take a few days now, and then a week or so at Christmas."

Violet tilted her head to the side to get a better view with her good eye.

"I wonder when Beth has off. Maybe we can go somewhere, like to Joel's cabin at Dale Hollow. Wouldn't that be fun?" Joel had offered the use of his lakeside cabin whenever she wanted it, and she made a mental note to ask him later if she could use it in December.

"You like Beth, don't you?" By now, she recognized the glint in her Grammaw's eye as her best effort to smile. "I like her too. In fact, I told her last night that I loved her. Can you believe that? I never said that to anybody before. It's true, though. One minute we were friends, the next minute I couldn't get enough of her. And we owe all that to you, you know. It's hard to imagine something good could come out of you going into the nursing home, but it did. Did you know Beth practically raised her little sister, the one I played basketball with?"

She went on to relate what Beth had told her about becoming Kelly's legal guardian. "I can't imagine having all that responsibility at her age. Heck, I probably couldn't do something like that now."

"Hmmpf." That was Violet's way of disagreeing.

"You're right. I'm better than I used to be." She thought about it for a minute and realized she had grown quite a bit more responsible, especially since she and Beth had become friends. "I actually own my own home now, and I'm doing a pretty good job of taking care of it, if I must say so myself. I've kept up with all the bills and I even clean the whole house every Monday. And before you know it, I'll be starting a job that pays a lot more than I'm making now, and Oscar says it could be a career job." Also, she had smoked pot only twice in the past three weeks, both times over at Dennis's house, but Grammaw didn't need to know about that particular mark of maturity.

"I guess the biggest change is Beth, though." Beth was all she really wanted to talk about, but there was only so much she could share with her grandmother. "I've never felt like this about anybody before, Grammaw. She makes me want to . . . I don't know, do things right. I feel like if I don't she'll think I'm still a kid or something."

She wasn't the only one who was changing. It was as if Beth was meeting her partway. "I'm showing her a few things too. I finally got her to come out with me to that club I go to in Nashville. We danced and drank a couple of margaritas. We had a good time."

She thought again about how Beth had described her life when Kelly was in high school, how she wasn't able to go out in the evening or on weekends. "I was lucky that you and Grampaw let me go out with my friends. I know I worried you sometimes, especially that time you caught me drinking when I was only eighteen. I hope I never did anything else to make you ashamed of me."

"Hmmpf."

Audie looked up to see her Grammaw's fingers wiggling. She grasped them and felt a squeeze. "I love you too."

Tears clouded their eyes as they stared at each other, locked in a moment filled with both sorrow and joy.

"Hey, ladies. Am I interrupting anything?"

"Joel! Grammaw, look who's here." She raced around the bed to give her friend a hug, stronger than usual since her emotions were on overload.

"How are you doing, Mrs. Pippin?"

206

"Mmmm."

"That means not too shabby," Audie said, her Grammaw's weak smile a confirmation of her translation.

He leaned over her bed and gave her a pat on the arm. "I was here to see one of my patients and I thought I'd drop by and say hello, and maybe talk your granddaughter into having lunch with me down in the cafeteria."

Audie made a face.

"I know, it's awful. But I bet you haven't had anything to eat all day." He was right about that.

"I can probably find something that won't kill me." With a promise to return soon, they headed for the elevator. "I guess you got my message."

"Yeah. I called Chuck Hill before I came over to get his take on things. I hope you don't mind."

"Of course I don't. He talked to me this morning after he looked at her. What did he say to you?"

"Probably the same thing he told you. He said this was a major event, and that she appears to have lost all function on her left side."

"But he also said she might get some of it back." They joined several others on the elevator and tabled their conversation until they reached the cafeteria.

"She might get something back, Audie, but that's probably a long shot. She didn't recover a lot of function after her first stroke, did she?"

Audie looked away in defeat. She knew her Grammaw's condition was serious.

"If it makes you feel better, I have a lot of confidence in Chuck. He's well respected in Sumter, so you don't have to worry about what kind of care she's getting."

"Hello, Dr. Petrone," a woman said, her voice dripping with invitation. It was one of the nurses Audie had seen in the emergency room. If only she knew.

"Hi"—he peered at her nametag—"Nurse Tyler."

"Call me Sarah, please."

"That always cracks me up," Audie said when they were out of earshot.

"I can't help it if I'm a chick magnet." They reached the cashier and he paid for their lunch—soup and salad for him and a roast beef sandwich for Audie. "Speaking of chick magnets, how are things with you and Beth Hester?"

"Man, she's the chick magnet. At least she's a magnet for me."

"You got it that bad?"

"I've got it awful. I'm seriously whipped."

"Audie Pippin whipped? That's a news flash."

"Tell me about it. I can't stand to be away from her."

"I liked her. So did Dwayne."

"And Dennis?"

"You know Dennis. He likes everybody, but I think he's kind of bummed that he screwed things up with David, and you being with Beth reminds him about that. Plus, he sees all of his friends moving on, but he still wants to party like Peter Pan."

"There's more to life than partying."

"I know. And Dennis will find that out one of these days too. But for now, I think he's worried about not having anybody to get high with."

Audie shifted uncomfortably and looked to confirm that no one had overheard. "You know about that?"

"I'm not stupid, Audie. I've seen you two at the Gallery with your eyes looking like little red slits, laughing your asses off at stuff that isn't remotely funny."

That was disconcerting. She hoped her Grammaw never put all that together. "We don't do that as much anymore."

"That's good to hear. There are better ways to spend your time." He looked away to recognize another flirtatious woman, this one a doctor. "So tell me more about Beth. Are you two serious?"

Audie shrugged. "What does that even mean? It's not like we can get married or anything."

"I know. But if you're thinking about each other for the long term, you can move in together someday, make plans for your future."

"We haven't talked about stuff like that. All we've agreed to right now is that we won't see other people."

"That's a pretty good start."

"Yeah, and a good reason for me to stay out of the Gallery."

"Is Beth the jealous type?"

"I don't think so, but it doesn't matter. I'm not interested in anybody else."

"Maybe not, but you've always liked hanging out at the Gallery with your friends."

"Yeah, but I don't want to give people the wrong idea."

"You mean people like Regan?"

"Like Regan. Like Deanna. Like anybody. I don't want people to think I'm there to hook up with somebody." Audie slurped the rest of her soda through a straw.

"People won't think that . . . as long as you don't pull a Dennis and sneak off to the bathroom."

"I'd like to think I have more class than that."

"We all have more class than that. Seriously, as long as you behave yourself and act like you have somebody special, I don't think anyone will make a big deal out of you being there."

"Maybe. I just wish Beth liked it more so she'd come with me. Then there wouldn't be any doubts about who I wanted."

"Didn't she have fun the other night?"

"Yeah, but it's not really her thing."

"That's one thing about new relationships. You have a lot to work out about each other. You'll both make compromises here and there if you want things to work."

"I want things to work."

"Then that answers my first question. You're serious."

"I guess I am."

"You should bring her over for dinner sometime. Just the four of us. I'll get Dwayne to cook something fabulous."

"As long as fabulous doesn't mean . . . organic."

"Don't worry. We know your peculiarities, Audie. What about Beth?"

"She likes things like quiche. She and Dwayne are probably soul mates." She shoved the last bit of her sandwich into her mouth. "Oh, by the way . . . if Beth can get a week off before the end of the year, can we use your place at Dale Hollow?"

"Sure. Dwayne and I will be there at Thanksgiving and from Christmas to New Year's, but any other time you want it, it's yours."

"Great. Maybe I'll surprise her with a weekend or something."

Joel looked at his watch. "I have to go. Thanks for having lunch with me. And don't worry too much about your Grammaw."

"I don't know how I'm supposed to do that."

"Just trust that she's in good hands, Audie. Things happen the way they're supposed to, you know."

She nodded. That's what her Grammaw had said when her Grampaw died. "Thanks for coming by. It makes her happy."

"No problem."

"Hey, do me a favor. Call Dennis and tell him to get his ass over here when he gets off work."

Beth walked into the room to find Audie asleep in the chair, her slender form awkwardly slumped with one foot on the windowsill. She tiptoed closer and saw that Miss Violet was awake.

"How are you feeling?" she whispered, slipping her fingers into Violet's hand. "I see that Audie finally gave out."

Violet nodded and squeezed Beth's hand.

"I'll take her home later and put her to bed." Out of habit, she checked the monitors and IV, satisfied that all was normal. "I don't want you to worry about Audie, Miss Violet. I'll be taking good care of her and making sure she eats right and gets plenty of rest."

Violet struggled to slide her mask to her side, causing Beth to catch her hand.

"You shouldn't do that."

Violet ignored her and pushed it away, mumbling something low. Beth leaned close to hear it.

"Say it one more time," she whispered.

"Audie loves you." The words, though garbled, were unmistakable this time.

"I know. It makes me so happy, Miss Violet. You can't imagine what it means to me that she feels that way." Beth wanted to tell her that she loved Audie too, but Audie deserved to hear that first. "She's one of the sweetest people I've ever known."

Audie's foot dropped from the sill with a loud thump.

"Look who's awake," Beth said, shooting Audie a bright smile. "Her ears must have been burning."

"Are you two talking about me?"

"Yes. I was just telling your Grammaw that I was going to take you home and put you to bed."

"I'm okay. I've had a little sleep."

"It doesn't count if you're still sitting up. Did you get something to eat?"

Audie stood and stretched, then leaned over and surprised Beth with a quick kiss. "Joel came by and dragged me down to the cafeteria."

"Good. Glad to know there are other people looking out for you too."

"You must be tired. I told Grammaw that you were here all night with me."

"I am tired, but Hazel had me chained to the desk all day doing paperwork, so at least I wasn't running around. That reminds me, I got some news today."

"Oh yeah?"

"Guess who passed her nursing boards on the first try?" She knew Audie would be happy for her, but she didn't expect to be lifted off her feet and twirled around.

"That's fantastic!"

"And I'm getting promoted to charge nurse as soon as the certification goes through."

"Doesn't that mean you'll have weekends off?"

"I hadn't thought about that. I guess it does."

"So will I when I start the outreach job. Then we won't have any excuses for not going out dancing on Friday nights."

"Well . . . except maybe old age."

"That's not going to fly, Nurse Hester. You might as well give it up now."

Beth grinned and looked at Violet. "Is she always this bossy?"

"Mmmm."

"Hey, is this a private party, or can anyone come?"

Beth looked up to see Audie's friend Dennis, who appeared genuinely bashful about coming in.

"It's private, but we'll make an exception for your sorry butt," Audie said, chucking him with her elbow.

"I didn't come to see you," Dennis proclaimed, pushing his way toward the bed, where he gave Violet a kiss on her forehead. "I came to see this sweetie pie right here."

Audie rolled her eyes and addressed Beth. "Remember that old TV show that had the kid who was always obnoxiously polite to grown-ups, but a jerk otherwise?"

"I think I know who you're talking about." Audie jerked her thumb in Dennis's direction and Beth laughed. "I think I'll head on home so Dennis can visit."

"I'll walk you out," Audie said, and waited at the door while Beth said goodbye. "I found a supply closet down this hall if you're still having fantasies."

Beth chuckled. "Don't tempt me. Will you come over tonight?"

"I don't think so. I really need to spend some time with Buster. I feel bad about neglecting him so much."

"I understand." She pushed the elevator button. "What if I came over to your place tonight? You could call me when you got home."

"I'd love that."

"And I'll bring you something to eat, because I know you won't bother."

Audie pulled her into a hug as the elevator door opened and

212

closed, continuing on its destination without its passenger. "I told Grammaw all about you today. I even told her that I loved you."

Beth took her hand and pulled her into the corner of the waiting room, far enough from the hall traffic to give the illusion of privacy. "You know, when you said that last night, it just . . . I wanted to tell you too, but I didn't want you to think I said it just because you did."

"Said what?"

Beth was startled at first until she saw the teasing grin.

"That I love you."

"I'm sorry. I didn't hear that. Could you say it again, please?"

"I love you." Beth enunciated each word slowly. "Did you hear it that time?"

"I think so. I might have to hear it again a few times." As she had when she heard about the test score, she scooped Beth up and twirled her around.

"I'm sorry I didn't find a more romantic place for that declaration, but I've wanted to tell you all day."

"That's all right. You can tell me again when you come over tonight."

"I will, but I doubt I'll be awake long enough to show you."

"So the honeymoon's over, huh?"

"Hardly. But I have to live long enough to get through your list at least once, and I won't do that without sleep."

Chapter 19

"Are you glad to be back, Grammaw?" Audie opened the blinds to let a little light into the room. Dr. Hill had warned her this stroke might leave her Grammaw depressed, so she was determined to be as cheerful as possible.

"Mmm-hmm." She had difficulty speaking, but Audie had encouraged her to keep trying. "I missed my room."

"I missed seeing the pretty nurses, one in particular." Her Grammaw answered, but Audie couldn't make out what she said. "One more time, Grammaw."

"I said I don't want to go back."

"I don't want you to go back either. So you better stay healthy."

"Audie . . . I don't want to go back." This time her voice was firm, and Audie understood the implications. "I don't want to leave here again."

"I know, Grammaw. I know." She sat on the edge of the bed and took her grandmother's hand. "It's hard to be away like that, isn't it?"

"I don't want them to take me next time. Tell them not to."

"Just stay well, and you won't have to go again. I promise."

Beth entered the room with lunch and set it on the serving tray. "Do you know how nice it is for me to walk into this room and see two of my favorite people in the whole world?" She pressed a button on the remote to raise the bed to a sitting position.

Audie knew her Grammaw would love hearing that. "My two favorite people are in the room too, Grammaw."

"Mine too," her grandmother said.

"I'm going to let Audie help with your lunch, Miss Violet." Their eyes met and Audie signaled her agreement. "I'll be back in a few minutes, okay?"

"I bet you missed the food here too, didn't you? I wonder if they have a ward in the hospital just for people who get sick eating there." She rolled the lunch tray alongside. "Now we get to guess what everything is. This light green stuff looks like butter beans." She scooped up a spoonful and held it to her Grammaw's mouth.

"That's it."

"Wonder what this mystery meat is."

Violet sampled it and swallowed. "Turkey . . . or chicken," she mumbled.

Audie chuckled. "I can go sneak a peek next door and see what it looked like before they pulverized it."

"Creamed corn," Violet said, pointing toward a yellow mash.

"I guess putting that in the blender would have been overkill." Audie dished out a spoonful. "And dessert looks like some kind of pudding. Of course, everything on your plate looks like some kind of pudding." Bit by bit, the food disappeared.

Audie used the napkin to gently wipe her Grammaw's chin. She was trying her best to be casual about the change in diet, not wanting to cause any upset or worry. She knew what a humiliating experience it must be for her Grammaw to be fed like a baby. But Audie weighed that against how much she would hate making a mess, because that would embarrass her and cause more work for the staff. At least this way, they got to spend the time together.

"Beth brought her cat over to the house last night to meet

Buster. You should have seen them. BD walked all around the house jumping from one piece of furniture to the next. Drove Buster crazy. He got too close once and BD took a swipe at his nose."

"Was he good after that?"

"Yeah, they finally left each other alone. BD even slept on the bed with us."

At that moment, Beth returned.

"I was just telling Grammaw about us sleeping together. Hope that's all right."

"Oh, sure. I told the mailman and the folks down at the bank."

"Very funny."

"Miss Violet, I promised you I'd get her in bed by ten thirty, didn't I?"

"Yes." Even though she tried to smile, it was obvious from the lilt in her voice that Violet was tired.

"I think I'm going to go home for a while, Grammaw, and let you rest. I didn't have a chance to clean the house yesterday, and I have to go back to work tomorrow. I'm going to start going in earlier so I can get off to help with lunch and dinner. Beth said she'd call me if they needed help with breakfast. I can be here"—she snapped her fingers—"just like that."

"You're sweet, Audie."

Audie kissed her forehead. "I'll see you later then."

"I'll walk you out." Beth squeezed Violet's hand and walked with Audie into the hallway.

"Grammaw's really depressed today."

"That's normal when they come back from the hospital, especially when they've been through something serious or debilitating like she has."

"That's what Dr. Hill said, but I don't understand why they aren't just happy to be back here."

"They usually are. But when they get back, it signals the end of the episode. They think about the whole experience and they start to imagine what the next one will be like."

"Grammaw says she doesn't want to go back to the hospital."

"I'm sure it was hard on her." They leaned against the wall opposite Violet's room. "But you know we'll take care of her."

"I'm so glad she ended up here." Audie looked up and down the hallway to verify they were alone. "Remember what an asshole I was that first day?"

Beth smiled at her with a look of real affection. "I started falling in love with you that day."

"Oh, yeah?"

She pointed toward the door that opened onto the back lawn. "Right out there. You were trying so hard not to cry and all I wanted to do was wrap my arms around you."

"And I wanted to pinch your butt and see if it was as soft as it looked."

"You did not." Beth punched her gently on the shoulder. "I have class tonight so I guess I won't see you until tomorrow."

"How will I ever survive?" Audie stole a quick kiss when she saw no one around.

"Don't do that here. You'll get me in trouble," Beth scolded, guiding her through the double doors and out into the parking lot to stand next to the Xterra. "What are you doing tonight?"

"Dennis called me a little while ago and asked me to go with him to the Gallery, but I didn't feel like it, so he's coming over to watch a movie or something instead."

"Why didn't you want to go? I thought you liked going out with the guys during the week."

Audie shrugged, not quite knowing how to explain that the dance club had suddenly lost its appeal unless Beth was with her. "You've ruined me. I can't stay up that late anymore."

Beth laughed. "Oh, yes you can. You just need the proper incentive."

"Then how about coming over when you get out of class? I'd stay awake all night for you."

"I'm not sure I could, though. Sharing a bed with you has a deleterious effect on the amount of sleep I get."

"But regular practice builds stamina and helps you recover quickly." Audie scanned the parking lot and grabbed both of Beth's hands. "I've got an uncontrollable urge to throw you over the hood of your car and have my way with you out here in front of everybody."

"You'd really do that?"

"You bet."

"Something tells me I should believe you." She gently pulled her hands away. "I'll call you later when we get a break, okay?"

"I'll be waiting."

"Tell Dennis hi for me."

Audie watched her walk back toward the building, admiring the way her hips swayed with every step. And what lovely hips they were.

Beth finished writing her comments in the last patient file, noting that her shift was up in three minutes. She had spent the whole afternoon at the nurses' station, but was determined not to get behind in paperwork as Francine had.

Audie would probably be back in another hour or so to help her Grammaw with dinner, but she couldn't wait around that long. She needed to go home and finish some reading before class.

A buzzer sounded and she looked up, startled to see Miss Violet's signal illuminated. She had never called for help before. Beth rushed down the hall and into the room.

"What is it, Miss Violet? Are you all right?" She hurriedly checked for signs of distress.

"I want . . ." Her last words were too garbled to understand.

"What is it? I didn't hear."

"DNR."

Beth's heart skipped a beat. "Are you feeling okay? Are you worried about something?" She had to ask Violet to repeat her answer twice.

"I'm fine . . . but I don't want to go back to the hospital."

"Why not? Sometimes they can make you feel better." She sat on the edge of the bed, taking Violet's hand.

"I don't want to live . . . if somebody has to take care of me."

So that was it, Beth thought. Violet was feeling guilty about all of the attention she now required. "But we're here to take care of you. Audie wants to take care of you, and so do I. Let me call her and she'll come right here and tell you that."

"No!"

The force of Violet's response surprised her.

"This is too hard for Audie."

"No, it isn't. She loves you and she wants you with her."

"Audie has you now," she rasped. "And I want to go be with Lewis, but it's too hard for Audie to let me go."

Tears suddenly welled in Beth's eyes as she realized the sincerity of the request. Miss Violet wanted this for herself, and she wanted to spare Audie the difficult decision.

"Miss Violet, I know you're sad today, and sometimes that makes people feel like giving up. I don't want you to do this when you're sad, okay? Please wait and think about it some more."

"I have." The old woman's look was desperate. She squeezed Beth's hand and enunciated her words slowly. "I don't want to leave this place again."

Beth couldn't let her do this. Maybe Clara would help talk her out of it. It would break Audie's heart just to know her Grammaw was even thinking about this. "I tell you what. I'll ask Clara to come talk it over with you. She'll explain what it—"

"I know what I'm doing, Beth. I need you to help me."

"Not me, Miss Violet. Please don't ask me. Audie would never forgive me."

"It has to be you." Violet clenched her hand to the point of pain. "She trusts you. Only you."

Beth suddenly realized her position. This was exactly the sort of circumstance Hazel had warned her about, a situation in which she had to choose between what was best for her patient, Violet Pippin, or what was best for Audie. And Miss Violet was right that Audie would be distrustful of anyone but her. "I don't want to do this, Miss Violet."

"Please help me."

Her heart sank as she thought of how devastated Audie would be, but she owed her allegiance to Miss Violet. Still fighting back tears, she finally nodded. "I need to get the papers from Clara. You can sign them and she and I will witness your signature."

"Thank you."

"Are you sure this is what you want?"

"Yes."

Wiping her eyes, Beth headed toward Clara's office. At first, she hoped to find her on the phone or otherwise busy so she could postpone this and give Violet time to change her mind. Then she realized a delay of even a few minutes might mean Audie would walk in and discover what they were doing. That was the last thing she wanted.

"Clara?"

The social worker looked up from her desk. "Are you still here? Your shift is over."

"I had some things to finish up. Miss Violet's asking for a DNR, but she just got back from the hospital and she's depressed. I think we should try to talk her into waiting a few days."

Clara located a form in her drawer. "I don't think it'll make any difference. She asked me about it last week, even before she went in the hospital. I think her mind's made up and she wants to hurry in case something else happens."

"Wait a minute." Beth shut the door so she wouldn't be over-heard. "If she had signed one of these last week, she wouldn't even be here."

"Maybe she doesn't want to be here, Beth. Maybe she can't stand not being able to do things on her own. She's entitled to make that decision."

"So why didn't you give it to her last week?" If she had, maybe someone else would have signed it and Beth wouldn't have had to face this.

"She didn't ask for one. She just asked me who she could get to sign it besides Audie."

So Violet had been planning this. "Do you remember what day that was?"

"I do, because it was so weird the way it happened. It was Wednesday, and she seemed all happy about something. She had her stroke that same night."

Wednesday was the day Audie had told her about their relationship. Now it made sense. Violet was happy that day because Audie was happy. And she could leave knowing Audie would be taken care of.

"Let's go get this over with."

Ten minutes later, she signed her name beneath Clara's as a second witness to orders not to resuscitate should Violet's heart cease again.

"Beth?" Clara nudged her back into the office.

"Yeah?"

"I know I don't have to tell you this, but what we just did has to be kept private, even from Audie."

She was momentarily surprised at the reference to Audie, but realized it was silly not to expect word of their relationship to travel through the nursing home quickly. "Even if Audie has her power of attorney?"

"This trumps a POA if her heart stops. We agreed by our signatures that Miss Violet was mentally capable of making this decision for herself."

It wasn't as if Beth was hearing this policy for the first time. She knew it well, but never before had it affected her so personally. Audie would find out eventually about the paperwork, and she would know Beth's role in it. All she could hope was that Miss Violet was right, that Audie would trust her and believe it was what her Grammaw had wanted.

◈

"Where did you get this stuff?" Audie asked, lighting the one-hitter to draw the smoke deep into her lungs.

"You're going to laugh your ass off when I tell you."

"I'm going to laugh my ass off anyway."

Dennis began to giggle and Audie followed right along. "Shit, you're so funny when I'm fucked up," he said, which set off another round of laughter.

"So." Audie knocked the residue into an ashtray. Somewhere in the recesses of her mind, she knew that something was unfinished, something that had seemed incredibly important only moments ago. "What did I just ask you?"

"How the fuck would I know? You're the one that asked it to me."

"I know. But you're the one I asked it to." She stopped to ponder whether she had said that right. "Don't you listen . . . when I ask things . . . to you?"

"Apparently, I do not," Dennis answered formally.

Again, they burst into fits of giggles.

Audie stopped abruptly. "I remember!"

"Fuck, don't yell like that!" He shifted on the couch to sit farther away. "You fucking scared the shit out of me."

"You're so paranoid. What I asked you was where you got this shit."

"From Buddy Mickel."

"The preacher's kid?" Audie remembered how they used to joke about PKs being the wildest of all.

"That's right."

"Well, praise Jesus! This is good shit." She stuffed the bowl again.

"I bet all three of us go straight to—" Again, he jumped, this time because of the ringing phone.

Audie studied the phone on the end table as though she expected it to move toward her. On the fourth ring, she reached out to answer it. "Hello."

"Hi, sweetheart."

"Beth!" Instinctively, Audie sat up straight and pushed the

plastic bag of marijuana underneath a pillow on the couch. "Are you . . . where are you?"

"I'm at class. We're on break."

"Oh." She glanced at Dennis, who was contemplating his navel—literally—as he picked it clean of lint. She watched him, probably for too long as she left Beth hanging on the phone.

"Are you watching a movie with Dennis?"

"No." Audie held her tongue for fear she would begin a sentence and forget what she was saying in the middle. It would not be good for Beth to know how totally fucked up she was right this minute.

"Is Dennis still there?"

Audie almost described the navel action but stopped herself. That would just start her laughing again. "Yeah."

"What are you two doing?"

"Mmmm . . . nothing. Sitting."

"Is everything all right?"

That was the question she had dreaded, since it meant she had failed at acting normal. "We're . . . a little . . . fucked up . . . just a little." It seemed as though nine minutes passed before Beth responded.

"I see." Another eternity passed. "I'll let you get back to what you were doing."

Again, Audie looked at Dennis, who didn't seem to be paying much attention to her conversation. "Are you going to come over when you get out of class?"

"I don't think so, Audie. I should go home by myself and leave you and Dennis to each other."

"You want me to come to your place?"

"No. I think you should stay where you are for tonight. You don't have any business out on the roads."

Audie was sure she heard irritation in Beth's voice, but she was in no shape to explore it. Instead, she said what she hoped would make everything all right. "I love you," she mumbled, covering her mouth with her hand.

"What?"

Audie cleared her throat. "I said I love you." She flipped her middle finger at Dennis when he rolled his eyes.

"I'll see you tomorrow, Audie."

They said goodbye and Audie hung up, immediately anxious about the conversation that had just transpired. Beth should have said she loved her too. Unless she didn't.

"You're so whipped."

"Am not." Audie knew that was a lie. Why else would her stomach be knotting? "So what the fuck if I am?"

Dennis laughed. "I don't get you two. Beth Hester is nothing like any of the girls . . ." He waved his hand in a circle to finish his thought.

"All you have to get is that I'm in love with her, dickhead," she shot back, instantly aware that she was very close to losing her temper. If he said anything bad about Beth, she would have to get up and kick his ass. She took a deep breath and continued evenly. "I like that she's not one of the Gallery crowd. There's more to her than that."

"But you hardly ever do shit anymore," he whined.

"I know." She recalled what Joel had said about Dennis at the hospital, that he felt like his fun and friends were slipping away. "I told you, though, you're my best friend. My being with Beth doesn't have to change that. I'm still going to hang out with you, but my days of getting high and staying out half the night are just about over. I have a lot more responsibility now than I used to."

"Would you be saying all this bullshit if it weren't for her? Because I think it would suck if you were changing your whole life just for a little pussy."

"That's not what she is, shithead," Audie snapped, not at all happy to notice that her nice little buzz was fading fast. She took another calming breath to keep her temper in check. "If I'm changing, it's because I have to. I have things to lose now, like a house and a new job that pays good money. I can't just screw around like I used to."

Dennis snorted. "Look, I don't mean to make you mad or anything, but I don't see what it is about Beth Hester that's got you creaming your jeans."

Audie leaned forward and gave him her most menacing look. "If you really don't mean to make me mad, then you better shut the fuck up."

"I'm not saying she's bad looking or anything. She's not. But it's like you're going out with your mother or something."

"My mother was probably a whore, asshole. And she ran off and left me, so forgive me if I can't see your analogy."

Clearly deflated, Dennis slumped on the couch. "It sucks, Audie."

"Everything's a trade off, Tinkerbell. But I don't want to have to choose between doing the things I have to do and hanging with my friends."

Dennis stood and pulled on his jacket. "Seems to me you already have."

"What's that supposed to mean? I'm sitting here with you, aren't I?"

"Yeah, but only because your girlfriend's got class tonight. I'm not stupid."

Audie couldn't argue with that. Any other night, she would rather be with Beth. "I'm not sleeping with you, dude. It's different."

"I know. But you're basically saying the hell with everybody else."

"I am not. Shit, Dennis, I can't help how I feel. You're supposed to be my friend too. That means you should want me to be happy."

"Whatever. All I know is I got shit from you for being all ga-ga over David. Then I got shit for doing Alan Edwards. All I get from you any more is shit until you have an opening on your busy schedule. Then you want good old Dennis to come by and get you high."

"Poor, mistreated Dennis. Let me get some hats so we can have a pity party."

"Go fuck yourself, Audie."

Beth shifted to her side, prompting BD to stand and stretch before moving to a distant corner at the foot of the bed. She was determined not to watch the green digital display of her alarm clock for one minute more. Six a.m. would get here soon enough.

For the first time since she and Audie had become lovers, she was losing sleep over an argument, one Audie probably didn't even realize had taken place. Obviously, Beth had been too subtle about her attitude toward drugs when they talked that day out at Sumter Point. Either that, or Audie didn't care how she felt, at least not enough to give up her own pleasures.

That wasn't a road Beth wanted to travel with a partner again, being with someone who always put her own wants and needs first. Thanks to Shelby, this was familiar territory for Beth. Shelby was always the more forceful, which meant she usually did whatever she wanted and made decisions for both of them. Whenever Beth complained, Shelby said it was her own fault for not speaking up sooner.

She wasn't going to repeat that mistake with Audie. There weren't many things she felt strongly about, but drugs were right up there near the top of her list. Audie needed to know that, even if it meant sending a forceful message.

Chapter 20

Audie popped a mint into her mouth as she scanned the hallway for Beth. She didn't feel hung over today—she had drunk only three beers last night after Dennis left—but she wasn't taking any chances on having Beth pick up a whiff of anything.

Last night was supposed to have been a relaxing evening with a friend, a chance for her to catch up with Dennis on what she had missed with the Gallery crowd since her love life had taken off. Instead, the whole evening had turned into a train wreck. She was probably going to have to go crawling back to Dennis to make up for that pity party crack.

And if things with Dennis weren't bad enough, something was going on with Beth. According to her Grammaw, Beth had already come by to perform her midday check of vitals and dispense medications. She usually waited until Audie got there to do that so they could see each other and have a chance to talk while her Grammaw ate lunch. That probably meant Beth was pissed about something, like her getting stoned last night. Audie hoped she hadn't phased out on the phone and said something stupid she couldn't remember.

Whatever it was, they needed to talk to straighten things out. Beth hadn't been around her before when she was high, so she felt she needed to explain how it wasn't all that big a deal . . . she hadn't been driving . . . yada yada yada. She would try harder to keep that part of her life separate from their relationship if Beth had a problem with it. It didn't have to come between them.

Audie wandered back into her grandmother's room aimlessly and slumped into the recliner.

"Did you two have a fight?" Violet asked.

"No, we're okay, Grammaw." Even if they had been fighting, Audie wouldn't want her Grammaw to know about it. "I was with Dennis last night and she called me. We couldn't talk very long, so I don't know what's bugging her. You sure you don't want more of your lunch?"

Before her grandmother could answer, Audie heard Beth's voice in the hall and sprang from the chair to intercept her as she went past. "Beth?"

"Audie . . . hello."

"Hello?" Audie closed the distance between them and lowered her voice. "Is everything okay?"

"I'm really busy right now." Beth tried to push past her, but Audie blocked her path.

"What's wrong?"

Beth glanced nervously toward the nurses' station, where most of the staff seemed to be gathered. "I didn't like you getting stoned last night," she whispered, "but I don't want to talk about that sort of thing here."

"What didn't you like? Did I do something?"

"I told you I'm uncomfortable with that."

"No, you didn't. You said you didn't understand the appeal. That's different."

"It's not something grown-ups do, Audie." Again, Beth tried in vain to escape the conversation. "I need to go to work."

Audie stepped back, unable to stem the flow of anger that seemed to boil up out of nowhere. It was one thing for Beth not to like her getting high with her friends, but to imply she wasn't grown up was outrageous. "You know, Dennis was right. You really are more like a mother than a girlfriend." She spun toward her grandmother's room, resisting the urge to bang the door as she went through. "I have to go, Grammaw," she said, her voice shaking. "I'll be back to help you with dinner."

"Audie?"

"I can't stay any longer. I love you."

She turned away from the nurses' station to exit the side door of the building. This time, she tried her best to slam it, but the hydraulic closer caught the heavy door and allowed it to gently latch.

Beth pulled the laundry door closed behind her and flung her pen across the room in frustration. When she decided last night to be forceful in making her views known, being called a mother wasn't exactly what she had in mind. Her so-called serious resolve had come off as patronizing and bossy. No wonder Audie had said what she did.

And now the truth was out. Audie—or at least Audie's friends—had reservations about the difference in their ages. Audie was young and carefree, maybe even reckless sometimes. Beth was older and responsible. And prudish, she admitted, running both hands through her hair. If they were going to bridge the gap, they needed to find common ground somewhere in the middle. Otherwise, their relationship had nowhere to go.

She checked her watch. Audie would be at work for the next four or five hours, then back at the nursing home to feed Miss Violet her dinner. That was too long to let things seethe. At the very least, she should call and try to smooth things over for now. Maybe Audie would be willing to talk it all out tonight.

Beth exited the laundry room and almost collided with Wanda. "There you are. Miss Violet was looking for you."

Beth steeled herself and made her way back down the hall. "My ears were burning, Miss Violet. I thought I'd better come see what that was about."

The old woman waved her over to the bed without even a greeting. "Tell me what's wrong with you and Audie."

Beth knew it was useless to pretend things were fine, but this particular subject was one they needed to keep private, especially from Miss Violet. Especially from everyone, actually. "We just need to talk some things out, Miss Violet. It's hard to do that here with everybody around."

"Audie can be stubborn. I told you that the first day I moved in here."

"I think it was my fault this time, not Audie's." Beth went through the mindless motions of clearing the lunch tray and filling the water pitcher. "We're just not communicating very well."

"You still love each other, don't you?"

The anxious tone of her question was unmistakable. Violet wanted them together and happy.

"I love her very much, Miss Violet. Everything will work out. I promise." She hoped.

Audie wished she could rewind the last two hours. Why had she popped off about Beth being like a mother? That was Dennis talking, not her.

She had never experienced this kind of inner turmoil. Ever since she left the nursing home, she had made herself sick imagining what her life would be like if this fight ended their relationship. It wasn't as if she could just go back to being the person she was a few weeks ago. It would tear her heart out to walk away . . . or worse, to have Beth walk away.

The clock on the wall seemed to be stuck. She couldn't even try to talk to Beth again for another hour and a half when she left the nursing home. This wasn't the sort of thing they should be talking about in public, and Beth had tried to make her see that. Instead, she had pushed it to a breaking point and both of them had lost their tempers.

At least Dennis wasn't pissed anymore. He said he owed her a free pass after being such a shit recently, but that she had better not push her luck. She called him a dickhead, signifying things between them were back to normal.

Oscar opened the door from the hallway and entered the technician's room, setting off a round of excited barking from the twelve dogs who called the shelter their temporary home. "I've got a job for you on Monday, Audie."

"Monday? That's my day off." She slid a water bowl into a crate that housed a yappy terrier mix.

"What if I gave you Saturday and Sunday instead . . . from now on?"

Audie shot him a sidelong glance to convey her suspicions. "What's the catch?"

"No catch. But I hired that friend of Dennis's and two other techs this morning, so we can start scheduling you for a few of those outreach events."

She didn't really want this now, not when her whole life might be on the verge of being turned upside down again. On the other hand, it was a chance to step up and show Beth she could be responsible. "Okay, but I thought it wasn't going to start until December."

"That was the plan, but they want to do this on Monday."

"What do I have to do?"

"Talk to third graders at Sumter Creek Elementary School. Tell them what we do here and how they can help."

"I've never talked to third graders before." Automatically, she thought of Dennis.

"Sure you have. You do it all the time when they come in here to pick out a dog or cat. Just do the same thing, but with thirty of them."

Her cell phone began to ring inside her backpack, but she ignored it. It was probably Dennis again. "What do I have to wear?"

Oscar looked at her and grinned. "Well, I guess there is a catch. Isn't that your cell phone?"

"It's nobody. So what's the dress code?"

"Do you have some pants besides blue jeans?"

Audie thought at once of her leather hip-huggers, but she was sure Oscar meant something else.

"I can probably get your bump in pay to start next week," he went on. "You can plan a few events to do here and there while you bring the new techs up to speed."

"Does this mean I don't get to sleep late anymore?"

"Eight to five, but we can fudge it a little so you can get out to the nursing home in time for dinner."

Audie sighed. First the house. Now the job. Next would be giving up all her bad habits. "Can I have this Saturday off? I have to go buy some pants."

"Sure. You ought to look at your vacation schedule too. You need to use those hours before the end of the year or you'll lose them." With that, he disappeared back into the hallway.

A chirping sound announced a voicemail, and she dug her phone from her backpack. Now that she and Dennis were pals again, he probably wanted to go out to the Gallery. These last few weeks, her penchant for partying seemed to be causing more problems than it was worth, what with the police pulling her over, the fights with Dennis, and now with Beth. It was time to take a step back. She would start with telling Dennis no, even if it meant getting grief.

She dialed her voicemail and pressed the phone to her ear. She was startled to hear not Dennis but Beth.

"Audie . . . I don't know about you, but I'm not feeling so good right now. Obviously, we both need to find a better way to express ourselves when we disagree about something. I was a jerk and I apologize. So . . . maybe we could talk all this out at my place when you get off work."

Audie heard her draw a deep breath and exhale. *"In the meantime, I'd appreciate it if you would just call me at home and leave a message telling me you still love me. Then I'd quit having such a bad day."*

Audie smiled as her whole body relaxed. Everything was going to be okay, not because they had magically worked out their differences—they hadn't—but because they still loved each other. She dialed Beth's home number as instructed and waited for the machine to pick up.

"I got your message . . . and thanks to you, I just quit having a bad day too. I love you, and I'll see you about five thirty."

"There's Audie, BD," Beth said, stretching across the sink to pet the cat in the windowsill. The yellow SUV was pulling into the space next to her Mazda. She and Audie had so much to talk about, not just the drugs issue, but the way they both had handled things today at the nursing home. They had to learn to talk to each other rationally and respectfully . . . like grown-ups, she thought dismally.

Why had she said that about what grown-ups do? She was just begging for Audie's mother remark, and it had stung her like a wet whip. She walked to the front door to wait, and when she heard footsteps, she opened it and held her arms wide. "Don't say anything yet. Just hold me for a little while."

Audie enveloped her in a bear hug. "I'm sorry."

"Shhh . . . I love you."

They stood in the entry in a quiet embrace for several minutes. Then Audie dipped her head and began a series of soft kisses that finally found Beth's lips. Beth couldn't remember a kiss so tender, and it gave her confidence they would weather this storm together. Finally they broke, resting their foreheads together as each let out a soft sigh.

"What do you say we skip the talking and just make out instead?" Audie asked, nuzzling Beth's ear.

"Tempting, isn't it?"

"I really am sorry, Beth. I don't know why I said that about you acting like a mother."

"Because that's pretty much what I was doing. There's plenty of blame to go around."

"But I don't think of you that way."

"And I don't think of you as a kid." They exchanged sheepish looks as she took Audie's hand and led her to the couch. "I need to tell you about something . . . something I haven't told many people."

"Okay."

"Remember that day we were out at Sumter Point when we smelled the marijuana?"

Audie nodded, sinking against the back of the couch to hear the tale. Beth joined her, tucking a knee underneath as she turned sideways.

"I wanted to get out of there so bad. I just can't be around that kind of thing. It's not worth the risk to me."

"What risk are you talking about?"

"Back when Kelly was sixteen, one of her friends in Nashville got caught smoking pot behind the mall. The police got her to name the people she knew who used drugs and they showed up at our apartment with a search warrant. They found a bag of pot in Kelly's room and arrested both of us."

"You got arrested?" Audie suddenly sat up straight, her mouth agape.

"Hazel went to bat for me and helped me get my charges dropped. But since I was Kelly's guardian, I was responsible for everything she did. She got probation and community service, and I got monitored by family services until she turned eighteen."

"I had no idea."

"Believe me, we kept it as quiet as possible. That's why I can't be around it. They wouldn't be lenient if it happened again. And I'd probably lose my job."

"Why didn't you tell me any of this?"

"We didn't know each other that well back then. I never even told Shelby."

"So you're afraid if I get caught, it'll make you look bad."

"That's part of it. The other part is what if I was with you when it happened?" She studied Audie's pensive look, afraid she might go on the defensive. "I know you'd never mean for it to—"

"I'm always careful. We don't even have it in the car anymore, just at home with the doors locked."

"Is it that important to you?"

Audie shrugged, not making eye contact as she struggled with her answer. "I wouldn't want you to break up with me because of it."

"And I don't want to be making rules for how you should live. You have to be the one to decide. I promise you we won't break up over this, but try to imagine what would happen to us if you did get caught. I'd be mad as hell and you'd feel so guilty it would probably tear us up anyway."

Audie wiped her sweaty palms on her jeans, a sure sign she was uncomfortable with the conversation.

"Look, Audie . . . like I said, I won't make rules for you. And I won't force you to make them for yourself. Just please be careful."

"I am careful."

"Okay. That's all I ask."

"So are we done?"

Beth chuckled, breaking the tension for them both. She had a hunch she could extract a promise from Audie if she put more pressure on her, and the temptation to do that was great. But she didn't want Audie to give up smoking pot only because she was asking. It had to be something she did for herself.

"We can be done with that. But I want to ask you about something else."

Audie frowned and looked at her suspiciously. "What else have I done?"

"Nothing. But I want to know if it bothers you to have your friends saying I might be too old for you?"

"No! No way. You're not too old."

Beth was glad to hear the vehemence of Audie's denial. "That's good, since we can't do a thing about it."

"Do you ever think I'm too young?"

She almost answered with similar forcefulness, but caught herself. They needed to be honest with each other. "I never think you're too young for me. But sometimes I worry that I might be too . . . I don't know, too boring."

"Why? Because you don't go out every night?"

"Because I hardly go out at all."

"That's not a big deal. I don't have to go either."

"Audie, that's not fair. You like it. I don't want you to stay home every night because of me. You should go whenever you want to."

"I do like it, but what I want is to be with you, whether it's here or at the Gallery. Of course, if you would come out with me once in a while that would be the best of both worlds."

"Are you sure you want me there with all your friends?" The last thing Beth wanted was for Audie's pals to sit watching them in judgment.

"What kind of ridiculous question is that? My friends like you."

"Even Dennis?"

"Don't worry about Dennis. Talk about somebody who needs to grow up!"

"But he's your best friend."

"He won't be if he tries to come between you and me. It's as simple as that."

"I don't want that to happen, Audie."

"Me neither. But it's up to Dennis, not you. He'll come around once he realizes you're not going anywhere."

Beth scooted over on the couch to straddle Audie's lap. "You're right about that. I'm not going anywhere."

"Now are we finished?"

"I guess so, unless you have a deep, dark secret or two you want to share."

"You already know my secrets . . . except that I didn't tell you about Dennis and me getting stopped a few weeks ago by the cops and me having to eat a joint so they wouldn't find it."

"Audie!"

"I know. It scared the shit out of both of us."

Beth listened in disbelief as Audie related the details of her traffic stop. "It scares me just to hear about it. I can't believe you ate a joint."

"Me neither. It made me sick all day the next day."

"That would have been the least of your problems. You could have gone to jail. You would have lost your job. Your Grammaw would have—" She was startled by Audie's hand as it abruptly covered her mouth.

"It didn't happen. We learned a lesson. I'll never have drugs in my car again, I promise." She removed her hand and kissed Beth on the tip of her nose. "Now, let's please talk about something else."

Beth wiggled from side to side to settle herself more firmly onto Audie's lap. "I'm so glad you came over tonight. I would have gone crazy if you hadn't."

"I can't stand having something between us."

"Me neither."

"And I feel better knowing we don't have any secrets now," Audie said.

It was all Beth could do not to look away to hide her guilt. Their argument today was minor compared to the one they would probably have when Audie discovered her grandmother's DNR. "There are always things people need to keep to themselves, sweetheart. But no matter what the circumstances, I want you to know that I would never intentionally hurt you by keeping a secret." It was a fine distinction, but it was true.

"I know you wouldn't. And I wouldn't hurt you either."

No longer able to maintain eye contact, Beth gripped Audie's head and pulled it to her chest. She needed to talk to Violet again, to beg her to change her mind.

Chapter 21

Audie stirred the spaghetti, checking to be sure there weren't any big chunks of ground beef or tomatoes. "Why don't you bring your bed up, Grammaw?"

Violet leaned forward as the electric motor raised her bed to a sitting position. "How did you get the whole day off, sugar?"

"I just told Oscar you wanted me to take care of a few things at home today, and he said it was okay. He's been after me to use my vacation time."

"He always has to get after you at the end of the year."

"I know. I asked Joel if Beth and me could use their cabin for a few days and he said yes."

"Beth and I."

"Oh, you want to go too?" She gave her grandmother a playful wink. "You were right about Estelle, Grammaw. Your winter coat fit her just right," she said, pulling the dinner tray closer. "And her daughter tried on one of the sweaters and took them all."

"What about the dresses?"

"Those too. You wouldn't believe how happy they both were."

"I knew they would be."

"And you should have seen Estelle's face when I told her Tommy could come and get the Buick. She kept saying it was too much. But I told her you wanted them to have it."

"I've got no use for it anymore."

Either her Grammaw's speech had improved a bit, or Audie had gotten better at deciphering it. "You've been helping out the Tuckers for as long as I can remember," she said, presenting the first spoonful of dinner.

"They were poor, but they always worked hard."

"Estelle said she'd get Tommy to bring her out here for a visit tomorrow when they come for the car. Would that be all right with you?"

"No!" Violet shook her head vehemently. "I don't want people to see me looking like this."

"Aw, Grammaw, Estelle won't care how you look. She just wants a chance to visit and say thank you."

"I said no. Tell her no." Her anger seemed to be escalating.

Audie hated it when her Grammaw got upset, and she didn't want to push her further. It was her fourth such outburst in the past three days, all of which had left Audie feeling guilty and frustrated. Her efforts to cheer her Grammaw sometimes seemed to have the opposite effect. She chalked it up to Dr. Hill's prediction that she would be depressed for a while, but Audie had expected things to get better after a few days, not worse. "Okay, I'll tell her you're not up for visitors right now. Maybe you'll feel like seeing her in a couple of weeks."

Audie continued to feed her the spaghetti, but in silence as her Grammaw calmed down from her flare-up.

"That's enough," Violet said, turning her head aside like a child.

"But you've hardly touched it. How about some of this cobbler?"

"No."

239

"It's peach. That's your favorite."

"No! Leave me alone."

Audie fought a rush of tears. It hurt like hell when her Grammaw spoke to her this way, but she knew she wasn't herself. She would snap out of this depression soon.

"Okay, let's get this tray out of your way." She rolled it toward the door and returned to sit on the edge of the bed. "Beth and I are going to take Buster for a walk out to Sumter Point before it gets dark." The mention of either Beth or Buster usually brightened her Grammaw's mood and thankfully, today was no exception. "She and BD came over and stayed at the house last night. I can't stay too much at her place because they don't allow big dogs and I don't want to leave Buster by himself."

"Do they fight?"

"No, they get along just fine. But Buster's decided he likes cat food better than dog food, so we have to keep BD's bowl on the kitchen table." She knew that would get a rise out of her Grammaw.

"Audrey Jane!"

Audie grinned at finally seeing a smile. "I was kidding. I know you'd come home and kick my tail if I fed an animal on the table. We keep it on top of the dryer."

"You're wicked the way you tease me."

"I know." She looked at her watch. "I guess I'll go on and pick up Beth so we can get there in time for the sunset. I'll be back at breakfast, okay?"

"Okay, sweetie." Violet reached out a hand to cup Audie's face as she bent forward for her usual goodbye kiss. "I'm sorry if I was mean to you."

The apology brought fresh tears that Audie couldn't stop and she hurriedly wiped them away. "You weren't, Grammaw. I know you don't feel so good right now. I'm sorry I kept pushing you."

"I love you, Audie."

"I love you, too."

She sighed deeply as she walked out to her car. She needed for something good to happen.

Beth could see that Audie was hurting today. It had nothing to do with yesterday's argument, she knew. They had worked that out last night. This probably had more to do with her Grammaw. She wore a faraway look when she tried to push things out of her mind. Beth wanted to take her in her arms and comfort her, stroke her head and give her soft, reassuring kisses. But Audie didn't need that just yet.

She was just beginning to understand the nuances of how Audie dealt with little things that got under her skin. First, she needed a little space in her head to work through whatever it was. She wanted to be strong enough to handle things on her own, but eventually she would reach out for support. Beth had to wait for that moment. In the meantime, she decided on a compromise, a physical gesture to let Audie know she was there for her. As they walked along the path to the river's edge, she linked her fingers loosely with Audie's and gave a small squeeze.

"I love you, Beth."

Beth raised the fingers to her lips and delivered a soft kiss. Then she tucked both of their hands into the warm pocket of her jacket. "That's because I'm now the girl of your dreams. Remember?"

"I do." Audie unclipped Buster's leash with her other hand and tossed the ragged Frisbee ahead on the path. "I'm worried about Grammaw."

"I know. I could tell it was bothering you."

"She isn't happy anymore. She's acting like she's getting ready to leave me."

Beth had come to the same conclusion last week when she had been asked to sign the DNR. Still, she was watching Miss Violet carefully for signs her depression was subsiding, looking for a chance to talk to her about rescinding the form for Audie's sake. "I think she's having a hard time adjusting to the total loss of movement on her left side. She's not as independent as she was, and she's not the kind of person who likes to ask for help."

"Tell me about it. I had to practically force her to let me adjust her bed this afternoon. I couldn't believe it when she told me to call Estelle Tucker. She's always given Estelle her hand-me-downs, but she wanted me to give her everything today—all of her dresses and sweaters, even her winter coat."

"Maybe she was thinking about winter coming on, and she realized Estelle might need that stuff."

"And then she told me to give the old Buick to Estelle's son. She even said they could have her bedroom furniture if they wanted it, but I said no, that I wanted to keep it."

"Old people go through times like this, Audie, at least the ones whose minds are still sharp. Your Grammaw had a scare with her last stroke and I think she feels like she needs to get her affairs in order. But it doesn't have to mean she's finished with living." Audie didn't answer, but Beth could tell from the thumb stroking her hand that her words were comforting. "It might help her to do all of this. Maybe it'll make her feel like she's back in control."

"I hope so." She pulled the Frisbee from Buster's teeth and tossed it again. "I can't stand it when she yells at me."

"I don't believe it's you she's yelling at. I think she's just frustrated at not being able to do things for herself anymore. She hates that you have to come to feed her, but—"

"I don't have to. I want to."

"I know you do. But she feels bad that you changed your work schedule to come back at dinner."

"Oscar doesn't care when I work, especially now that I'm going on a regular workday. He even told me it would be okay to skip out a little early every day and do dinner."

"That's good. But what your Grammaw sees is that you had to make special arrangements. She feels bad about that. The thing she really hates is being a burden on the staff."

"But that's why she's in the nursing home in the first place."

"I know, but she still wants to be independent. She wouldn't even call for help to go to the bathroom, so we just put it on the

242

schedule to take her every three hours, whether she asks or not. We're all trying to get her to feel normal about things again."

They reached the point just as the sun was starting to dip and discovered they were alone. Audie helped Beth up onto a boulder where they wrapped themselves in a flannel blanket to watch the blazing sky.

"How do I get her to snap out of it? I swear the only thing that even brings a smile to her face is when I talk about you or Buster."

"So try to do that as much as you can. I will too."

"She's so happy about you and me."

Beth laid her head on Audie's shoulder. "That's because she's knows what a catch I am."

Audie chuckled and wrapped an arm around her, pulling her close. "I don't know where I would have been without you these last few months. Even before I knew I loved you, you were already there for me."

Each time Audie spoke her heart like this, Beth savored the sweetness of their new love. She couldn't remember a time when simple words—anyone's words—had made her feel so grand. The more she got to know Audie, the easier it was to reconcile this softer side with that brash young woman who hid her heartache for her beloved grandmother behind a wild, angry front. Audie was all of these things, a dynamic, multi-layered woman whose appetite for fun was exceeded only by her capacity for tenderness. And Beth was undeniably, irrevocably in love with her. "What can I do to make things easier?"

"Just be here with me." She scooted behind Beth on the boulder and spread her legs, pulling her snugly to the cushion of her chest. "Let's watch the sky and talk about something a little less depressing."

Beth relaxed and gave in to the embrace. Buster scrambled onto the boulder to lie down next to their outstretched legs. "You want me to talk about how good it feels when you put your arms around me like this?"

"That could be nice. Or you could murmur sweet nothings when I kiss your neck like this." Audie nuzzled her behind her ear.

"I love that," she said, allowing her head to drop to the side. Being close to Audie this way was incredible. It wasn't as much their sensuous connection—Audie oozed sex appeal, so it was easy to relate to her that way. What was special about their relationship was the growing emotional bond, something that only a few short months ago had seemed far-fetched. "When did you first know you loved me?"

Audie took a few moments to think about her answer, reaching down to scratch Buster on his back before wrapping her arms around Beth again. "I think the first time I realized it was really love was when I said it out loud that night in your bed. Maybe after I had that dream about us and decided I wanted it to come true."

"And now it has." Beth turned and they shared a long kiss, relishing their privacy at this special place.

"I remember the first time I thought about kissing you. It was that night I stopped by your place on my way out to the Gallery. You had on those gray sweatpants, and when you bent over to pick up your keys I checked out your lovely ass."

"I remember that night. You looked so hot I would have done you on the floor."

Audie chuckled. "Sure wish I'd known that."

"It's a good thing you didn't. I would have failed my nursing boards."

"I doubt that."

They watched the sun sink lower in the southwestern sky, sending shimmers off the river to sparkle in the golden trees.

"Thanks for bringing me out here again, Audie. It's beautiful."

"I needed this today, to be with you out here away from everybody."

"I think we both did," Beth said. Sumter Point was peaceful and romantic, better for serious conversation than at home, where they tended to get sidetracked by spurious lovemaking whenever they began to share deep emotions. "You know, after Shelby left, I thought I could get used to being by myself, maybe even get so I wouldn't want anyone else that close again."

"And what do you think now?"

"Now I can't imagine not having you like this. I thought about that yesterday and it scared me half to death."

"I thought about it too," Audie said. "But I'm not going to be that easy to get rid of."

"I don't ever want to lose you."

"I'm not going anywhere." They both sat mesmerized as the last sliver of sun disappeared. "I'm kind of new at this, but if this is how it feels to be in love, I hope it never ends."

The words, solemn and heartfelt, were like music to Beth's ears. Without turning around, she said, "It doesn't have to end, Audie. I could see myself being with you for a long time."

"I hope so. Sometimes I get so scared of being alone." Whether they talked about it or not, it was obvious her anguish was still close to the surface.

"You won't ever be alone." Beth turned around to find Audie near tears. Now was the moment of transition she had thought about earlier, when Audie let go of her feelings and looked to her to be the strong one. "There are so many people who love you."

"I know."

"Look at me, sweetheart." She tipped Audie's chin upward and wiped a tear with her thumb. "You won't ever be alone as long as I'm around, I promise. No matter what happens to us a year from now or twenty years from now, I'm going to love you, and I'll always be there for you." She didn't care if it sounded like a lofty vow, it was true. "Okay?"

Audie nodded, her expression tentative. "What do you think will happen to us?"

"I want to be part of you for a long, long time—however long it takes to really know your soul and have you know mine."

"What if that takes forever? Will you stay with me that long?"

"Yes, I would stay with you that long." Beth's heart skipped a beat as she realized what she was saying. But she was undeniably ready to make Audie Pippin the center of her life. "It's a big step for us to be talking like this, Audie. Maybe we ought to wait until there's not so much going on."

"Why, are you going to change your mind?"

Beth gave her a reassuring smile. "No, I'm not. I can make that kind of promise right now, but can you?"

"I've never felt like this about anybody before. It's like the ground's been shifting under me all this time and you've given me something to stand on."

"Oh, Audie." Beth wrapped her arms around Audie's neck and hugged her tightly. "For somebody who claims to be new at this, you've sure got the heart-stopping lingo down."

They held each other for several minutes without saying a word before finally leaving their perch to return to the car. As they walked down the path in the waning light, Beth noticed that Audie's hand felt different from earlier when she tucked it in her pocket. This hand belonged to her now, and she wanted it to be the only one she would ever hold this way. "What's today?"

"November sixth."

She stopped walking and tugged on Audie's wrist, turning her so they faced each other. "I want this to be the day we mark our time, not when we met or when we first made love. I want our time to start when we both said we wanted to stay together forever."

Chapter 22

"Let me know when you're ready for me to help," Audie called through the crack in the bathroom door. She had gradually overcome her discomfort regarding her grandmother's personal needs. It seemed as normal now as helping her eat or put on her slippers.

"I'm almost done. What's for dinner?"

Audie stirred a bowl containing rice and minced meat. "I think it's chicken but I'm not a hundred percent sure. Mr. Wortman got a chicken leg with his. You want me to go steal it?"

Her grandmother laughed as she struggled through the doorway in her wheelchair to return to her bed. "Get his biscuit too."

Audie loved days like today when her Grammaw was talkative and in a good mood. She couldn't wait to share what she and Beth had talked about at Sumter Point. It was the first time in her life she was eager to talk with her grandmother about her personal life. She had always shared the superficial version, the one that skipped her partying lifestyle, but there was an even bigger reason she had never talked about a romantic relationship—she had never had one. The only person who had come close to being called a girlfriend was Maxine, and the details of their unhealthy attraction—the drugs, the alcohol, the rough sex—weren't exactly things her Grammaw would have appreciated. And there hadn't been any deep feelings to talk about.

That's what was different about Beth. Audie was bursting to talk about her feelings and dreams. She wanted an affirmation and a blessing for their life together from the only person whose opinion really mattered.

"Did you and Beth talk about anything today?" Audie served up a spoonful of the main course.

"She told me a little about her sister." Violet paused to take another bite and swallow. "She's like you. She didn't know her mama very well either."

It hadn't occurred to Audie before that she and Beth had that in common. "It was harder for her, though, because she didn't have anybody like you or Grampaw."

"Sounds like she had to grow up fast."

"She did." Audie thought little details like this made Beth a special person. "I was lucky to have you and Grampaw. Now I'm lucky to have Beth too." Audie held a sipping cup to her grandmother's lip. "You remember yesterday at supper when I told you I was going with Beth and Buster out to Sumter Point?"

"Mmm-hmm." Violet continued to eat as she listened.

"We talked about being together, Beth and me . . . staying together. We can't get married or anything like that, but I think we would if we could."

Audie waited nervously for what seemed like long minutes for a response. Finally, a pat from her grandmother's frail hand vanquished her doubts. "Beth's good for you."

"Do you think it's silly for us to feel like that already? We just started being friends three months ago."

"Does it seem silly to you?"

Audie chuckled. "No. But there's an old joke about lesbians who show up with a U-Haul on their second date because they fall in love so fast. I used to think that was funny, but now it's hitting a little close to home."

"Who's to say what's too soon? Just listen to what your heart's telling you."

"Is that what you did with Grampaw?" Audie scooped a spoonful of vegetables. "Here, try some of this."

Violet swallowed and Audie wiped her mouth. "Your Grampaw didn't waste any time, I'll tell you that. But I guess I didn't either."

"How long did you know each other before you decided to get married?"

"He came with some boys from the army to one of the dances we had at Peabody." She leaned back, motioning with her hand that she was finished with her dinner. "He was stationed at Fort Campbell. He wasn't the handsomest fellow, but he could talk sweet."

"Sounds just like Grampaw." Audie enjoyed the faraway smile on her Grammaw's face as she relived her memories. "So you met at a dance. Then what?"

"Then he came calling two weeks later to the dormitory. Said he couldn't get me off his mind. Truth was, I'd been thinking about him too, because he wasn't like the other soldier boys just looking to be with the women. He wanted to be with me. Your Grampaw was a good man. I knew it the first time we met."

"And that's when you started dating?"

"He took me out for a milkshake that night and told me he was shipping out to Korea and asked me if I would wait for him till he got back. I said no."

"You said no?" Audie couldn't believe she was hearing this story for the first time.

"I said I wasn't going to wait that long for anybody but my husband, so we slipped off that weekend and got married. Didn't tell a soul."

"Whoa! You got married after only one date and it lasted . . ."

"Forever, Audie. I still love that old man like I did the day we married."

Audie's heart swelled with hope. If her grandparents could build a whole life on only a dance and a milkshake, then she and Beth had as good a chance as anyone to make their love last. "How did you know Grampaw was the right one to marry?"

"Like I said, I knew he was a good man. You can't go wrong with that."

Audie nodded, understanding clearly what her grandmother was saying, because Beth was probably the most decent person she had ever met. "Is there a secret for making love last forever?"

"Just trust each other."

"Beth and I already do that."

"Trust her all the time, sweetie. She won't ever let you down."

The way she said that made it sound more like a warning than just grandmotherly advice. Audie doubted Beth would have said anything about their fight the other day, but she knew anyway whose side her Grammaw would have taken.

"Did you and Grampaw ever have a fight about something big?"

"Your Grampaw made me real mad once, but I listened to why he did what he did and I decided he was right." From the look in her eyes, she was remembering a time long past. "It was when your mama called from Las Vegas and he hung up on her without even letting me talk."

"You mean back when I was in the fifth grade?"

"That's right. He knew how bad I wanted to see your mama again, but he didn't trust her. She told him if we sent her the money, she'd take the bus back home so we'd all be together again. He was afraid she might come and try to take you away from us."

"I wouldn't have gone with her, you know."

"Dang right you wouldn't, because I wouldn't have let her have you. But your Grampaw wasn't going to take a chance. He told her she could just stay out there. We were through with her."

Audie was moved by the tears in her grandmother's eyes. "And you never heard from her again?"

Violet shook her head sadly. "No, that was the last time. And I was so mad at him, but after I had time to think about it, I knew he was right. We couldn't take a chance that she would come back to Sumter and tear us all apart. Your mama didn't love people, Audie. She just used them for her own good."

"I never have understood why she didn't like living here as much as I did."

"It wasn't just living in Sumter. It embarrassed her that your Grampaw and I were so much older than her friends' mamas and daddies. She never wanted us to come to school for anything and she wouldn't bring anyone over to the house. She got so she would stay out all night. We couldn't control her. She just couldn't wait to get away from us, and she went with the first man to take her."

Audie had never been curious about her mother. From the time she first understood that she had been left behind to be raised by her grandparents, she wrote it off. She always told herself she didn't want to know her mother at all. What she didn't like was that her mother had hurt the two people she loved most, her Grammaw and Grampaw.

"We got the best of your mama when she brought you to live with us. Your Grampaw and I were so worried you'd grow up to hate us like she did."

"No way. I always loved you and Grampaw."

"I know, sweetie. Watching you grow up into such a fine young lady made us so proud."

If her grandmother knew about her partying ways, she probably wouldn't feel that way. But with each day, Audie vowed to try harder to be the good person Beth and her grandparents believed her to be. "I always knew I was lucky to be with you and Grampaw and not with my mama. I never had to worry about somebody loving me, no matter how much I screwed up."

"You never messed up, Audie. You did some little things, but you never gave us more trouble than we could handle. We couldn't have asked for a better granddaughter."

"You're going to make me cry." Audie sniffed and wiped a tear from the corner of her eye. "I love you, and I loved Grampaw too."

"And now you're all grown up and you love Beth."

"I sure do."

"You take care of her, you hear me?"

"I will." On that note, their conversation had come full circle. "We're going out dancing tonight at the Gallery. Did she tell you that?"

"How did you talk her into it?"

"It was her idea, believe it or not. We had so much fun there on our first date that she wanted to go try it again."

"I hope it's fun for you girls again."

Audie noticed a lilt in her voice, and her eyes closed briefly. "I guess I'll go home and start to get ready. I love you, Grammaw."

"I love you too, sweetie."

"Sleep well tonight, and I'll see you at breakfast."

As she walked back to her car, Audie couldn't help but feel lighter than she had in days. Her Grammaw seemed to be doing better, and more important, she was happy again. And after their talk today, Audie felt closer to her than she ever had since her Grampaw died.

Beth smiled as the headlights from passing cars illuminated Audie in the driver's seat. Audie was her usual sexy self tonight, dressed in soft denim jeans that hugged her butt, and a tailored white shirt unbuttoned to expose part of a black bra.

"Damn, you look hot!"

Audie grinned at her lasciviously. "Good enough to eat?"

Beth groaned. "If that's what you were going for, you might as well turn this car around."

"No way. I want to dance."

"Okay, but if you start grinding on me out there, don't be surprised if I throw you down on the floor."

"Yeah, baby." Audie leaned over and slid her hand between Beth's legs. "What are you doing tomorrow?"

"Laundry. Why?"

"I want you to go shopping with me. I have to buy some new work clothes. Oscar has me down to do a talk at Sumter Creek Elementary School on Monday morning."

"I think that's great you're starting the new job. I'm so proud of you." Even in the dim light, Beth could see by the look on Audie's face that she was proud of herself too. "What kind of clothes are you looking for?"

"Something besides jeans that covers my tattoo . . . maybe something loose enough that I could actually put my hands in my pockets while I'm talking."

"Are you nervous?"

"Not so much with the third graders. But I might be when I have to talk at the Kiwanis Club or something like that."

"You're going to do great, Audie. You'll have them eating out of your hand."

They pulled into the parking lot next to the Gallery and Audie shut off the engine. "Thanks for coming with me tonight."

"It was my idea, remember?" Beth got out and met Audie at the back of the vehicle. "But if that Regan chick lays one finger on you, I'm going to bite it off."

"Don't worry about Regan. Yours are the only fingers I want."

They entered the club, where Beth immediately spotted Ginger and Mallory at a table with several women. "Where do you want to sit?"

"With the girls is fine. I'll say hi to the guys after while."

As they moved through the crowd, Beth felt Audie's hand slide into her back pocket and caress her rear. She liked the feel of it there, and she didn't care who saw it.

Ginger leapt from her chair and held out her arms. "I didn't know you were coming out."

"Surprise," Beth said, pulling Audie with her as she leaned forward for a hug.

"Is this going to be a regular thing now that you're off on the weekends?"

"Maybe. Audie has weekends off now too."

Audie pulled her hand from Beth's pocket and extended it to Ginger. "We'll be here whenever she wants."

"Good. Come dance with me."

Beth watched slack-jawed as Ginger pulled Audie out to the dance floor. Clearly, she was up to something.

"Pull up a chair, Beth." Mallory reached for the pitcher in the center of the table and an empty mug. "Have a beer."

"I can't. I'm driving us home tonight." She took the seat vacated by Ginger. "I figure since Ginger took my girlfriend, I can at least take her chair."

She watched as the song continued. Ginger and Audie were talking about something, but it didn't seem to be serious, since both were laughing. When the music ended, they shared a hug and returned to the table. Mallory slid a brimming mug to Audie, who caught it just before it reached the end of the table.

"That was close, Audie."

"She's very good with her hands," Beth offered, immediately slapping a hand to her own mouth. Everyone laughed and she joined in. "What I meant was—"

"They know what you meant, honey," Audie said as she leaned over and planted a kiss on Beth's temple. "It's our turn to dance. Are you ready?"

Beth held on to Audie's belt loop as they wound through the crowd to the center of the dance floor. The beat of the music was neither fast nor slow, and Audie chose to lead with an embrace.

"What was all that about with you and Ginger?"

"She just had a couple of things she wanted to talk about."

Audie's hands slid down her back, sparking a surge of arousal as their hips came together. "What kind of things?"

"She asked me if you were happy and I said yes."

She could tell from Audie's smirk there was more to it than that. "And what else?"

"That I'd better keep it that way or she'd break both my kneecaps."

Beth snorted with laughter, causing both of them to temporarily lose the beat of the music. "Did you believe her?"

"Totally. But I told her I had all the motivation I needed to keep you happy."

"And what's that?"

"Now you know I'd never give our secrets away."

"That's probably a good thing . . . a very good thing."

"Because then people would get jealous and I'd probably have to crack some heads."

The music changed to a techno beat and Audie gently disentangled to dance at arm's length. Beth focused on the belly button ring that peeked out below the last button of Audie's shirt. "We didn't last very long the last time we tried this," she shouted.

Audie grinned. "Because you got me hot."

"I think it was the other way around."

"Does it matter?" When the song ended, Audie took her elbow and led her back to the table, where Regan now sat drinking her beer.

"Come sit with me, Audie. Let's talk," Regan said playfully.

Beth stiffened at the proprietary way Regan draped her arm across the back of the chair next to her. Then she felt her whole body shift as Audie sat and scooped her onto her lap in one move.

"Looks like the rumors are true." Regan pushed the half-empty mug toward Audie and refilled it from the pitcher. "You're Beth, right?"

"Right, and you're Regan." She swiveled so they were all facing each other, and hooked both arms possessively around Audie's neck.

"I am. I hear you've taken Audie out of commission."

"She has," Audie answered.

"That's a pity." Regan looked at Audie, not Beth. "I guess if I were a good sport, I'd say best wishes or something."

"You could always get us a housewarming present," Audie suggested, batting her eyes innocently.

Beth couldn't believe her ears. Not that she hadn't been thinking that one of these days she would move into Audie's house and they would make it their home. She just couldn't believe Audie was talking about it so casually.

Regan leaned over and gave Audie a quick kiss on the cheek. "It's cheaper to give you best wishes. You too, Beth. Now, if you'll let me out of here, I think Deanna just got here."

She scooted out from behind the table and disappeared in the crowd that gathered near the door.

"So you think we're ready for housewarming presents?" Beth asked, tightening her grip around Audie's neck.

"Probably not just yet."

Beth wasn't quite ready yet either, but she found herself disappointed by Audie's quick reply until she went on to clarify.

"Maybe after I clean out the garage and get all the dirty dishes out of the sink."

"Yeah, you're definitely in charge of your own dirty dishes." The chair beside them was now empty, but Beth was content to stay right where she was—in Audie's lap. "Hey, isn't that Dennis out there dancing?"

Audie craned her neck to see. "Well, I'll be damned."

"Who's that guy he's with? He's cute."

"His name's David."

Chapter 23

" . . . and the other great thing about owning a pet is that you're always going to have a best friend, no matter what. If you have a hard day at school, they'll be right there when you get home to lick your face or sit in your lap. They don't care if you don't eat your vegetables or don't clean your room." The boys and girls giggled. "The only thing they care about is getting their ears scratched and hearing you say 'good boy' or 'good girl'."

Audie leaned with both hands on the back of the chair Mrs. Newman had provided at the front of her classroom. She was moments away from surviving her first outreach assignment. It had been relatively painless, once she got over the initial butterflies.

A boy's hand went up in the back of the room.

"Do you have a question?" she asked.

"Our dog got stuck to the neighbor's dog once. Daddy had to turn the hose on 'em to get 'em apart. Mama said they were making puppies."

Audie looked immediately at Mrs. Newman for a clue on how she should handle the remark. The teacher was blushing furiously, apparently mortified. Audie looked back at the boy, whose face was a mask of total innocence. "I'm glad you brought that up about puppies. One of the most important things we do is try to keep dogs and cats from having too many puppies or kittens."

"Why?"

"Well, because we have more puppies and kittens than we have good homes for them. We want good homes for all of them."

"I think everyone likes getting a new puppy or kitten," Mrs. Newman interjected. Audie almost laughed at her transparent effort to keep the discussion from drifting back to two dogs fucking.

"But when puppies and kittens come along, they're so much fun to play with that people sometimes stop paying attention to their older pets. For instance, there's my dog, Buster. He's three years old. He's not a puppy anymore, but he still needs me to play with him. And he's still my best friend."

A girl in the front row raised her hand.

"Yes?"

"Do you ever . . ."

She seemed unsure how to ask her question.

"Do we ever what?"

"My brother said when you can't find homes for them you have to kill them."

Audie knew this question might come up, and she had worried about how she was going to deal with such a sensitive subject with eight-year-olds. They deserved to know the truth, she thought, but not in a way that might cause them anguish.

"We used to do that, but not anymore. Now we try to find homes for all the animals that come to us, no matter how long it takes. We have a rule now that says every single cat or dog that comes to the shelter and needs a home gets to stay there until they find one."

"What if they're sick or something? My dad said we have to put them to sleep so they won't suffer."

Audie wasn't going to be able to avoid this. "Well, your dad's right sometimes. Once in a while, we get a dog or cat that's very sick or that has been injured so badly that they're suffering. We don't think it's right to let them suffer so we put them to sleep. It doesn't happen very often though. Only with dogs or cats that are too sick or hurt to go to good homes."

The boy who spoke before raised his hand and shouted his question simultaneously. "How do you kill them?"

Audie looked at the teacher again for guidance, but Mrs. Newman was raptly listening for an answer. "Well, it's like this. If we have to do it, we bring the dog or cat out of its crate and set it on the table. Dr. Martin—he's the vet—he's the one who gives the shots . . . two shots. The first one is just to calm them down so they won't be scared. While they're relaxing, I usually brush them real good and tell them how pretty they look. And I scratch their ears and say they're a good boy . . . or a good girl. And when they're nice and calm, Dr. Martin gives them the other shot and they go to sleep forever. I like to think the last thing they remember is a person being nice to them and telling them how wonderful they are."

Mrs. Newman was wiping her eyes, but the children seemed okay with everything she had said.

"Okay, thanks for inviting me to come. I brought some stickers for everybody. I'll leave those with Mrs. Newman."

"Class, let's show Miss Pippin how much we appreciate her talking to us today."

Audie blushed as the children clapped. She would have to figure out how to deal with being called Miss Pippin.

" . . . and then this one kid raised his hand and told all about seeing two dogs get stuck together when they were . . . you know. And his teacher looked like she wanted to just disappear through the floor."

Her grandmother laughed with obvious delight. Audie knew she would love hearing all the details of the first day on her new job. "So what did you do?"

"I just acted like it was a question about puppies and started talking about why we didn't want so many."

"You're smart, Audie."

Audie grinned. "Nah, just a fast thinker."

"Come here, honey." She held out her hand and Audie took it. "I'm so proud of you . . . for everything."

Audie had probably never been prouder of herself, and hearing it from her Grammaw meant more than anything could. "I think I'm really going to like it. At first I thought it was going to be hard, but it turned out to be fun." Her head was exploding with ideas. "I'm going to tell Oscar this afternoon about this idea I have for setting up little talks for all the elementary schools. It's a good way to—"

Her grandmother hadn't moved, but her right eye—the one that usually stayed focused—was fixed in a downward position.

"Grammaw?"

Audie's stomach dropped when she got no response.

"Grammaw? Wake up." Panicked, she yelled out. "Somebody come quick! Something's wrong." She groped beneath the covers for the emergency call button and pressed it several times in succession. "Beth!"

The next few moments went by in a blur as Beth and Wanda rushed headlong into the room. Neither even looked at Audie, but she didn't care. She wanted them to fix whatever was wrong as fast as they could.

"I was just talking to her and all of a sudden, she just . . ." She held her tongue as Beth grasped her grandmother's wrist and looked at her watch.

"Do you want me to get the crash cart?" Wanda asked anxiously.

"No. Get Hazel . . . and Clara," Beth answered crisply.

Audie's fear was ready to spiral out of control. "What are you going to do?"

"Hold your Grammaw's hand, Audie. Talk to her."

"Beth?"

"Tell her you love her, sweetheart. She wants to hear that."

Audie did as she was told, trying her best not to panic as Hazel Tipton entered and austerely walked around to the other side of the bed. She held her breath when Hazel opened the top two buttons of her grandmother's gown and pressed a stethoscope against several spots on her chest. Several minutes passed, with Audie watching closely for the slightest movement, any sign at all that her Grammaw was still with them.

"I'm not getting a heartbeat," she said softly.

"Do something!"

"Audie . . . sweetheart." Beth put a hand on her shoulder. "Your Grammaw wouldn't want that . . . not this time."

What was Beth saying?

"Audie, I'm so very sorry," Hazel said, pocketing her stethoscope before she respectfully closed the gown and gently closed her grandmother's eyes. "I can't say for certain, but it looks like she had a major stroke."

"Can't you . . . ? Something . . . anything."

"She asked us for a DNR, Audie," Beth finally said. "It's what she wanted."

"No." Audie wouldn't believe it. "I never signed it."

"She asked for it on her own, sweetie."

There had to be some mistake. Her Grammaw didn't want to leave.

"Beth, why don't you take Audie down to the sunroom for a few minutes while we prepare things here?" Hazel met Audie's eyes with a somber look of her own. "You can come back in a few minutes and wait with her if you like."

Audie didn't want to let go of her Grammaw's hand. She wanted to be there when she woke up.

"Come on, Audie. We have to leave the room for a few minutes." Beth nudged her gently toward the door and into the hall.

Audie broke down in tears and felt an arm go around her waist as she struggled to stand on her own.

"Come on, sweetie. Let's just go sit here for a little while."

With Beth's help, she made it to the sunroom, where she collapsed into a vinyl chair. "What are they doing?"

"They're just cleaning her up a little . . . putting her in a fresh gown." Beth was kneeling in front of her, gently rubbing her hands and arms. "We can go back in when they finish."

Suddenly it hit her what was happening. "She doesn't want to die, Beth. I know it. Go back and make them save her."

Beth was crying now, and shaking her head. "She didn't want to go back to the hospital, Audie. She didn't want to lose anymore control."

Audie sobbed and sniffed. "She never meant for you to let her die."

Beth's hands cradled her face. "Honey, this is what she wanted. She told me so. I tried to talk her out of it—"

"You knew?" Audie jerked her head out of Beth's grasp. "You knew about this and you didn't tell me?"

"I couldn't."

Audie felt her whole world spinning out of control, and she strained to stand up, but Beth had her pinned in the chair.

"Listen to me, Audie. Please, listen."

She had no choice.

"Your Grammaw said you would only trust one person . . . one person, Audie."

"To do what?"

"To tell you it was what she truly wanted. She didn't want you to doubt it, on account of your Grampaw, so she asked me to be the one to witness it. I told her I didn't want to do it, but she said I was the only one who could."

Audie slumped against the chair back, defeated and heartbroken. Her beloved Grammaw had chosen to leave her.

Hazel stepped into the hall and motioned that it was okay for her to return.

"I don't want to go back in there."

"You need to, honey. You have to say goodbye." Beth stood up and took her hand. "We can wait until they come for her. Then I'll come home with you."

"No . . . no, I just . . . I'll come say goodbye, but . . ." She felt Beth's hand squeeze hers and she gripped it tightly. "Will you stay and wait with her?"

"Where will you go?"

"I have to . . ." They stopped in the hallway outside the door and she took several deep breaths. "I have to call Oscar . . . and Joel and Dennis."

"Are you sure you're okay to drive?"

Audie nodded.

"Okay, let's go do this and I'll wait with her. But I'm coming to find you as soon as Hazel lets me out of here."

Beth drew a sigh of relief when she saw the yellow Xterra in the lot at Sumter Point. When she had reached the house only forty minutes after Audie left the nursing home, she assumed Audie would be here because Buster was gone. It worried her to think Audie might have come here to get away from her, angry about the DNR.

She parked and got out, wishing she had more to ward off the chilly autumn air than the sweater she had worn to work. But she warmed up as she briskly walked along the path toward the point. When she rounded the last curve, Buster barked and jumped down from the boulder to meet her.

"Hey, boy. You looking after Audie?"

She continued tentatively to the rock, where Audie sat with her knees pulled to her chin. Her eyes, nose and mouth were swollen and red from crying.

"Audie, I'm so sorry." A quick glance was the only indication Audie heard her. She scooted up from behind and began a gentle massage of Audie's shoulders. The fact that Audie wasn't pulling away was a good sign. "Your grandmother loved you so much."

"I feel like I failed her."

"No, you didn't. She was so proud of you."

"I mean with that form. She needed me to do that and I couldn't."

Beth slid around to sit where she and Audie could see each other's faces. "Your Grammaw never meant for you to be the one to do that. But she was afraid you might think somebody pressured her or tricked her into signing it."

"She told me just the other day to trust you. She said you wouldn't let me down."

"I won't."

"You're all I have now."

Beth's heart was breaking for Audie's grief, but it soared at the simple understanding that they would see this life through together. "You'll always have me."

Chapter 24

"You look tired. Why don't you take a load off?" Joel offered, pointing to one of the small antique chairs in the corner of the little-used parlor.

"Thanks," Beth said, taking a seat for what seemed like the first time in three days. "I am tired. I don't know what Audie's running on."

From their vantage point, they could see her in the hallway by the door, greeting guests one by one. After more than two hours of condolences, she was answering with an almost robotic cadence.

"Has she eaten anything?"

"Not much. I fixed her a plate and put it in the kitchen for later, though."

"Good. Maybe all of us can sit down together when these people are gone."

Dennis came in to collect a load of plates and cups from around the room.

"I should see if they need a hand in the kitchen." She started to stand, but Joel gently pushed her back into her seat.

"Dwayne and Dennis have it all under control. You just take it easy."

It felt good to sit, but Beth felt guilty at seeing Audie still on her feet. Neither of them had slept well since Violet died, with Audie walking the house every night and sitting for hours in her grandmother's bedroom.

Joel grabbed a newly vacated chair and pulled it next to Beth's. "Audie says she feels bad about her Grammaw giving up."

"I don't think it was like that. I told Audie I thought she needed to leave on her own terms, when she still had some control."

"I know she feels good about her Grammaw being taken care of all the way to the end."

"And she was happy, Joel. She loved seeing Audie and me together." Beth swallowed hard, the knot nearly piercing her throat as she considered the weight of Audie's loss. "I think her last days were happy."

"That's what counts, isn't it? I don't know about you, but I want to go exactly the same way."

"I wish everyone could." It was definitely what Miss Violet had wanted, Beth reminded herself. Even Audie had come to accept that.

"I haven't said anything to Audie yet, but Dwayne and I are going to be fixing Thanksgiving dinner at our cabin in Dale Hollow. We'd like for you guys to come."

Beth usually made the holiday trip to Knoxville to have dinner with Kelly and her husband, but she wanted to be with Audie and her friends this year. "That sounds good. I'll talk to her about it and we'll let you know."

"We have an extra bedroom if you want to stay over. We can put Dennis on the couch."

Beth snorted. "I'm sure he'll like that." She looked up to see Dennis whispering something into Audie's ear. Audie gave him a nod before turning and locking eyes with her for a brief moment. "I don't think Dennis likes me very much."

"Why do you say that?"

"Just some things Audie said. I think Dennis feels like I might be . . . too old for her."

Joel shrugged. "I wouldn't worry about it. Dennis just figured out he's the last one left in Never Never Land."

"I don't want to come between Audie and her friends, though. She loves Dennis."

"She loves you more."

"But it doesn't have to be a competition."

"Dennis is the one who needs to realize that, not you." He leaned closer and rested his hand on her knee. "Beth, I've known Audie for eight years, and I've never seen her settled like this before. She always looked around, but she didn't have a clue what she was looking for. Now she acts like she's found something with her name on it, and she's ready to take her life in a whole new direction. She's very happy with you."

"This has my name on it too, Joel."

"I'm glad to hear it. You're good for her, especially now, so she won't have to feel like she's alone."

"She's not alone. I won't let her be."

"And I won't let Dennis screw that up. I'll talk to him."

"You don't have to do that. I just need to reach out and show him that he's not going to lose Audie as a friend."

"Okay, but if you need an ally, let me know. I can reason with him better than most."

"Thanks."

The last group of visitors walked out the door and Audie slumped immediately onto a bench in the hallway, obviously exhausted. Beth hurried to her side.

"I guess it's all over," Audie said, heaving a sigh.

"That's right. It's just your friends here now."

"Are Joel and Dwayne still here?"

"They're in the kitchen with Dennis, cleaning up. I saved you something to eat."

"I'm not really hungry."

"I know, but you need to eat anyway."

Audie tugged at the lapels on her black jacket. "What I need is to get out of this suit."

"Let's go put on our jeans and come back down and have dinner with the guys. Then we can just relax tonight, maybe watch some TV or something."

"If it's okay with you, I think I'll go over to Dennis's house tonight. I need a change of scenery. I feel like these walls are closing in on me."

Beth drew in a breath. It wasn't a change of scenery that Audie needed. She was probably going with Dennis so they could get high. That was the invitation he had whispered into her ear earlier.

"We could go over to Oscar's and get Buster . . . maybe walk down to Sumter Point if you want to get out."

"Nah, it'll be dark soon."

"Do you want to stay at my place tonight? We can sneak Buster in if you want to."

"No, I just . . . I need to . . . he says he has a bottle of tequila . . ."

Among other things, Beth thought. "You don't have to say anymore." In spite of her insistence to Joel that she and Dennis were not in competition, Beth felt jealous that Audie was choosing to spend this emotional time with Dennis. It wasn't just his company that Audie wanted though. She was following her wild side.

"Look, Beth. I don't have to go if you don't want me to. I just thought . . ."

"It's okay, Audie. You should go and relax with Dennis if that's what you feel like doing. Just promise you'll call me to come get you if you guys get messed up."

Audie nodded.

"I mean it. Promise me."

"I promise. Where will you be?"

"I'm going to pick up Buster and BD and bring them both back here. Is that okay?"

"That's perfect. I won't stay out late."

"And you have to eat before you go." Audie started to protest, but Beth held up her hand. "Not negotiable."

"You're looking out for me, just like Grammaw told you to."

"And I'm never going to stop."

That earned her a kiss, her first real kiss in three days.

"I don't know how you drink that shit," Dennis said, gesturing toward the plastic pitcher of margaritas Audie had mixed in the kitchen. "Tequila kicks my ass for three days."

"Mine too. But at least it doesn't give me beer farts."

"Mine are usually gone by lunchtime."

"And everyone in your office is dead. That's the real reason Jackie wanted to come to work at the shelter, isn't it? She'd rather shovel dog shit than smell your beer farts." Audie swirled her drink and took a swig. "How come every time I'm with you, we end up talking about either your dick or your ass?"

Dennis laughed so hard that beer came out his nose. "God, I've missed hanging with you, Audie. I wish we could have"—Dennis pounded his fist on his chest and belched—"dickheads' night out or something. You should come with us tomorrow night. They're doing Eighties karaoke."

"Think Dwayne will get up there and moonwalk again?"

"Probably. So you'll come?"

"I doubt it. Beth has to go back to work tomorrow. She won't be able to stay out that late." She braced herself for a snarky reply but it didn't come.

"I have to be at work at eight. What's the big deal?"

"You're taking loan applications, shithead. She's got people's lives in her hands."

"Oh . . . right."

"Speaking of the Gallery, what were you up to with David the other night?"

Dennis shrugged noncommittally. "We're talking again."

"What brought that on?"

"He came over to where I was with Joel and Dwayne. We danced a couple of times, then went outside and talked."

Audie fished an ice cube out of her drink and threw it at him. "I can't believe you're making me drag this out of you. What's up?"

Dennis sighed. "He said he had something to tell me about . . . you know, before. I said I'd listen so we went outside. He told me that the reason we couldn't fuck back then wasn't really because he wanted to take things slow. He said he was still stuck on this other guy, his old boyfriend. He kept thinking they might get back together, so he didn't want to do anything to mess that up."

"That piece of shit!"

"Nah, he's all right. I kind of get why he'd do that."

"Huh?" Audie figured if she didn't get it, Dennis couldn't possibly get it either. "He was jerking you around."

"Yeah, but the way he explained it, I sort of understand. What if Beth all of a sudden told you she needed a little space, that she wanted to take some time for herself? Would you go out and screw around with somebody while you were waiting to see if you two were going to get back together?"

"No, but I wouldn't be making out with somebody else in front of a couple hundred people at the Gallery either."

"See, that's the really weird part. I don't think David thought he would either. But we really hit it off. It was more than I ever clicked with anybody."

"So what's going to happen now?"

"We'll see where it goes. His old boyfriend decided he didn't need all that space after all and moved in with some other stromo."

"Do I even want to know what a stromo is?"

"They're faggots who want everybody to think they're straight."

"Ahhhh." Audie chuckled to herself as she thought of Beth's tales about Shelby. "I'm going to have to tell Beth about that one."

"So you and Beth . . . you two are like . . . together for sure, right?"

Her first instinct was to toss back a sarcastic reply, but this was the first time Dennis had even mentioned Beth in a way that wasn't hostile or condescending. "Yeah, I love her. I want you to get to know her better. You guys don't have much in common, but I think you'd really like her."

"But would she be willing to talk about my dick or my ass?" He grinned as he pulled a tin box from beneath his couch and worked the lid off with his fingernails. Inside were two plastic bags of marijuana and the necessary paraphernalia—pipes, papers and butane lighters. He held up one of the bags. "I've got some more of that shit from Buddy Mickel if you want it."

Audie hesitated before waving him off. "Nah, I'm good."

"And I've still got some of what we smoked last time I came over."

She sighed. "I think I'm about done with all that."

"What do you mean done?" Dennis reached into the bag and crumbled the leaves, pinching just enough to fill his small pipe.

Audie didn't want to get into another argument with Dennis about Beth. "I just don't think I want to be getting fucked up anymore."

"Not ever?"

Audie chugged her drink and grabbed the pitcher to pour another. "Do you ever get the feeling somebody is trying to tell you something?"

"Yeah, but it's usually you or Joel, so I've learned to tune you both out."

"Isn't that the truth!" She tossed another ice cube at him. "It started with me sucking up all those roaches in the ashtray that day I cleaned my car. Then we got pulled over and I had to eat that joint. Then we both got high over at my place last week and Beth and I had a big fight about it."

Dennis started to protest, but Audie held up her hand. "She was right. I'm not going to tell you what all that was about, but she was a hundred percent right. So I was already thinking I probably shouldn't do it anymore." She fought the waver in her voice. "Then Grammaw died."

"Audie, your Grammaw didn't die because of anything you did."

"I know. It's just . . ." If he made fun of what she was about to say, she was going to tear his head off and stuff it up his ass. "I feel like she can see me now . . . that she knows everything I do."

Without a word, Dennis dropped the unlit pipe back into the tin box and closed the lid. "That's kind of creepy if you think about it that way."

Audie chuckled. "Tell me about it."

Beth warily scanned the dark neighborhood, wondering if she dared leave the safety of her car to go to Dennis's door. It was jolting to realize that her new circle of friends now included drug users who lived in seedy neighborhoods. At least Audie was a drug user who lived in a good neighborhood.

She double-parked in the street, as close as she could to the second door from the end, the only unit where the porch light was out, its fixture dangling from the wall beside the door.

Nervously, she rapped lightly on the door and waited.

Audie met her at the door, already wearing her coat. "Hey, baby."

"You ready?" The odor of alcohol was pervasive.

"I'm a little drunk."

"It's okay." She took Audie's elbow and walked with her in silence to the car. Behind them, Dennis was watching from the door. "Go ahead and get in the car. I'll be right back."

She walked back to the apartment, where Dennis stood in the doorway, his arms folded across his chest. This was Audie's best friend. She would have to find a way for them to be friends too, because she didn't think Dennis would take the initiative.

"Thanks, Dennis. I don't know what she'd do without friends like you."

The look of surprise on his face was priceless, as he had clearly expected a scolding for his hand in Audie's condition. "I just thought she needed to relax a little."

"I think that's exactly what she needed. She's been so wired these last few days. It looks like she's finally going to get a good night's sleep."

Dennis shoved his hands into his pockets and looked at his feet, seemingly uncomfortable with the praise. "Probably. She's pretty mellow. Half a bottle of tequila does that."

"I bet."

"Good thing we didn't get stoned or she'd be a zombie."

"You didn't . . . she didn't smoke anything?"

"Said she was done with it. She didn't want her Grammaw to see her."

Beth felt a rush of tears, but she didn't know if it was pride for Audie's newfound conviction or sorrow for her heartbreak. Either way, she hid her eyes from Dennis when she shocked him with a hug. "Thanks for being there for her. She's going to need all of us now."

Chapter 25

Audie steered her nimble vehicle around the ruts in the dirt drive, finally coming to rest in front of a log cabin with a wide covered porch.

"Wow. This is gorgeous," Beth said, opening the passenger door even before the Xterra had come to a halt.

"You think this is something, wait till you see the lake." Audie stretched behind the front seat to retrieve her backpack. "Just leave the bags for now. I'll come back and get them. I want to show you around."

Buster jumped through the opening over the console and bounded out the driver's door, running immediately to the edge of the woods to pee.

"I can see why Joel and Dwayne love it here."

"Yeah, and it's all ours until Wednesday. Think you can handle being alone in the woods with me for five days?"

Beth snagged Audie's hand as they started up the steps. "I plan on handling you for five days. It wouldn't matter where we were."

Audie grinned. "I always wondered what it would be like to have a handler." She turned the key in the lock and gave the heavy door a push.

They entered a rustic hallway with a door on each side.

"This is our room over here." Audie stepped into the small bedroom on the right and dropped her backpack on the braided rug. "Cozy, huh?"

"I bet it's more room than we'll need." Beth was immediately charmed by the antique bed and dresser, the only two pieces of furniture in the room. "Is that a bathroom?"

Audie flicked a light switch inside the tiled room. "It's pretty small, but it's private."

"It's perfect."

"I knew you'd like it. Come see the rest." She pulled Beth by the hand down the hall into a great room where sliding glass doors opened onto a deck that overlooked the lake. A stone fireplace filled the wall opposite the kitchen.

"This is beautiful. I can't believe they aren't out here every weekend."

"They would be if Joel had his way. But Dwayne likes to go dancing on the weekends so they only get out here once or twice a month." Audie opened the sliding glass door and led the way outside to the deck. "I told you you'd love it."

"You were right." Beth stepped under Audie's outstretched arm and wrapped her own arm around Audie's waist. "We could have a place like this someday if we really wanted it."

"Yeah, maybe when I'm fifty and get Oscar's job."

"It's not that much of a stretch. All we have to do is save our nickels and look for a good deal." Beth could teach Audie all the things she had learned about making her money work harder. Together, they could have quite a comfortable life.

"You could always save some nickels by moving in with me. You're practically living there now as it is."

Moving in together was definitely in their future, but Beth wanted to give Audie a little more time to go through her Grammaw's things and get used to thinking of the house as her own.

"I'd have to find a good renter for my condo."

"I bet Dennis would rent it if you'd let him paint it something besides beige."

Beth laughed. "I think if Dennis moved in, wall colors would be the least of my worries."

"Can you imagine?"

"I'd rather not."

Buster suddenly darted past in pursuit of a squirrel that made it safely to a tree before turning to taunt his tormentor.

"Speaking of your partner in crime, is he coming for Thanksgiving dinner?"

"No, you're not going to believe this. David talked him into helping serve dinner at a homeless shelter."

Beth opened her mouth in disbelief. "Our Dennis?"

"Our Tinkerbell. I think David's a good influence on him . . . sort of like somebody I know is on me."

"Somebody you know, huh?" Beth turned and leaned against the rail. She was awestruck by how beautiful Audie looked with the sun on her face.

"Just a woman I met."

"That's such a coincidence. I met a woman too who's been a good influence on me."

"From the way you were dancing last night at the Gallery, I'd say she tapped into your wild side." Audie lunged forward and thrust her hips into Beth's. "Do you call that a good influence?"

"I call that just what I needed." She pressed her mouth hard into Audie's for a long, hungry kiss.

Audie looked at her skeptically. "You actually expect me to believe I'm good for you?"

"Yes, I do." She took Audie's hands and looked directly into her eyes. "I didn't get to have a lot of fun when I was your age because of Kelly. With you, it's like I get to rewind my whole life and have that part over."

"Your sister's going to freak out when I walk in the door with you on Friday."

"I imagine we'll all freak out a little, but we might as well get it over with. You're part of the family now."

"And you're part of mine . . . such as it is." Audie gestured toward the cabin, an apparent indication that she thought of Joel and Dwayne as family.

"It's a good family to be in."

A gentle breeze stirred the trees and caused the water to ripple across the lake. Beth loved how Audie's long hair fluttered around her face.

"You want to walk down to the water?" Audie asked.

"Sure, but I want to take your picture first. Stay right here."

Audie watched as Beth disappeared through the sliding glass door. "The camera's in my backpack," she yelled.

She rested her arms on the rail and stared out across the lake. Her Grammaw had been right about Beth, about how lucky they were to find each other. Beth was probably right that her Grammaw had died happy knowing they were in love and committed to having a life together. She took a lot of comfort in that.

Beth was everything to her—a fun-loving friend, an exciting lover and a faithful partner. Audie had always envied her friends who had that, but she had never thought she would find it herself. Whatever it took, she wanted that with Beth forever.

"Ahem."

Audie turned her head to see why Beth was clearing her throat and broke into a monstrous grin. "That was supposed to be a surprise."

"Oh, I'm sure I'll be plenty surprised." Beth leaned in the doorway, sensuously fingering the lime green Dual-Do. "Which end of this is mine?"

"You can have either . . . or if you're really good, you can have both."

"And if I'm really bad?"

Audie's eyes widened as Beth reached forward and tugged at the zipper on her jeans. "If you're really bad, then I can have both."

"I have a feeling that over the next five days, my behavior is going to vacillate."

"That's a mighty big word, vacillate."

"Let's go back inside and I'll demonstrate what it means."

Audie smiled and followed her future back into the cabin. It was definitely the season to be thankful.

BEHIND THE PINE CURTAIN by Gerri Hill. 280 pp. Jacqueline returns home after her father's death and comes face-to-face with her first crush.   1-59493-057-0 $13.95

18TH & CASTRO by Karin Kallmaker. 200 pp. *Halloween Night, San Francisco* . . . and this steamy collection of stories explores it like no other.   1-59493-066-X $13.95

JUST THIS ONCE by KG MacGregor. 200 pp. Wynne Connelly struggles to resist Paula McKenzies's fascination and allure . . .   1-59493-087-2 $13.95

ANTICIPATION by Terri Breneman. 240 pp. Toni and the female investigator assigned to protect her try to remain professional while searching for a killer.   1-59493-055-4 $13.95

OBSESSION by Jackie Calhoun. 240 pp. Lindsey thought she was happy with her husband and children until Sarah loaned her a copy of *Desert Hearts* . . .   1-59493-058-9 $13.95

BENEATH THE WILLOW by Kenna White. 240 pp. Paris lost both her love and her will to love on 9/11, then a childhood friend re-entered her life . . .   1-59493-053-8 $13.95

SISTER LOST, SISTER FOUND by Jeanne G'fellers. 224 pp. The highly anticipated sequel to No Sister of Mine.   1-59493-056-2 $13.95

THE WEEKEND VISITOR by Jessica Thomas. 240 pp. The third Alex Peres mystery.   1-59493-054-6 $13.95

THE KILLING ROOM by Gerri Hill. 392 pp. How can two women forget and go their separate ways?   1-59493-050-3 $12.95

PASSIONATE KISSES by Megan Carter. 240 pp. Will two old friends run from love?   1-59493-051-1 $12.95

ALWAYS AND FOREVER by Lyn Denison. 224 pp. The girl next door turns Shannon's world upside down.   1-59493-049-X $12.95

BACK TALK by Saxon Bennett. 200 pp. Can a talk show host find love after heartbreak?   1-59493-028-7 $12.95

THE PERFECT VALENTINE: EROTIC LESBIAN VALENTINE STORIES edited by Barbara Johnson and Therese Szymanski—from Bella After Dark. 328 pp. Stories from the hottest writers around.   1-59493-061-9 $14.95

MURDER AT RANDOM by Claire McNab. 200 pp. The Sixth Denise Cleever Thriller. Denise realizes the fate of thousands is in her hands.   1-59493-047-3 $12.95

THE TIDES OF PASSION by Diana Tremain Braund. 240 pp. Will Susan be able to hold it all together and find the one woman who touches her soul?   1-59493-048-1 $12.95

JUST LIKE THAT by Karin Kallmaker. 240 pp. Disliking each other—and everything they stand for—even before they meet, Toni and Syrah find feelings can change, just like that.
1-59493-025-2 $12.95

WHEN FIRST WE PRACTICE by Therese Szymanski. 200 pp. Brett and Allie are once again caught in the middle of murder and intrigue.   1-59493-045-7 $12.95

REUNION by Jane Frances. 240 pp. Cathy Braithwaite seems to have it all: good looks, money and a thriving accounting practice . . .   1-59493-046-5 $12.95

BELL, BOOK & DYKE: NEW EXPLOITS OF MAGICAL LESBIANS by Kallmaker, Watts, Johnson and Szymanski. 360 pp. Reluctant witches, tempting spells and skyclad beauties—delve into the mysteries of love, lust and power in this quartet of novellas.
1-59493-023-6 $14.95

ARTIST'S DREAM by Gerri Hill. 320 pp. When Cassie meets Luke Winston, she can no longer deny her attraction to women . . .   1-59493-042-2 $12.95

NO EVIDENCE by Nancy Sanra. 240 pp. Private Investigator Tally McGinnis once again returns to the horror-filled world of a serial killer.   1-59493-043-04 $12.95

WHEN LOVE FINDS A HOME by Megan Carter. 280 pp. What will it take for Anna and Rona to find their way back to each other again?   1-59493-041-4 $12.95

MEMORIES TO DIE FOR by Adrian Gold. 240 pp. Rachel attempts to avoid her attraction to the charms of Anna Sigurdson . . .   1-59493-038-4 $12.95

SILENT HEART by Claire McNab. 280 pp. Exotic lesbian romance.

1-59493-044-9 $12.95

MIDNIGHT RAIN by Peggy J. Herring. 240 pp. Bridget McBee is determined to find the woman who saved her life.   1-59493-021-X $12.95

THE MISSING PAGE A Brenda Strange Mystery by Patty G. Henderson. 240 pp. Brenda investigates her client's murder . . .   1-59493-004-X $12.95

WHISPERS ON THE WIND by Frankie J. Jones. 240 pp. Dixon thinks she and her best friend, Elizabeth Colter, would make the perfect couple . . .   1-59493-037-6 $12.95

CALL OF THE DARK: EROTIC LESBIAN TALES OF THE SUPERNATURAL edited by Therese Szymanski—from Bella After Dark. 320 pp.   1-59493-040-6 $14.95

A TIME TO CAST AWAY A Helen Black Mystery by Pat Welch. 240 pp. Helen stops by Alice's apartment—only to find the woman dead . . .   1-59493-036-8 $12.95

DESERT OF THE HEART by Jane Rule. 224 pp. The book that launched the most popular lesbian movie of all time is back.   1-1-59493-035-X $12.95

THE NEXT WORLD by Ursula Steck. 240 pp. Anna's friend Mido is threatened and eventually disappears . . .   1-59493-024-4 $12.95

CALL SHOTGUN by Jaime Clevenger. 240 pp. Kelly gets pulled back into the world of private investigation . . .   1-59493-016-3 $12.95

52 PICKUP by Bonnie J. Morris and E.B. Casey. 240 pp. 52 hot, romantic tales—one for every Saturday night of the year.   1-59493-026-0 $12.95

GOLD FEVER by Lyn Denison. 240 pp. Kate's first love, Ashley, returns to their home town, where Kate now lives . . .   1-1-59493-039-2 $12.95

RISKY INVESTMENT by Beth Moore. 240 pp. Lynn's best friend and roommate needs her to pretend Chris is his fiancé. But nothing is ever easy.   1-59493-019-8 $12.95

HUNTER'S WAY by Gerri Hill. 240 pp. Homicide detective Tori Hunter is forced to team up with the hot-tempered Samantha Kennedy.   1-59493-018-X $12.95

CAR POOL by Karin Kallmaker. 240 pp. Soft shoulders, merging traffic and slippery when wet . . . Anthea and Shay find love in the car pool.   1-59493-013-9 $12.95

NO SISTER OF MINE by Jeanne G'Fellers. 240 pp. Telepathic women fight to coexist with a patriarchal society that wishes their eradication.   ISBN 1-59493-017-1 $12.95

ON THE WINGS OF LOVE by Megan Carter. 240 pp. Stacie's reporting career is on the rocks. She has to interview bestselling author Cheryl, or else! ISBN 1-59493-027-9 $12.95

WICKED GOOD TIME by Diana Tremain Braund. 224 pp. Does Christina need Miki as a protector . . . or want her as a lover?   ISBN 1-59493-031-7 $12.95

THOSE WHO WAIT by Peggy J. Herring. 240 pp. Two brilliant sisters—in love with the same woman!   ISBN 1-59493-032-5 $12.95

ABBY'S PASSION by Jackie Calhoun. 240 pp. Abby's bipolar sister helps turn her world upside down, so she must decide what's most important.   ISBN 1-59493-014-7 $12.95

PICTURE PERFECT by Jane Vollbrecht. 240 pp. Kate is reintroduced to Casey, the daughter of an old friend. Can they withstand Kate's career? ISBN 1-59493-015-5 $12.95

PAPERBACK ROMANCE by Karin Kallmaker. 240 pp. Carolyn falls for tall, dark and . . . female . . . in this classic lesbian romance.   ISBN 1-59493-033-3 $12.95

DAWN OF CHANGE by Gerri Hill. 240 pp. Susan ran away to find peace in remote Kings Canyon—then she met Shawn . . .   ISBN 1-59493-011-2 $12.95

DOWN THE RABBIT HOLE by Lynne Jamneck. 240 pp. Is a killer holding a grudge against FBI Agent Samantha Skellar?   ISBN 1-59493-012-0 $12.95

SEASONS OF THE HEART by Jackie Calhoun. 240 pp. Overwhelmed, Sara saw only one way out—leaving . . .   ISBN 1-59493-030-9 $12.95

TURNING THE TABLES by Jessica Thomas. 240 pp. The 2nd Alex Peres Mystery. *From ghosties and ghoulies and long leggity beasties* . . .   ISBN 1-59493-009-0 $12.95

FOR EVERY SEASON by Frankie Jones. 240 pp. Andi, who is investigating a 65-year-old murder, meets Janice, a charming district attorney . . .   ISBN 1-59493-010-4 $12.95

LOVE ON THE LINE by Laura DeHart Young. 240 pp. Kay leaves a younger woman behind to go on a mission to Alaska . . . will she regret it?   ISBN 1-59493-008-2 $12.95

UNDER THE SOUTHERN CROSS by Claire McNab. 200 pp. Lee, an American travel agent, goes down under and meets Australian Alex, and the sparks fly under the Southern Cross.   ISBN 1-59493-029-5 $12.95

SUGAR by Karin Kallmaker. 240 pp. Three women want sugar from Sugar, who can't make up her mind.   ISBN 1-59493-001-5 $12.95

FALL GUY by Claire McNab. 200 pp. 16th Detective Inspector Carol Ashton Mystery.   ISBN 1-59493-000-7 $12.95

ONE SUMMER NIGHT by Gerri Hill. 232 pp. Johanna swore to never fall in love again— but then she met the charming Kelly . . .   ISBN 1-59493-007-4 $12.95

TALK OF THE TOWN TOO by Saxon Bennett. 181 pp. Second in the series about wild and fun loving friends.   ISBN 1-931513-77-5 $12.95

LOVE SPEAKS HER NAME by Laura DeHart Young. 170 pp. Love and friendship, desire and intrigue, spark this exciting sequel to *Forever and the Night.*
ISBN 1-59493-002-3 $12.95

TO HAVE AND TO HOLD by Peggy J. Herring. 184 pp. By finally letting down her defenses, will Dorian be opening herself to a devastating betrayal?
ISBN 1-59493-005-8 $12.95

WILD THINGS by Karin Kallmaker. 228 pp. Dutiful daughter Faith has met the perfect man. There's just one problem: she's in love with his sister.   ISBN 1-931513-64-3 $12.95

SHARED WINDS by Kenna White. 216 pp. Can Emma rebuild more than just Lanny's marina?
ISBN 1-59493-006-6 $12.95

THE UNKNOWN MILE by Jaime Clevenger. 253 pp. Kelly's world is getting more and more complicated every moment.
ISBN 1-931513-57-0 $12.95

TREASURED PAST by Linda Hill. 189 pp. A shared passion for antiques leads to love.
ISBN 1-59493-003-1 $12.95

SIERRA CITY by Gerri Hill. 284 pp. Chris and Jesse cannot deny their growing attraction . . .
ISBN 1-931513-98-8 $12.95

ALL THE WRONG PLACES by Karin Kallmaker. 174 pp. Sex and the single girl—Brandy is looking for love and usually she finds it. Karin Kallmaker's first *After Dark* erotic novel.
ISBN 1-931513-76-7 $12.95

WHEN THE CORPSE LIES A Motor City Thriller by Therese Szymanski. 328 pp. Butch bad-girl Brett Higgins is used to waking up next to beautiful women she hardly knows. Problem is, this one's dead.
ISBN 1-931513-74-0 $12.95

GUARDED HEARTS by Hannah Rickard. 240 pp. Someone's reminding Alyssa about her secret past, and then she becomes the suspect in a series of burglaries.
ISBN 1-931513-99-6 $12.95

ONCE MORE WITH FEELING by Peggy J. Herring. 184 pp. Lighthearted, loving, romantic adventure.
ISBN 1-931513-60-0 $12.95

TANGLED AND DARK A Brenda Strange Mystery by Patty G. Henderson. 240 pp. When investigating a local death, Brenda finds two possible killers—one diagnosed with Multiple Personality Disorder.
ISBN 1-931513-75-9 $12.95

WHITE LACE AND PROMISES by Peggy J. Herring. 240 pp. Maxine and Betina realize sex may not be the most important thing in their lives.   ISBN 1-931513-73-2 $12.95

UNFORGETTABLE by Karin Kallmaker. 288 pp. Can Rett find love with the cheerleader who broke her heart so many years ago?
ISBN 1-931513-63-5 $12.95

HIGHER GROUND by Saxon Bennett. 280 pp. A delightfully complex reflection of the successful, high society lives of a small group of women.   ISBN 1-931513-69-4 $12.95

LAST CALL A Detective Franco Mystery by Baxter Clare. 240 pp. Frank overlooks all else to try to solve a cold case of two murdered children . . .   ISBN 1-931513-70-8 $12.95

ONCE UPON A DYKE: NEW EXPLOITS OF FAIRY-TALE LESBIANS by Karin Kallmaker, Julia Watts, Barbara Johnson & Therese Szymanski. 320 pp. You've never read fairy tales like these before! From Bella After Dark.
ISBN 1-931513-71-6 $14.95